Reluctantly in Love
with a Viscount

Book Two: The Barrington Saga

Teresa Sweeney

Courting Romance Publishing
California

Copyright 2025 by Teresa Sweeney

Library of Congress Control Number: 2025919977

Published in the United States by Courting Romance Publishing

ISBN 978-1-940319-10-0

First Edition

Cover Models: Nicole and Lawrence Sweeney III

By Teresa Sweeney

Always Rebecca

The Brentwood Tales
A Love Match, Indeed!
An Uncommon Affair
Only a Captain Will Do

The Reluctant Series
The Reluctant Viscount
A Very Reluctant Lady

The Barrington Saga
A Reluctant Debut
Reluctantly in Love with a Viscount

To my beautiful and amazing grandchildren:
Harrison, Donovan,
Lorenzo, Maria, Ana,
Bella, Lawrence IV, Roman,
soon to arrive baby Sweeney,
and Talia

A Note on the French Text

I learned while having my French phrases reviewed by my good friend Elizabeth Cooper that a space is generally put before an exclamation point and question mark. Elizabeth is a retired French Teacher with a Masters in the language and an avid reader. She asked her friend, Chantal Vandemaële, to also review the French dialogue in my manuscript. After all, a slight phrasing can make the difference between "I speak French fluently," to "I speak it fluently."

So, dear reader, these spaces before exclamation points and question marks in the French text are not typos, but are intentional. Any errors or misunderstandings are mine.

Reluctantly in Love with a Viscount

Book Two: The Barrington Saga

Chapter One

Miss Arabella Barrington's bum smarted from landing hard on her thinly-padded coach seat. She yowled and would have bellowed a bloody curse, if the wind was not knocked out of her. Her relic of a coach was racing along the king's highway and she was being tossed about like a bag of goods every time her coach hit a rut.

She was at fault for her burgeoning bruises. After all, she was the one who did not cavil when her escort Viscount Thomas Bolton suggested the coachman give the horses their heads. Of course, she did not know the borrowed coach she was to travel in was not as well-sprung or appointed as the viscount's. The vehicle, of which she had knowledge, was carrying her sister Rebecca to London to meet the Earl and Countess of Belcrave.

Rebecca was married to Thomas' brother Harry and when the Earl of Belcrave learned his son married a girl mired in scandal he ordered his heir to collect Harry and his bride and bring them to London. The scandal tainting the Barrington name derived from the fatal duel involving her father and their neighbor Baron Damburten. Mr. Barrington and his son Nathaniel had tracked the baron to London after the villain viciously assaulted Rebecca. Nathaniel stood witness for his father on the dueling field.

The duel, with its rules of conduct, even if illegal, was the gentlemanly way to settle an affront. A tradition hailing from the days of chivalry where combatants, in a fight to the death, let the divine justice of God determine the righteous. But Damburten was no gallant knight, nor did he adhere to any code of ethics. He was a coward who turned and discharged his weapon at Barrington before he completed the required ten dueling steps. The bullet, without warning, hit Barrington in the back. Barrington fell forward to the ground with the evidence of his fatal wound saturating the back of his coat.

Grief-stricken, Nathaniel had rushed to his father's side, praying he could help him, but there was nothing he could do. His father was dead. In an all-consuming rage, he had picked up his father's unspent pistol and fired it at Damburten. The baron clutched his bleeding chest and crumbled to the ground. Shocked at what he did, Nathaniel fled the field.

The deaths of the duelists and the flight of Nathaniel after he shot Damburten burst through every Mayfair residence like a devastating flood: fast and relentless without consideration to the lives it ruined. The gossip barely died from lack of new information when

Harry's marriage to Rebecca reignited the months old scandal. Ladies in their Mayfair parlours and gentlemen in their St. James clubs wagged their tongues shamelessly to slander the Bolton name. *How exactly was the new Mrs. Harry Bolton accosted? Was the attack to her person or character?* No one knew.

Some dared to whisper in Belgrave's presence whether his spare would take up the sword to protect his wife's honor. By the time the earl returned home from his club, he blustered to no one in particular, "Barringtons may be speculated upon, but a Bolton is not fodder for gossip!"

He fumed at the audacity of his peers to besmirch his family name and was determined to stop it by introducing his new daughter-by-marriage at a ball held in her honor. He would remind his peers of the power he wielded in Parliament, business, and through his noble lineage. Anyone thinking to bandy about his family name would learn there were dour consequences to doing it. He ordered his eldest son Thomas to collect the newly married couple.

Thomas had traveled to the Barrington cottage where Harry and his new wife lived with different intentions than what his father bid. He planned to extricate Harry from his union, should he learn his brother was bamboozled into it. What other reason could make Harry enter into an ill-advised marriage? It took a matter of days in the couple's company to learn theirs was a love-match. While Thomas was not one to subscribe to the folly, he did not have any qualms bringing the couple to London and offering his support since the marriage made Harry happy.

However, a promise Harry made to Rebecca delayed their departure. Rebecca needed answers only her brother knew and Harry promised to get them for her. He placed his wife and her sister in Thomas' care while he was gone, but an anxious letter from the Countess of Belcrave changed Thomas' plans. He could not wait for his brother to return before he left for London.

The countess wrote the ball's invitations were generating more speculation than responses; and could not combat any of it unless Rebecca was at hand. Thomas easily read between the lines of his mother's letter and understood she needed to show a number of her peers Rebecca was indeed a lady and worthy of association. Nothing would be more ruinous than to host a ball where the leading members of Society did not attend. Thomas gave orders for their immediate departure and was uncharacteristically surprised to learn Rebecca refused to go without Harry.

He was not used to having his edicts denied. His temper rose when nothing he said moved Rebecca to change her mind, not even his offer to find and replace Harry in his search for Nathaniel. Rebecca explained with equal fervor Thomas could not act in Harry's stead because the questions Harry was to ask on her behalf were private. Thomas' patience finally expired when Arabella suggested she could accompany him since she was in her sister's confidence. He adamantly refused the improper notion.

Thomas expounded he did not want to be caught in a parson's noose because it was discovered he traveled with her without benefit of chaperone. He reasoned she, more so than he, should be concerned about her reputation being ruined. Arabella scoffed at his concern. She was insulted he thought marriage to her an abomination. She countered he should be so lucky to have her for wife and when his expression hardened in fury at her flippancy, she laughed.

"Heavens!" she exclaimed, "I have no designs on you, Bolton, so put your wild presumptions to rest."

Their fervent exchange was one of many. Ever since their first infamous meeting when Thomas mistook her for a maid, they bantered like fencing partners, silently acknowledging a hit when one outsmarted the other. Arabella thought Thomas arrogant and her refusal to submit to his authority infuriated him. Thomas found her bold, stubborn, and unable to withhold her opinion. She often acted without regard to decorum and more times than not, he took steps to protect her from her own folly.

Regardless of Arabella's denial, Thomas was not sure if her motive to travel with him was not self-serving. He had years of experience protecting himself from those who would scheme to call him family. More than one mother with an unmarried daughter tried to catch him in a compromising situation, but he always ignored the urgent notes sending him to isolated locations and empty libraries. He never responded to an unmarried lady's overture. He was careful not to find himself alone with one, so after years of being diligent, he was not going to be caught because of a good deed.

He would fulfill his duty to produce the next heir when he wanted. He definitely would not be bamboozled into it or pressured into it by his father. When the time came he would contract a marriage of convenience with a lady of childbearing years who would be obedient to his will. He was resolute to not subject himself to those emotions involved in marrying for love.

He once overheard a young debutante he admired in his first Season speak of how she would gladly suffer his intimacies to become his future countess and eavesdropping upon her confession made him rethink the notion of love. It was a hard lesson to learn why the Season was called the marriage mart. Love was not a factor among the titled where rank, property and wealth precluded everything else in marrying.

Debutantes sought gentlemen to increase their own position in society and their family's stature. They were tutored at a young age to attract and bring the most eligible bachelors *up to scratch*, and were preached about the consequences of failing. Those who entered a second Season suffered as the lady who did not take. Their names were often coupled with biting remarks, *"Why would I want what others found lacking?"*

Thomas was in no rush to marry. There was plenty of time for him to start his nursery. He certainly did not want to marry a lady who challenged him at every turn. Never in his life did he argue with a commoner, much less a woman. It vexed him when Arabella did not submit to his authority. The tediousness of having to negotiate with a person unequal to him in consequence continually tried his patience.

He could not believe she suggested he hire a chaperone so they could travel together. He kept his voice from escalating into a shout when he reminded her Nathaniel was a fugitive and he did not want anyone to bear witness he aided and abetted a felon.

Thomas did not know where to search for Harry, much less Nathaniel. The servants he sent to follow his brother had not reported. His best guess to search was in and around Truro where Nathaniel might have fled. Rebecca's father once worked as a clerk in Truro and the Barringtons lived just outside the city, but without the sisters' knowledge of Nathaniel's childhood friends, his haunts, and the location of their grandfather's cottage he was hard-pressed to find Harry. He was hindered by time and by not having Rebecca's confidence. He could not seek the answers Rebecca wanted if he did not know the questions to ask.

His arguments for Rebecca to entrust him to find Nathaniel and ask her questions were futile. The Barrington sisters were not easily swayed; especially Arabella and it was she who rattled him. She was an obstinate minx who piqued his temper as often as his amusement and no sooner did he refuse one idea than she concocted another. Part of him marveled at her persistence and determination not to waver, and part of him was vexed she did not bend to his will.

He watched her eyes race as if searching the corners of her mind for an idea and when they twinkled in delight. He asked with reservation, "Well, what harebrained idea are you ready to suggest now?"

"I shall travel with you disguised as a man," she announced.

Thomas pressed his lips together to keep himself from ranting at her and then raised his hand to halt her next words. He was done trying to rationalize with her and her sister. Using all the authority a man of his station held, he left believing his departure settled the matter. He was wrong.

He could not complain she would hinder him. Arabella was resilient and fearless as evidenced by the way she took over the responsibility for her sister and farm when her father died and her brother fled. She managed to keep the farm when the debt collectors arrived using her father's reserved monies to settle the accounts. She nursed Rebecca from her wounds, cared for her through their difficult time, and pushed her to venture into society when all Rebecca wanted to do was hide. Harry praised her capabilities in managing the farm, and since Thomas' first meeting with her, he came to admire her strength, enjoy her wit, and cringe at her tenacity.

Reluctantly, he agreed to take her with him, but only on his terms. She was to use his married sister's name, since it was completely acceptable for a brother and sister to travel together. Thomas' sister, Lady Margaret MacDougall lived in Scotland with her husband and children. Her last appearance in London was when she made her debut and met her husband. No one would remember her aside she looked like a Bolton with dark brown hair and classic features. Arabella fit the description easily enough with her oval face, straight nose and full lips. Her rich brown hair made it easy to call her family. Only her light brown eyes called out the lie. Boltons were noted for either having blue or hazel eyes.

Regardless, at four and twenty she was old enough to pass for his sister. As an unmarried lady some might say Arabella was *long in the tooth*, but Thomas believed her beauty, intellect, strength, and compassion were more than enough to recommend her for marriage. She was still of childbearing years and Thomas hoped she would take advantage of the Season to find a husband when she went to London, and thereby, unburden Harry of her care.

"Ow!" screeched Arabella when the coach hit another rut. She was wedged into the corner of the carriage to keep from flying off her seat. Her shoulder and arm hurt from being rubbed against the coach's side whenever the bumpy and furrowed road jerked her up and down. She mumbled an oath for agreeing to travel at the reckless speed; but enough was enough, and so she would tell Thomas.

She moved forward on her seat and dropped the glass pane of the coach window. A cloud of dust flew in her face. She coughed, quickly turned her head into the coach to take a deep breath and then put her head out the window to find Thomas. She did not see him and realized he probably was riding ahead of the carriage so as not to suffer, as she was, from the dust kicked up by the horses' hooves and the carriage's wheels.

She tried yelling out to the driver to slow the coach and ended with a mouth full of grit. Frustrated and resigned, she quickly pulled her head back inside and pulled the glass pane up to close the window. She was not prepared when the coach jerked again. She fell onto the floor and tried to grapple for purchase among the seats to rise, but the jarring kept throwing her back on her bum. Tired from her attempts to reseat herself on the coach's bench, she reconciled to rattling about like a child's toy, until the carriage came to a stop.

Chapter Two

Thomas cantered into the Crown Inn courtyard and brought his stallion to an immediate stop. His horse shook its head and blew out its nose the moment the reins loosened. Thomas gave his loyal steed a pat for a job well done and waited for it to settle into a stand before dismounting.

In one fluid movement he swung his leg over his saddle and descended into the billowing dust caused by his horse's hooves. He searched the courtyard until his eyes fell upon an earnest stable boy eagerly waiting for a customer. Thomas beckoned the lad forward and was pleased the boy was attentive to his instructions regarding the care of his horse. He handed over the reins and rewarded him generously.

Satisfied, his mount was to be well-attended he looked to his own care. He was covered in layers of dust. He rode hard to make this first stop on his way to Truro and the effort made him tired and gritty. As if to validate his own findings, a rain of dirt showered his head when he removed his tall beaver hat. He quickly shook his head to rid himself of the grit and then ran his fingers through his hair before he replaced his hat.

He began to slap away the dust from his multi-caped greatcoat until he remembered Miss Barrington. Disgust marred his features when he looked back at the road and saw the weary and dated black traveling coach. The coach's previous owner was a neglectful one, leaving the carriage to age without improvement.

The carriage's center sagged like a man with a full belly. The body, without benefit of a coat of lacquer or refurbishment, was dull and scratched. The vehicle rocked into the courtyard looking like it carried a heavy burden. He never would have purchased the relic if another choice was available, but yesterday he was lucky to find it.

His own posh traveling coach was on its way to London carrying Harry's wife, Rebecca, as were several other well-appointed carriages in the area he attempted to borrow or buy from their owners. Time constrained him from searching farther afield and forced him to purchase the sorry excuse for a vehicle. He was so mortified to present the coach to Arabella when they were ready to leave he left her to be assisted by his footman into the carriage. He mounted his horse and galloped away before he bore witness to the door's warped frame.

The relic with a whirl of dust came to a jerky stop in the courtyard. Thomas waited for the dust to settle and for an ostler to grab the lead horses' bridles before he came near the carriage. His servant traveling with the coach brought forth the stepping stool and was ready to place it before the door once it was opened. Thomas grasped the door handle and pulled. His fingers slipped from the handle. He grabbed the door more firmly and pulled again, only to stumble back when the jammed door did not budge.

Embarrassed, he stayed his servant with his open hand and set his stance to leverage his weight into the pull. This time, the door flew wide and out of his grasp. He staggered back and knocked his hat off his head when his arms windmilled. If not for his agility, the force would have thrown him on his backside. He straightened his spine and then scowled at his servant for chuckling. Satisfied, he was no longer an object of ridicule he turned his eyes to the inside of the coach and swore.

There on the floor lay a sleeping and sprawled Arabella. Her head rested against one of the seat's thinly-padded squabs and her limbs were at odd angles lodged between the two bench seats. At least, he hoped she was asleep. He could not tell if her chest rose.

Frantic, he started to lean into the carriage, until he realized he would likely fall upon her if he tried. Instead, to rattle her awake, he grabbed the foot stuck under the bench seat nearest to him. The trim ankle he held in his hand was warm and he let the breath he did not know he held loose. He unconsciously rubbed his thumb over Arabella's smooth skin in relief of learning she was not dead. He began to note the perfection of her ankle and then, dropped her leg like a hot coal before his thoughts turned inappropriate. Shocked, he berated himself for where his mind began to trespass.

Arabella once accused him of being in the petticoat line and he retorted, "What man is not?" he took offense at her accusation. She gave it scornfully and he took it disrespectfully, since at the time they did not know each other well-enough to draw each other's character. He indeed enjoyed the company of women, but no lady ever called him a brute or uncaring. If anything, his attentions were sought-after for being a handsome and charming man. He exuded strength. His witty repartee could, if he chose, bring laughter to any situation and when he chose to be quiet his companions were equally content just to be by his side. He was a viscount, after all.

His hair was nearly black and contrasted beautifully with his bright blue eyes. One lady remarked his likeness to a Greek statue with his high cheekbones, noble nose, and strong chin. He corrected, "Surely, you mean god," which drew her to laugh, leading them into a merry evening. No one could ever accuse him of playing them false for he was honest about seeking only companionship.

Arabella witnessed firsthand how he treated his ex-lovers. The *modiste* who fashioned her new clothes was one of Thomas' old flames whom the viscount set up in business when he ended their affair. Arabella saw how he respectfully treated Mademoiselle Lavigne. There were no intimate whispers or touches. There was only the type of courtesy one offered to a person completing a service commissioned. Arabella would never have known Mademoiselle Lavigne was once the viscount's mistress or the lady wished to be so again if she had not eavesdropped on their private conversation. The little morsel Arabella overheard had put a blush to her cheeks and earned her a severe scold from the viscount when he caught her snooping.

Thomas picked up Arabella's leg again and shook it to wake her up. He jabbed her in the shoulder with his riding crop and prodded her again when she remained unresponsive. He called out her name and was about to prod her again when she groaned. Concerned, he asked, "Are you well, Miss Barrington?"

Arabella's eyes shot wide in outrage at hearing his ridiculous query. She lifted her head from the seat and scolded, "Do I look well, Bolton!" She tried to push herself up, but her shoulder was jammed under the seat and her arms proved useless. She wailed, "Don't just stand there! Help get me out of here. I believe my arms and legs are asleep and I cannot manage on my own."

"No need to spew your venom at me, Miss Barrington," he retorted, affronted how she placed the blame on him. "I was not the foolish one to take a seat on the floor."

He straightened out her legs, frowning at the impropriety of his actions, especially when he realized he enjoyed touching her more than he should. Irritated, he reached in, roughly grabbed her hands, and pulled her to a sitting position. Her cry shocked him into releasing her hands. He immediately felt remorse for his manhandling and flippancy.

Taking greater care, Thomas quickly extricated her from the carriage and set her on her feet. She began to fall when he removed his support, so he quickly grabbed hold of her. He lifted her into his arms when she looked like she was about to cry again. The servant who traveled before them to secure rooms raced up to his side, picking up his employer's tall hat on the way.

"Milord," his servant Timothy asked, "What can I do? Shall I carry her?"

Timothy was one of the many soldiers Thomas hired at the end of the war with France to use as runners, guards, and for reconnaissance work. The young man was six and ten when he joined the infantry in answer to his country calling able countrymen to defeat Napoleon. He suffered a saber cut to his leg for his bravery and the injury put a hitch in his gait. He was unable to find work when he returned home, until he heard Viscount Bolton hired ex-soldiers.

Timothy's confidence in his own abilities impressed Thomas into hiring him on the spot. Timothy proved he was agile, quick-witted, and capable of any task the viscount assigned him. His youthful look made him blend easily into crowds where the more ominous and hardened man usually stood out. Some of those men were also in the viscount's pay, but Timothy's discretion and good sense made him invaluable.

Thomas commanded, "Have a bath ordered for Mi...my sister and make sure the mistress of the inn is there to help, but first show me to her room."

Timothy was in his lordship's confidence and knew the lady was not his sister. He did as he was told and led his employer into the inn, up the staircase and into Arabella's room, before leaving to find the publican's wife.

Thomas gently placed Arabella on the bed and noted her distress. She was biting her bottom lip to keep from sobbing. Her expression and the way her hair escaped her coif made her look younger than her four and twenty years. It reminded him of her custom of breaking her morning fast before styling her hair. A habit she would have to break when she resided in London where parlours were not private, but often intruded upon by visitors.

She looked far from the combatant he commonly engaged in banter. Pain marred her features. Worried he asked, "Shall I send for a doctor?"

"No," she groaned out in agony. "I am sore and my limbs feel like they are being pricked with needles, but once they wake and I can begin to move them, I shall be fine. A hot bath will be sufficient and I am sure the mistress shall have some salve for my scrapes and bruises."

Thomas apologized, "I am sorry, Miss Barrington. I should have checked on you, instead of pushing us to great speeds. Forgive me, my focus was on Harry instead of your well-being, but I shall do better. Shall I have a tray sent to your room?"

"No, thank you, Bolton," she replied brusquely, "I must move about or I will suffer for it tomorrow. May I meet you downstairs in half the hour?"

"Of course," he replied, pleased to see she was becoming annoyed with him; clear evidence she was already improving, "but I wish you would reconsider entrusting me to find Nathaniel and discover whatever your sister needs learned. I could leave you here until you are fit to travel to London."

"You know I cannot, Bolton. Rebecca trusted me to speak with Nathaniel. What news he has is hers to share or not."

Thomas gave a curt nod and took his leave. He saw the publican's wife making her way up the stairs and informed her to provide everything "his sister" wanted.

A smidgeon of regret creased Arabella's features as the publican's wife closed the buttons on the back of her ponoma striped muslin dress. Her short puffy sleeves and high-waist bodice were all trimmed with ruching of the same sea green material. It was one of the garments Thomas commissioned for her and her sister. Playing with the long ribbons circling beneath her bodice and falling down the back of her dress reminded her of Thomas' generous nature. She regretted venting her anger at him for her injuries.

Her bruises were not the viscount's fault. While she was sorry she ranted at him, she was not sorry for what she gained. He promised to be attentive to her while they traveled. She preferred his company in the carriage to help make the time pass, but she would settle for his courtesy.

The warm bath and the salve the publican's wife rubbed into her shoulders eased her pain. She thanked the good wife and then made her way to the private parlour where she was told she would find Thomas. A sense of anticipation overcame her. She could not deny she liked spending time with the viscount or the sense of womanhood she felt when she was with him. The tenuous feelings he evoked were different from anything she ever felt.

She looked forward to engaging in their usual witty repartee. Sparks often flew when they bantered and mischievous notions crossed her mind to whether she could pique or fluster his temper. She expected a host of other ladies of his acquaintance experienced the same titillation of sparring words with him. After her atrocious carriage ride she was hoping for an entertaining dinner.

She checked her giddiness before she entered the parlour. Viscount Bolton was too handsome for his own good and too charming when he chose to be. The last thing she wanted was to inflate his ego for he was too arrogant not to know he was admired by many, even her.

He might not be attracted to her. He might even resent being saddled with her on this trip, but it did not matter. After months of sorrow, she was having an adventure. For the first time since her father's death, life was not sad, dreary and burdensome. The viscount was stirring new and invigorating feelings in her. She was a woman, not a daughter or sister, and she planned to enjoy the sentiment for as long as it lasted.

Chapter Three

Thomas swirled the whiskey in his snifter. He sat at the head of an oak planked table in the inn's private parlour awaiting Arabella. The liquor he sipped came from a bottle he brought from his own reserves, something he initiated doing after suffering the pitiful excuse his brother offered him at Barrington Farm.

Thomas laughed. His brother called his tastes too discriminating and practically dared him to sip the pale concoction. Well, pride and good manners made him taste the unaged liquor, but his flavor palette kept him from finishing the drink. He vowed to never suffer the like again and now traveled with a bottle of his finest whiskey.

He raised the balloon-shaped stemmed glass to his nose and breathed in the aromatic and smoky fragrance of the well-aged caramel-colored whiskey before he savored a sip. His anger kept him from enjoying it and he cursed when he slammed his heavy snifter on the table. He ran his hand over his head before upbraiding himself for not personally seeing to Arabella's comfort during their journey. He could not remember a time he was so inconsiderate. The moment they left his manor, he rode ahead of the coach and assumed his coachman stopped at intervals. *But what if his driver hadn't? Besides the bumpy ride, were Arabella's basic needs also neglected?*

He lifted his glass and took another sip of his whiskey. He pressed his lips tight and then popped them open to curse again, "Blast and damnation!" He shook his head in self-reproach. He could not believe he ordered his coachman to gallop the horses without thought to Arabella's well-being.

Granted, he asked her if he could do so and she complied, but to not check on her throughout the journey was unlike him in thought and manner. He was so single-minded in his determination to get to their first stop for the night he utterly neglected her care. Swearing again, he pushed his glass away and stared at the closed door.

The innkeeper charged a fee for the small room where patrons could eat in private. The wealthy often reserved one for dining when they traveled or to conduct a meeting; especially with persons they did not want to welcome into their manor homes. The Crown Inn's private room was bare, aside for the table and the chairs situated around it; and the one window the occupant could open.

Thomas ordered supper after he settled Arabella in her room to be made ready and served in thirty minutes. True to his command a number of dishes and two place settings were brought in and now covered the table.

Thomas only awaited Arabella's arrival to dine. Most inns, especially those near the king's highway, were crowded with travelers and locals looking for a pint of ale or a meal. Nothing drew their attention faster than nobility making an appearance. Both the upper and lower classes enjoyed gossiping and the sighting of a man or lady of quality, what they were doing, and with whom, placed the peer and their party under scrutiny.

A private room offered the only respite from the loud noises, stares, and unruly behavior of patrons. Bawdry remarks and blasphemous outbursts from the bar were not uncommon, nor were unwanted advances upon a lady. The indulgence of privacy was so coveted it was not unheard to hear how one peer was ousted to give way to a gentleman of higher rank, nor was it uncommon to give sanction to any lady should the public dining parlour turn too unruly.

Thomas hoped the bath soothed Arabella's pains. His mind pictured the scenario. The corners of his lips turned up into a grin as his portrait became more detailed with Arabella lathering a bar of soap in the tin bath. He might have indulged further in his scenario if his imagination did not recall it was Arabella he was picturing. Even in his illusion, the scene quickly turned from her beckoning him to being reprimanded by her steely eyes and enraged voice for intruding upon her privacy.

Now, that was a vision he could believe and even though he was a man who enjoyed the company of woman in all states of dress, he did not engage in affairs with innocents. His amorous liaisons marked him a rake in Polite Society, but even with the moniker, he was one of the *ton's* most eligible bachelors.

Mothers warned their young daughters to stay away from him with one admonishing finger, while their other fingers beckoned him forward at every ball. He refused their blatant overtures to ensnare him by being the arrogant lord Arabella accused him. He ignored those mothers with marriageable daughters gesturing to him. The *ton* liked a lofty lord, and took no offense with his rebuff; since he treated all the debutantes the same.

Returning his mind to a fully-clothed Arabella, he did not blame himself for his wicked thoughts; especially after having knowledge of her trim and slender ankle. His response was natural for any healthy male. *What man would not be moved by her silky skin and fine features?*

Her face was classically perfect with high cheek bones, a straight nose rounded at the end and full lips. Rich chocolate brown hair, of which he knew fell to her waist, framed her symmetrical oval face. Her almond-shaped eyes were light brown in color and made more beguiling by her long thick eyelashes and naturally arched brows.

If not for her stubborn streak and quick to flare temper he might think her exquisite. Unfortunately, no matter how pretty was she, there was no denying Arabella riled him by constantly acting counter to his wishes. She always seemed to forget her station and spoke to him as if she was his equal. Since their first meeting, she imposed upon him, tested his patience, and asked him to fulfill her every wish. The audacity of the chit sometimes made him laugh, but more times than not, she angered him to distraction.

The creak of the door opening halted his musings and his pulse quickened in anticipation to see Arabella. He was anxious to learn how she fared. He began to push back his chair to rise and greet her, until he saw it was not Arabella at the door. To his surprise, his friend and fellow rogue, Edward Constantine Fairowe, the Earl of Fairgrove, stepped into the room.

"What's this I hear?" Edward asked closing the door behind him, disappointed to find his friend alone.

Thomas raised his brows at his friend, but did not speak. He and Edward were one of a group of men owning the moniker Dark Rogues. Most thought the name referred to a club in which the gentlemen were members, but they were simply friends who knew each other since boarding school. They all came of age together and participated in those activities all young men engaged in while attending the Season.

Their good looks and devil may care attitude brought them more successes with women than most, but their nickname came from their dark hair and charm, not from living a reprobate lifestyle. As a group, the Dark Rogues were tall, handsome, and fit. They were known to be gallant, notorious, even frightening when they asserted their strength and power; but most of all, they were known for their loyalty to one another. Even though

Thomas knew he could trust Edward with the truth of his journey, he also knew he could not disclose what was not his to tell.

"Well, Bolton," asked Edward. "Where is your ladybird? The publican said you booked rooms for you and your sister, but I know very well all your siblings visit Maggie during the Season. You have no sister here I would wager."

Before Thomas could chastise his friend for his informal use of his sister's name, the door opened to admit Arabella. She looked revived from her bath and bright-eyed at seeing supper already placed on the table. Thomas knew she owned a healthy appetite having suffered her short temper whenever she was hungry. He stood and was about to greet her when Edward reached out to grab her.

His arm startled Arabella and just as Thomas taught her, she grabbed Edward's finger and pulled it back. Her maneuver surprised and pained the earl into letting out a yelp. She was so pleased with her result she unconsciously relaxed her hold when she looked at Thomas for praise and was catapulted over Edward's shoulder before she knew what happened.

A breath swooshed out of her when her stomach hit his shoulder and then a gasp followed when he slapped her bottom. He chuckled and promised, "You will pay for that, my pretty vixen."

Outraged, Arabella pushed off Edward's back, but she and Edward immediately stopped their battling when Thomas spoke. His barely controlled rage brooked no argument, "I suggest you release her immediately, Fairgrove, and gently lest I call you out. She is not one for your amusement."

Astonished, Edward carefully placed Arabella on her feet and replied, "It is not like you to be possessive of your ladybirds, Bolton."

Arabella stood transfixed watching the heated scene. Her nerves made her fuss over her skirt. It was clear Thomas knew the man to call him by name, but she was not sure to what degree. *Is he friend or foe?* The gentleman was meticulously and fashionably dressed. Her lips twitched to offer the handsome earl a smile when she surreptitiously took his measure. His eyes were spectacular, as deep as the blue sea, and they pulled her into their depths, until she recalled the man called her a doxy. The insult made her dip her chin and blush.

"I beg your pardon, Miss..." stuttered Edward after her head dropped in embarrassment.

Thomas sighed at his friend's stutter and went to stand by Arabella to rectify the ill-timed meeting. He said, "Fairgrove, may I present Miss Arabella Barrington, Harry's sister-by-marriage. Miss Barrington, meet my longtime and ill-mannered friend Edward Constantine Fairowe, the Earl of Fairgrove."

Arabella shyly made her curtsey, turning a deeper crimson under the earl's inspection of her stylish dress and slender form. Thomas chuckled at her uncommon timidity and said, "Do not turn missive now, Miss Barrington."

Edward raised his eyebrows and opened his mouth to rebuke his friend, but Thomas raised his hand to stop him and said, "You do not know her as I, Fairgrove, so do not be her champion when she is in need of none."

Affronted to be scolded in front of Arabella, Edward retorted, "Perhaps, Bolton, but her champion I am."

Arabella looked at the earl gleefully and gave him a beaming smile for his gallantry. She did not see Thomas frown at her because she was too captivated by the act of Edward taking her hand, kissing the back of it, and saying, "I did not mean to keep you from your meal, Miss Barrington."

Edward winged out his arm for her to take. She was not used to such attention from a stranger, so a moment passed before she threaded her hand around his arm. He walked her to her chair and pulled it out for her to sit. It amused her to see him sit next to her rather than across. *Is this what it is like to be courted?*

Thomas shook his head at his friend's dallying and returned to his seat at the head of the table. He suggested, "You may take your leave anytime, Fairgrove. I have no wish to detain you from your amusements."

Edward grinned and replied, "I have no plans, Bolton. Besides, I am sure your tale will prove more amusing than anything I can manage this evening to divert myself."

Thomas sighed and said, "Then, ring the bell cord and order a plate and service for yourself, since there is no getting rid of you. You will be disappointed to learn there is no tale. We are on our way to collect Harry. His wife wishes him to be with her."

The name of Barrington finally registered with Fairgrove and he pressed his lips together from laughing. Thomas noted his friend's amusement and raised his brows in question.

"Am I to meet the former Miss Rebecca Barrington connected with Damburten's death?"

Affronted by Edward's mocking jibe, Arabella pushed back her chair and rose. She announced, "I am not staying, Bolton. I will have a tray sent up and will see you in the morning."

Arabella turned to leave but Thomas halted her with his stern words, "I did not teach you defense moves to act recklessly and gloat, Miss Barrington. Doing so put you in jeopardy. Do not make the mistake again, less I be inclined to teach you another lesson."

Arabella jutted out her chin in anger at not just being reprimanded in front of a stranger, but because like a child, she was being threatened to not misbehave in the future. She rebutted, "I did so only because you were at hand, Bolton. I would never have engaged Fairgrove if a true threat existed. It is no fault but your own I feel well-protected in your company." She turned and strode out of the room as if she was greatly wronged.

Edward laughed and remarked, "Well, she put you in your place, Bolton. Does she always speak to you in the familiar?"

"I fear so, Fairgrove," he replied, "unlike you, to whom she made her curtsey; she gives no thought to my consequence."

"I do hope my offense did not cause her departure. Forgive me, Bolton. I would never act so shamelessly if you did not register her as your sister. Why did you?"

"I would think it obvious, Fairgrove. You are astute enough to note Miss Barrington travels without benefit of chaperone. She uses my sister's name to protect her reputation, which I trust is not at risk from meeting you today."

"Rest assured, Bolton," replied Edward. "I would never endanger our friendship by telling tales."

"Thank you, Fairgrove. You are indeed a trusted friend."

Chapter Four

Thomas waited for Arabella to exit the inn. He stood by the new black traveling coach he purchased for her and was anxious to present it. The pristine lacquered carriage practically sparkled in the courtyard and his attendance to it was drawing attention. He was beginning to feel like a footman which stirred his temper.

Yesterday, after leaving Arabella to the publican wife's ministrations, he ordered Timothy to search out the local estates to find a carriage with springs and appointments worthy of his station. He did not quibble at the exorbitant price the local squire wanted for it.

His guilt had disturbed him. Even while keeping company with Fairgrove, he had silently chastised himself for his neglect of her. He worried so much he began to wonder, why? He reasoned it came from the responsibility he assumed in bringing her along and once he deposited her back into Harry's care his fretting would stop. This burgeoning concern for her made him uneasy. Even now, his disposition chafed at how much she was on his mind and her tardiness was beginning to make him angry. *Does the minx not understand the concept of an early start?* He shuffled his foot in the graveled courtyard deciding whether to go see what kept her when she appeared.

She exited the inn, much like a little girl trying to escape her afternoon nap, looking in all directions for the nurse who would return her to bed if caught. Arabella was too pretty in her long sapphire blue merino redingote trimmed with a black collar and black cuffs to go unnoticed. The coat's front panels were closed with the braided curlicue black frog fastenings, much like a Hussar's uniform, currently *á la mode* in women fashions.

Her form easily drew a man's eyes, but a lady turned her attention to Arabella because she looked like one of Ackerman's fashion plates. Thomas was enthralled and stepped forward to offer his compliments, until he saw her frantically inspect the courtyard. His protective instincts immediately searched for a possible threat.

Everyone in the courtyard was preoccupied with their own business of loading passengers and luggage to have any interest in Arabella, aside from admiration. Coachmen were perched on their box seats with reins in hand. Ostlers held onto the lead bridles of the carriage horses while servants loaded luggage. Gentlemen proffered their hands to aid their ladies step up into their traveling carriages and then joined them.

Nothing seemed amiss, so he returned his attention back to Arabella in time to see her stumble. His quick response rushed him forward to catch her by the elbow to keep her from falling to the ground. Concern marked his query, "Are you well, Miss Barrington?"

"Is Lord Fairgrove here?" she whispered, not seeming to hear his question.

Thomas' eyebrows drew up in surprise and he immediately came to an unflattering reason to why she might ask. Angry, he asked, "Why? Did Fairgrove give offense?"

Arabella looked at Thomas and all thoughts left her mind when she saw the rigid set of his mouth. He was angry and the idea he was mad on her behalf surprisingly pleased her. She did not want to cause trouble between him and his friend; especially since the affront she felt was not made intentionally. Fairgrove's tone was flippant not mean, though drawing amusement at someone else's expense was far from kind.

Aside from him manhandling her when he thought her a doxy, she took no offense of him. He was charming, amiable, and handsome enough to leave any lady in a stupor. Her good opinion of him changed when he made a mockery of her sister's connection to Damburten; especially since it enlightened her to how her sister's assault was cruelly discussed in Society. She took umbrage to the unfair speculation and immediately rose from the table and left because she did not want to share a meal with a man who made fun over her family's tragedy.

"Of course not," she answered Thomas curtly while searching the courtyard again.

Thomas narrowed his eyes at her. He did not tolerate lies. If they were in a private arena he would sit her down and lecture her on the consequences of playing him false. Instead, he pacified his temper by recalling he was in Fairgrove's company until the earl left. His friend did not have any opportunity to injure her.

Of course, mistaking her for his doxy was enough to offend, as was the slap he delivered to her bottom, but he remembered Arabella seemed quite smitten with his friend after the misunderstanding was corrected. In fact, she responded like a girl just let out of the school room, all agape at meeting a handsome titled man.

Edward was right to remark it was not like him to be possessive of a woman in his company, but Arabella was not like any other lady of his acquaintance. Their exchanges were not driven for obtaining a lover or connived by a debutant to bring him *up to scratch*, even though he once accused her of it. He could not think of one lady of his acquaintance, other than family, who did not covet what he could give them, be it a coronet or a *carte blanche*.

He was used to protecting his bachelorhood and because his brother married Arabella's sister and he was in Arabella's company more often than not, he tended to treat her like family, jesting and admonishing like an older brother. Perhaps, it was why he did not like Edward flirting with her. He would not like Edward flirting with his younger sister Charlotte. It did not matter. Before long, he and Arabella would part company.

He could at least ease Arabella's mind by inform-
ing, "He is not here, Miss Barrington. I saw him off late last
night."

"He traveled in the dark!" she exclaimed with
concern.

"He did not have far to travel," he explained annoyed by her obvious distress, until he saw her blush at
deducing the earl had an assignation. *Ha!* He silently
laughed, enjoying his friend's fall from her good opinion.

"Exactly," he conferred before escorting her over to
his newly acquired carriage where he quickly placed her
inside and shut the door. He leaned against the opened
window and advised, "Be assured, Miss Barrington, I shall
check on you throughout our journey."

Arabella watched him turn away from her and
stride over to mount his horse. He sat the beast beautifully
in one fluid swing and then pushed the sides of his caped
greatcoat behind his muscular legs to drape on each side
of his horse. She watched mesmerized, admiring his handsome form as he sat tall in his saddle and before she could
turn her head away from being caught gawking, he turned
and looked at her. He tipped his tall beaver hat, gave his
mount his heels and galloped away.

She was still staring at his departing form when
she was jolted forward in her seat. The start of the carriage
blinked her to alertness and she quickly turned her body
to pull the window pane up to keep the dust from swirling
inside. She gave herself a slight admonishment for her
woolgathering over a very contrary lord. The man was all

sugar and spice. In one moment, he charmed her with enough sweetness to give her a toothache, and in another, he reprimanded her with enough heat to make her own temper rise.

The carriage hit a rut and Arabella quickly settled back onto the plush squab, feeling the soft cushioned leather beneath her. The horses were not racing, but yesterday's ordeal was still too fresh in her mind to chance she might be tossed to the floor if she was not careful. The luxury traveling coach Bolton acquired for her comfort was more than she could imagine and the idea he acquired it for her specific use simply astounded her.

He considered her every comfort. There were heated bricks on the floor to warm her feet and a lap blanket for her body. A basket of food and a ceramic pitcher of lemonade were secured with a rope under the seat opposite her. A rosebud in a sterling silver vase was attached to the carriage wall and a small book of poems was placed on the seat beside her. It appeared Thomas was making amends to her for yesterday's neglect and she was so pleased her face broke out in a big smile. She picked up the poetry book to halt her ridiculous thought. *Might Thomas care for me?*

True to his word, Thomas came back on a number of occasions to inquire to her comfort. Arabella began to watch for him. She fought her impulse to ask him to ride inside with her. She would love to spar words with him, but she did not bother to ask knowing his strong sense of protocol would make him decline.

The carriage picked up speed on the straight lanes and unlike yesterday's ordeal, Arabella enjoyed a smooth ride. The traveling coach was well-sprung and even at the brisk speed she traveled, not once was she tossed about or injured. She took enjoyment in reading her poetry book and in the verdant landscape she saw through her clear glass window pane. She even slept at intervals having no companion to engage with discourse. By the time she arrived at the White Hart in Truro she was awake, hungry, and anxious to stretch her legs.

Thomas expected to hear word from Harry, but Arabella was not sure how he was to receive it until she saw Timothy. Once again, the viscount's servant journeyed ahead of them to secure their rooms, and it seemed to check for messages, since he ran up to Thomas and handed him a letter. Words were exchanged making Thomas shake his head. Thomas quickly opened and read the letter. Then, he looked back to the road from where they came as if he hoped Harry would appear.

Arabella could wait no longer to learn what news Thomas received and banged the carriage door open. The noise turned Thomas' attention to her and a curse of "bloody, stubborn, woman," left his mouth as he ran forward to catch her as she stepped into air. She forgot to wait for the carriage step.

Her cheeks bloomed pink and she felt the warmth of embarrassment spread through her as her body brushed his chest. He placed her on the ground, but still steadied her with his hands on her waist. She kept her face down so he could not witness her flushed face until she heard him chuckle.

Arabella planted her hands on his chest and pushed. She huffed and her blush turned a heated red from anger. "You are a rogue, Bolton," she fumed knowing he knew he discomposed her.

"Perhaps," he retorted. "But I prefer you mad than embarrassed. I meant no offense, Miss Barrington, but in the future please restrain from jumping out of the carriage. If not to protect your own reputation as a lady, then, do it to maintain my sister's."

Arabella was ready to make a derisive comment to his sarcasm when she remembered the letter. She asked anxiously, "Was the letter from Harry? How did he find you?"

"All in good time, Miss Barrington," replied Thomas. "Let us get settled and we will speak after our meal." Without waiting for a response, he commanded Timothy to escort Arabella to her room while he sought out one of the men he sent to trail his brother.

Thomas left the coachman to see their luggage was brought into the inn and then to drive the carriage to the stables where he was headed. He walked his own horse down the street and strode into the stables the inn used for its guests. He saw Hugh brushing down his horse and went to greet him.

Hugh heard him approach, looked up and took off his woolen cap to respectfully greet his employer, and take hold of the viscount's horse.

"Finish up with your own mount," commanded Bolton, "then meet me outside where we can speak in private." Hugh nodded and got on with his work, while Thomas headed through the back door of the stable to await his servant. Hugh did not keep his employer waiting long and found him leaning by the stable's wall. He removed his hat and began his report.

"Sorry, milord, but your brother caught on to us trailing him right away. Usually, no one gives us any thought, but Harry knows your tactics too well and once he saw our faces, he heeled his horse into a run and blooming waited around a bend for us to catch up. At first, Rees and I thought we ran into a bandit hearing the shout, 'Stand and deliver,' but once we saw it was Harry, we bloody well cursed to see him laugh at us.

"Your brother ordered us to help him. I know he had no authority to do so, but Rees and I figured our job was to keep him safe and there was no better way to do it than to stay with him. Even when we separated to cover more ground in our search of Nathaniel, we knew he would be where we were expected to meet to report our findings. There really was nothing to report until now, so Rees and I figured we were following your orders. Were we wrong?"

Bolton scrutinized his servant and decided the man was being sincere. He replied, "In the future I will want a daily report as I have a network among the inns to transport them, but I find no fault with your actions.

Harry's safety was my primary concern. Is Harry positive Nathaniel is not hiding in Truro?"

"Yes, milord, we spoke with everyone where he once lived and followed up on some ideas that came forth. The brother is not here. We would have searched for the grandfather, but Harry did not know where the man lived and he was too worried about his wife. He didn't want her fretting and decided to leave the search until after his wife's debut ball. Rees rode with him. I was readying to make my way to you and report, checking at all the inns to see if you sent orders as you instructed when I spied Timothy. Right glad I did before I left."

"Me, too, Hugh, we will talk again later after I dine with Miss Barrington and have speech with her. I believe we will continue the search and I will need your help."

"Right, milord, I am your man," Hugh replied. "I'll see to your mount, until you send for me."

Chapter Five

Thomas was glad to be rid of the layer of dirt, grime, and stench covering him after a full day of riding. His bath revived him and while his valet would cringe at his wrinkled shirt and simply knotted cravat, he was not so fastidious to let it put him out of sorts. There were many Englishmen who sided with the old proverb *vestis virum facit*. Thomas always disagreed with the premise that clothes made the man. He never allowed anything or anyone to diminish his stature; certainly not his wardrobe. Satisfied with his appearance, he left his room dressed in a superfine navy tailcoat over an embroidered grey vest and buff breeches. His boots might not shine, but at least, they did not leave a track of dirt when he walked down the hall.

The news of his brother making his way to London made his task easier with only Nathaniel to find. He no longer needed to chase after Harry and could focus his energies on finding Arabella's brother, who undoubtedly left a footprint in the small village of Cadgwith. He preferred to search for her grandfather on his own, but lest he forget, only Arabella knew what to ask Nathaniel. He had no choice but to keep her with him.

His thoughts pulled his attention to look towards Arabella's room in time to see her exit. She sparkled. Her dark brown hair was wet and glossy and rolled into a simple coil at the back of her head. Her cheeks glistened from cleanliness, and it pleased him to note, grew rosy when she saw him. She was quite pretty dressed in one of her new gowns of sprigged muslin with a silk floral fringed shawl wrapped around her shoulders. He felt his lips quirk into a smile even before she grasped her shawl against her bosom and ran to meet him at the top of the stairs like a hoyden.

"You look well, Miss Barrington," he remarked when she met him. "Have you recovered from yesterday's ordeal?"

"Indeed, Bolton," she replied looking up at him with glee. "Thank you for your concern but set your mind at ease. I am made of sterner stuff than to let a bump here and there discomfit me."

"You are stellar indeed, Miss Barrington," he complimented soberly, instantly realizing his glib response was born of truth. "Most ladies of the realm would lie abed for a week or more for their suffering."

"Well, I have no desire to repeat yesterday's ride, but rest assured today was quite enjoyable. I found amusement in the landscape and read the poetry book you gave me. Thank you for all the comforts. They did not go unnoticed. Not even the flower."

Thomas was pleased by her remarks, but he could not take credit for the book and informed, "The book was a gift from Fairgrove."

The revelation astonished Arabella. Thomas did not wait to see if a maidenly blush would color her cheeks again and quickly intruded upon her musings. He winged out his arm and proclaimed with one of authority, "Dinner awaits us, Miss Barrington. Allow me to escort you to our private parlour."

It was clear he would brook nothing but obedience and Arabella complied like a dog coming to heel. Her ire at being commanded instead of asked was about to reveal itself, except her shawl dropped to her elbows to show the deep blue and purple bruise she sported on her upper arm. Any anger she felt dissipated when he covered the hand she had on his arm with his own and apologized, "I am sorry, Miss Barrington."

Arabella turned her attention to the discoloration on her upper arm caused by yesterday's insufferable ride. She replied, "Truly, Bolton, the bruise is of little significance. Do not worry yourself for it looks worse than it feels." She jested, "If anything, your concern should be directed to my hunger. You were forewarned I become short-tempered when my stomach begs for food, so I suggest you focus on feeding me with haste."

Thomas blew out a chuckle. Usually, he demonstrated more panache in a lady's company, but he could not guard himself from Arabella. She always surprised him. No lady of his acquaintance would ever mention a body part while in the company of a gentleman. It was *beyond the pale*, but Arabella's honesty never ceased to amaze him. There appeared to be no boundaries of what they could speak about with one another. He was not sure if it was a good or bad thing, but he enjoyed the camaraderie of it.

"Hang on, Miss Barrington," he chuckled. "Substance is at hand to subdue your hunger before it sparks your temper."

He escorted her to the parlour he reserved and sat her at the table next to the seat he would take. Moments later, the innkeeper bustled in; an obsequious smile marking his middling and thick waist features. Two young serving maids followed carrying trays of covered dishes. The owner made a fanfare of telling the maids where to place and uncover the plates before he performed a flamboyant bow and took his leave.

The number of dishes spread out before them on the heavily scarred oak plank table smelled delicious. Aromas of herbs, garlic and onion filled the air. There was a crock of white soup made with veal stock, onions and crushed almonds; a full roasted duck garnished with steamed carrots and asparagus, a platter of baked salmon on a bed of green leeks, plus a loaf of freshly baked bread and a crock of butter. The cook outdid himself with fare not generally offered to the public in hope of receiving a significant vail. Thomas would not disappoint him.

"Shall we?" he asked Arabella.

"Oh Bolton, I am famished, but I cannot wait until after dinner to learn of what news you received. Was it from Harry? You will not keep me waiting, will you?"

Thomas replaced the glass of wine he just poured himself back on the table. He looked a bit vexed, but then his features relaxed and he replied, "I did not plan to speak of it over our meal, but since it is good news and cannot possibly upset our appetite, I will break with custom and tell you what I know."

"Did Harry find Nathaniel?"

"No, but the good news is Harry is on his way to London to be with your sister. Becca shall not be without his company for long. My man also informed me Harry completed a thorough search of Truro and all the possible locations your brother might have looked for sanctuary and could not find him. Which means the only other option for Nathaniel to seek help is from your grandfather. We will probably learn of Nathaniel's location once we speak with him."

"Papa once said the people of Cadgwith live among the cove's hillside in thatched roof cottages. He always remarked how everyone knew everyone, so grandfather should not be hard to find."

The loud rumble of Arabella's stomach made her eyes widen in embarrassment and Thomas grin. He commanded, "Eat your meal, Miss Barrington. I have no desire to suffer from your temper."

"I would exclaim 'unfair,' Bolton" she responded with a smile, "but I cannot since you witnessed how I am easily riled when hungry, but it is most ungentlemanly of you to remind me."

Thomas noted Arabella's appetite was as healthy as his own. The food was well-prepared and when the innkeeper returned with the same two serving maids, one carrying a plate piled high with peach tarts, and the other carrying a plate of fresh apple slices and cheese, he pulled out a number of coins, including two gold sovereigns. The maids placed the desserts on the table and then quickly cleared away the dinner service and refuse. The innkeeper waved them to exit before Thomas could hand out any vails. The man's eager expectation made Thomas decide to drop only one gold coin into the innkeeper's palm. Thomas offered his compliments and then added, "Rest assured, I shall praise and reward your maids and good cook personally."

The man did not look happy, but made his bow and left, pushing his gold sovereign deep into his pocket.

"I do not think he was pleased you did not trust him to give coin to his cook and maids," opined Arabella.

"It should not matter to him, unless it is his wife who is the cook and he fears she will not hand it over. No matter, the cook, be it he or she, is deserving of their vail, as are the maids, and they shall have it. Have you room for dessert?"

"Indeed, do not think to eat all the tarts on your own!"

Thomas laughed and said, "I would not think of such a thing. Take your fill. For now, I shall enjoy my wine."

Arabella asked, "How do we proceed, Bolton?"

Thomas put his glass down and said, "Yesterday, after I spoke with Hugh, I sent Timothy to journey ahead to Helston. His orders were to reconnoiter Cadgwith and its surrounding area tomorrow morning. He shall return to Helston and meet us at the town's inn to make his report. With luck, we will know the location of your grandfather's cottage. At a minimum he will tell me if the lanes can accommodate our coach. If not, then we will have to ride to Cadgwith, which means I must secure you a riding habit and sidesaddle in Helston. I do not remember if a habit was commissioned for you."

"No. I do not have one, but regardless, Bolton, I do not ride."

"Never?"

"I never learned, Bolton. I can hook up a horse to a cart and drive it, but I never rode a horse to command. Only Nathaniel was offered instruction. It was my father's greatest wish he aspire to the manners of a gentleman."

Arabella eyes began to water and Thomas interjected before her composure broke. "Well, I will consider the matter, Miss Barrington." Thomas saw her remove the small book Fairgrove gifted her from her dress pocket and asked, "Did you enjoy the poetry?"

"I have been thinking the earl did not mean the book for me. After all, Fairgrove did not know we would meet, nor did he have the time to purchase it after we met. However, the spine was unbroken and there were some uncut pages, so it is undoubtedly newly purchased, just not for me. It is not as though I left him with a high opinion of myself. I think the book was intended as a gift for another. What say you, Bolton?"

Thomas kept his lips tight from grinning. Arabella was a smart lady and he had witnessed her analytical mind in action on more than one occasion. He received great amusement watching her facial expressions while she worked out a problem. Every time, her eyes moved about as if she searched the corners of her mind for the answer like she did now.

She scraped her top teeth on her bottom lip until her eyes shot wide from coming up with the answer, causing Thomas to laugh when she remarked, "I think his lady was sorely disappointed he came empty-handed."

Thomas could not help but reply, "I do not think Fairgrove disappointed her. She had greater expectations than a book of poetry."

Arabella looked like she might quibble until understanding dawned. Embarrassed, she dropped her head the moment she felt her cheeks heat. She was sure they were blooming red and she was not about to amuse Bolton further. She waited for the warmth to leave her face before she lifted her head. Her calm reserve was thwarted when Thomas asked, "Has he caught your eye, Miss Barrington?"

The absurd question made her head jerk as if he took a swing at her. Thomas laughed at her shocked expression and inquired, "Is not every lady in need of a husband?"

"Not I, Bolton," she retorted with verve. "If you did not notice by now I am quite capable of taking care of myself. I need no one to govern me. Should I ever marry it will be someone who I have come to love and admire; someone who wishes to partner with me in all things."

"Then, Fairgrove, or I, for that matter would not suit you. I certainly will not marry for love, but above all things, you will be hard-pressed to find a gentleman of title and fortune willing to relent his authority over his wife. I know I shall expect obedience in mine."

"You would be surprised what a gentleman will forego to be with a lady he loves," she replied with conviction.

"You speak from experience, Miss Barrington?"

"No, but I have seen what two people can over-come when they love one another," she replied.

"You speak of your parents?"

"Indeed, but Harry and Becca are a more recent example. Would you not agree?"

Thomas lifted his glass to her winning argument. He could not disagree; especially knowing their siblings love would be tested under the *ton's* scrutiny. Thomas rolled his eyes and prayed for the best. The silence lingered for a moment until Thomas' curiosity pressed him to ask, "Is the reason you are unwed is because you did not find love?"

Arabella looked up at him quizzically, almost as if the thought never crossed her mind. She replied, "I suppose I never had the opportunity to search for it."

"Is love hidden, Miss Barrington?"

Arabella laughed and replied, "I cannot say, but I think like a treasure, love must be discovered, reflected upon, and cherished. The value of a chest full of plunder is not determined by its features, but on how much the plunder is cherished. Each item must be inspected to determine its worth. An uncaring man will not reap the benefits of one who cares."

"You are spouting rhetoric, Miss Barrington," criticized Thomas.

"Not at all, while our poets and playwrights over the centuries base many of their romances on love at first sight, I believe character and a host of other qualities; such as integrity and love of family, determine whether a couple's feelings will be lasting or fleeting. I do not disagree one can be attracted at first sight, but two people need more than handsome features to fall in love."

Thomas did not like where this conversation was going. It was too deep and far from what he wanted to know. He asked again, "You did not answer my question, Miss Barrington. Did you ever find love?"

"You are very persistent, Bolton. Almost to the point of annoyance," Arabella rebutted.

Thomas replied with a lifted brow.

"Very well, no, I did not find love, but there was never an opportunity for me to look for it. My mama fell ill when I came of age and after she passed, keeping my father from falling into a bottomless pit of grief consumed me and my siblings. It is heartbreaking to think the property supposed to uplift us was the root of my father's death and my brother's exile."

Chapter Six

They left Truro at sunrise for Helston. Hugh had recommended the food at the inn and it was the reason Thomas picked it to meet up with Timothy. He planned to let Arabella retire to a room for an hour while he heard Timothy's report.

The white two-storied inn in Helston was smaller than the White Hart Inn, but it offered a private dining parlour which suited Thomas' needs; especially if the fare was as good as Hugh praised. Timothy's report was unexpected. It meant he would have to engage stealth and disguise to smoke out Arabella's grandfather.

The door opened and interrupted Thomas from dispatching Timothy with his duties. This was not the first time someone intruded upon him and he now wished he chose another inn to break his journey. He thought the guinea he gave the publican to secure the room was sufficient to assure his privacy, but by the numerous intrusions, he determined the publican was palming some additional coin to let the locals trespass on his time. He checked his temper at his first intruder, a baron with the audacity to present a proposal needing an investor.

Thomas' reputation as a successful venture financier was well-known, so it was not uncommon for him to be solicited, not only by his peers, but by the local gentry when he traveled. This morning, he was already pressed upon by two unworthy candidates with obvious schemes to make use of his wealth.

He routed them immediately and began to wear his stern expression whenever anyone opened the door to dissuade them from entering. He was ready to browbeat the publican for letting these schemers impose upon him, but since he would be leaving soon he saw no need to cause a ruckus or to post Hugh as gatekeeper to the room.

Thomas was a responsible landowner who took care of his own people. He supported his manor's village with his patronage, and while he offered aid whenever a person he knew suffered unjustly, he did not throw his money around to be spent by others. Another knock piqued his temper. He was ready to rebuke his intruder, until he saw it was Arabella who entered.

"Am I interrupting, Bolton?" she asked.

"Not at all, Miss Barrington," he replied as he stood. He turned his attention to Timothy and ordered, "Collect what I require, then ready the horses for we will leave in half the hour."

"Yes, milord, I will see it done," replied Timothy before he left.

"Are we leaving, Bolton?" asked Arabella, taking Timothy's seat.

"Yes." Thomas looked at Arabella's bleak expression and asked, "Are you unwell, Miss Barrington? Do you need more time to rest before we continue our journey?"

"No, Bolton. I am just anxious. I realized if my grandfather does not know where Nathaniel is we will be hard-pressed to discover him."

"Well," Thomas responded, retaking his seat. "I fear it is worse than your grandfather not knowing Nathaniel's location. At this moment, we do not know where your grandfather lives. According to Timothy, there are no Barringtons residing in Cadgwith Cove."

"Impossible," challenged Arabella. "What can you possibly mean?"

"I mean, Miss Barrington, Timothy rode into Cadgwith and asked the local publican and others where Mr. Barrington lived. No one heard of him or his family. Timothy even tried using the moniker of *squire* you said the villagers called him, but no one acknowledged it. Timothy was thorough. He randomly knocked on a number of cottage doors, but was snubbed from the onset. The residents are not so many they do not know their own, but whatever they know they are not telling a stranger, not even a nice-looking man like Timothy. I fear we must suffer the journey to verify the results."

"I find it hard to believe my grandfather lied about where he settled his family to live. What purpose would it serve?"

"Timothy said there were a couple of excisemen milling around looking for smugglers and might be the reason behind the villagers having closed mouths. Regardless, your wish to dress as a man must be granted for I know you do not have a riding habit and we must ride. The lane to the cove is too narrow and steep for a coach and team.

"Timothy is borrowing a set of clothes from one of the stable lads for you to wear. They will still be large, but it will help disguise your identity. In the future, we will have to rectify your riding deficiency, Miss Barrington. For now, you may ride pillion and since I do not want to draw attention to my consequence, I shall also don serviceable clothes. I have no wish to stand and deliver!"

Astonished at the idea of being robbed, she asked, "Do you really think highwaymen are this far from the king's road?"

"No, but it would not surprise me to have a Free Trader apprehend and remove from my person anything of worth. They may be fishermen by trade, but disguised, they are known to create mischief for their betters. After all, if they find no fault in tricking our government so as not to pay taxes, why would they find fault in absconding from a nobleman's purse."

Arabella did not consider Free Trading immoral because her grandfather and uncles engaged in it, but using it as justification for other ill deeds sat wrong with her. Her frown began to deepen over the injustice of doing harm to a gentleman simply because he was a man of property and wealth. She heard Thomas chuckle and looked at him.

He asked, "Are you defending me in principle, Miss Barrington?"

Arabella grinned and said, "I believe I am, Bolton. Forgive me for my inattention, but it is not fair you suffer simply because you are an aristocrat."

"How very enlightened you are, Miss Barrington, but rest assured I am not one to suffer willingly."

"Oh," replied a wide-eyed Arabella. "Do you mean you will travel armed?"

"Most assuredly," he answered.

"May I as well?" grinned Arabella.

"No."

His abrupt reply turned her lips into a pout. She uncharacteristically whined, "But why? I should be capable enough if you show me how to shoot."

"You are dangerous enough, Miss Barrington," he said with mock sympathy. "Besides, you are under my protection and you may be confident I will not let anything happen to you. Do not forget Timothy and Hugh travel with us and it would be a foolish Free Trader to impose himself on my motley crew."

"Very well, Bolton," she replied disappointedly, adding, "but I shall add it to my list."

"And what list do you speak?"

"The one I am keeping to record all the things I wish for you to teach me."

"And why, I dare ask, am I to be your tutor in all things?"

Arabella grinned and said, "But who else, Bolton, dare I ask?"

Thomas shook his head and commanded. "Go to your room and wait for your clothes. Timothy should not be long and then, meet me out front. I will be there as soon as I change into my own disguise."

Arabella came down the stairs from her room and was bumped at the entrance of the inn by a couple of gentlemen who took no consideration to her person. She almost railed at them until she remembered she was disguised as a stable boy who could not scold his better without being backhanded for his impertinence.

Frightened of her own thoughts, she raced outside to look for Thomas. She knew he was also disguised and would look far from the manner of a lord, but she was sure she would recognize his broad-barreled stallion. The thoroughbred horse would stand out amongst the bays and coach horses congesting the street in front of the inn.

She caught the eyes of a peasant wearing a loose woolen jacket with pants that did nothing to promote his physique. A woolen cap was pulled low over his facial features and a wool muffler was wrapped around his neck. The man watched her and she glared at him until she saw it was Thomas dressed like the locals. She laughed. She did not know him at first glance or the sorrel to which he held the reins. She wondered why he was not riding his stallion.

She started forward, but was pulled to an abrupt stop when a hand grabbed her arm and slapped a pair of leather reins at her. Before she could decline the owner of the horse her service, she found Thomas at her side sternly remarking, "The lad is engaged, release him."

The gentleman took affront and tightened his hold on Arabella's arm. He admonished with all the authority given him as a man of means, "How dare you speak to your betters, thus. I will see you whipped for your impertinence."

Fury pulsed from Thomas and the man instinctively took a step back as if he was snarled by a feral animal, pulling Arabella along in front of him like a shield. Arabella released the horse's reins she still held in her hand and paled from the brewing tension. She did not want to be the cause of Thomas coming to harm. Her obvious fear made Thomas steel his eyes and step forward, forcing the man to step back with Arabella. Thomas matched the man step for step until the crowd at the inn's entrance blocked his escape.

The obvious confrontation was sparking speculation among the men at hand. *What's this? Is it a fisticuff over a stable lad?* Seething, Thomas used a quiet voice so the mischief makers would not encourage a melee for sport, or worse bolster the man's courage to start one. The last thing he wanted was for them to uncover Arabella was a woman in disguise, or for her to get hurt.

In his most threatening voice, he ordered, "Release the lad before I take measures to send you to the bone-setter if not the grave."

"Well, I," gasped the man in a thready voice before releasing Arabella.

"I expect not," returned Thomas turning away from the man while commanding Arabella to follow him.

He fumed, not just about Arabella's manhandling. He was angry he let his emotions overcome him. *Hell's bells! I almost planted a facer on the insolent man, instead of using my wits to bring him to heel.*

This was not the first time his emotions heated to a boiling point over someone pressing their attentions on Arabella. The first time he came to her rescue was when they broke their travel to his manor home to stay at the George Inn. He and his small party, made up of Harry, Rebecca and Arabella, took rooms for the night. He offered to escort Arabella to her room, but she tartly rebutted she could manage on her own, until she was accosted by a gentleman.

The incident was just a prelude to the type of trouble Arabella typically found herself. The offending gentleman, the son of an earl, grabbed her skirt in sport. He tried to pull her close after recognizing her name and the scandal associated with it. She screamed and Thomas raced to her side, pulling back on the assailant's fingers to release her. Lord Elwood, the miscreant, took affront at being injured; especially when he was accused of accosting a lady. Elwood argued Miss Barrington was no lady and in response, Thomas jabbed Elwood's jaw so hard it knocked him to the ground unconscious.

The duel tainting the Barrington name was a recurring *on dit* in Mayfair. The tragedy was recalled with relish over tea and biscuits since it involved the deaths of the dueling gentlemen and the reputation of a lady. It was at that moment, Thomas and Arabella realized the extent to which the Barrington name was sullied.

Like all vicious talk, innuendo regarding a lady's virtue became fact among the gossipmongers. Arabella, more so than Rebecca, was vulnerable to offense because she was unmarried, and had no father or brother to champion her. Rebecca, on the other hand, was well-protected under the Bolton name, if not by Harry himself. However, since Elwood's affront, it seemed Thomas was always at hand to come to Arabella's rescue.

Thomas would argue he acted as behooved a gentleman, but even he knew his particular interest in Arabella was far from gentlemanly. Only a dead man could ignore Arabella's inner and outer qualities and he was not dead. Unfortunately, Arabella was not a lady he could trifle without offering marriage.

He was determined to marry for convenience where emotion did not play into the equation. He did not want to be disappointed again in discovering it was the coronet, not the man loved. Besides, Arabella was not a suitable candidate for a future countess, nor was she likely to be obedient in a marriage. She was provoking and likely to drive him to act foolishly as proven by his desire to throttle the man who grabbed her.

Shivering from her fright, Arabella asked, "Where is your horse, Bolton?"

Ignoring her question, Thomas scolded through clenched teeth, "I thought I made it clear I did not want to attract attention. Nothing wags tongues faster than a peasant riding a nobleman's mount, aside from a melee over a stable lad."

"You are not being fair," she almost sobbed.

Thomas turned and saw her pale face and trembling body. His remorse at being angry at her softened his features and moved him to say, "No, I am not. Are you ready to ride?"

Startled, she asked, "With you?"

"Unless you prefer to ride astride with Timothy or Hugh?" he answered.

He did not allow her time to decide when she blinked in consideration, since he did not want her riding with anyone but him. He quickly lifted her up by the waist and tossed her onto the back of his horse to sit behind his saddle. His abrupt action surprised her into grabbing the leather cantle for purchase, lest she let her momentum toss her over the horse.

Thomas quickly mounted after her and was mindful not to push her off her seat as he settled himself into his saddle. He grabbed her wrists to bring her arms around his waist. The pull slammed her into his backside and drew an "oompf" from her. He grinned at giving her back a little for all the angst she caused him. Without a backward glance, he guided his horse down the street, assured Hugh and Timothy would follow.

They kept to a slow pace through the busy market town, but once they left it behind them, Thomas set his horse to a gallop. There were miles to go before they reached Cadgwith and he wanted to get there and back before night came; especially if they did not find Arabella's grandfather. He did not want to be stranded in a hostile community.

It continued to amaze Thomas how his concern for Arabella's comfort was constant. The moment he heard her groan he immediately began to look for a place to rest. No doubt, Arabella's legs and back were sore from their jarring ride; and most likely, she needed to answer nature's call.

He slowed his sorrel to a walk, before steering his horse to a small shaded area where only clover and leaves covered the ground among a cluster of trees. Those trees concerned him as they shielded any threat from his view, but he saw no other alternative for their stop. He swiftly dismounted and reached up for Arabella who practically fell from her perch into his arms. He held her steady until she gained her legs.

"Thank you, Bolton." Arabella did not wait for his reply, but hurried off to find some privacy among the trees. Thomas watched her go, feeling uneasy and impatient when she left his sight. He tried to see if any threat lurked in the trees and then gave up the effort.

He asked Timothy, "How much further before we leave this forestry?"

"No more than ten minutes and then you will see the coast. We have to descend over rocky ground to reach the cove. There are cottages all over the hill, but the pub and general store are on the flat."

Thomas gave a nod and then sent Hugh to scout the area, reminding him to stay clear of where Arabella went. He did not want him to intrude upon her. He untied the satchel of food the inn's cook prepared for him and then looked for a dry piece of land to sit. Timothy and Hugh brought their own satchels of food and would see to eating when they wished.

He was not the only one feeling as though eyes were upon them for Timothy also searched the surrounding woods. It made no sense to be wary in the light of day when other travelers would be using the road to come and go to Cadgwith. After all, bandits did not work in the light of day, but something was nudging him to be cautious. Perhaps, it was Hugh's tardiness to report back.

He quickly looked in the direction where Arabella went and strode forward. It mattered not if he intruded upon her privacy. Her safety overruled modesty. He called back to Timothy to be watchful, but his warning came too late. His servant's groan made Thomas turn around and draw his concealed pistol on the masked man who knocked Timothy out with a log.

He held his finger from pulling on the trigger when Arabella screeched and yelled, "Ow! There is no need to be so rough. I told you I would come along without force."

Thomas stepped back so he could keep both marauders in his sight. He knew he was at a disadvantage with Arabella held tightly by the second man. The bandit's features were concealed by the brim of his hat pulled low over his forehead and by a neck scarf covering his nose and mouth.

The bandit held Arabella tight with one hand on her arm positioned in front of him, while his other hand held his gun pointed into her side. He grinned and audaciously ordered, "Best drop your weapon. You would not want the young miss hurt."

Thomas asked Arabella, "Are you injured?"

"No, Bolton," she answered, "I am just bloody mad. He hit Hugh on the back of his head with his pistol and knocked him out. Poor Hugh did not even see him. He was too busy helping me with the cord I broke trying to get my pants off."

"What?!" yelled Thomas shocked by her words.

Arabella crimsoned and then yelled back, "I was desperate, Bolton, and did not have the wherewithal to untie the cord holding up my pants. I ended up breaking it. Hugh came upon me later when I was trying to retie the cord together using one hand to hold up my pants and the other to tie the cord. Hugh saw my dilemma and tried to help me when this ruffian hit him on the head. He made me leave Hugh and come with him. I don't know if Hugh's injury is serious and he wouldn't let me tend him!"

Thomas took a settling breath and then appraised his assailants. They looked more than capable of causing harm, especially the broad chested and thick limbed older man who held Arabella. He was not about to risk her being injured for the coin he carried, so he dropped his pistol and remarked, "Would it not have been easier to shout, 'Stand and Deliver'? Why all the dramatics if what you desire is my purse?"

The ruffian holding onto Arabella at gunpoint asked his partner, "Is this the *downy* one who asked all the questions? He sure has a way with words."

"Nope," replied the young marauder who hit Timothy. "The one I knocked out is the one who asked all the questions about the squire and even went around to the cottages looking for someone to squeal."

"Who are you?" demanded Thomas.

"None of your business," replied the ruffian who seemed in charge with all the questions he asked. "What we want to know is who are you and why you want to speak to the squire. No one calls him that but us, not even the excisemen, so start speaking."

"Are you friend or foe of the squire?" asked Thomas.

"What's it to you?" snarled the older man.

"Well, that depends on your answer."

The man began to look uncomfortable as if he erred in his judgment. He looked at his partner and said,

"Leave the bloke at your feet. This gent wants to see the squire. Well, let's see if the squire wants to see him." He pointed his gun at Thomas and told him to walk.

"My horse?" queried Thomas.

"No need. We will walk to where I need to take you." The man pushed Arabella to Thomas, mumbling over why a woman would dress as a man. Thomas took hold of Arabella and moved her away from the side where the ruffian walked.

"I hope Hugh and Timothy will not suffer much," she whispered to Thomas."

"They have seen worse," replied Thomas softly. "Trust me, they will be fine and then they will come to our aid."

"Oh I hope so, Bolton."

Chapter Seven

"Blast!" exclaimed Arabella.

Her curse drew Thomas' attention in time for him to see her pull on the pant leg on which she stepped. She was struggling to keep her pants from falling down. Without the cord to hold them in place she had relegated to folding her expansive waistband accordion style to hoist them off the ground. Thomas saw her dilemma immediately. Her grip could not keep the gathered material from slipping from her grasp.

He quickly came to her aid and unhooked his belt. Under Hugh's watchful gaze, he wrapped and tightened his belt around Arabella's waist under the closed fist of her gathered waistband. With great care, he evened out the material so it pulled the waistband over his belt to lift her pant legs off the ground.

Arabella smiled and thanked him, but before Thomas could reply with a "you're welcome," he was pushed from behind by the man in charge.

"That's good enough," the ruffian said. "Get going. We have a lot to do before sunset and coming upon you only added to our tasks."

Surprised, Thomas asked, "You were not lying in wait for us?"

"Not bloody likely," replied the ruffian. "I would have steered clear of you, but the youngster told me you were snooping around the cove and I can't have you reminding the excisemen why they are here."

"Aside from arresting smugglers, why are they here?"

His abductor replied, "Save your questions for the squire, if he chooses to speak to you,"

"And if he doesn't?"

"Well, then, I suppose you and the miss will be traveling abroad," the man answered smugly.

Thomas noted Arabella's tremor and almost turned to take a swing at the brute for scaring her. His good senses prevailed and he released the fist he clenched, knowing a better time would come. The cluster of trees, shaded the sun so it was difficult to determine in which direction they walked, but as time passed he smelled the sea's salty air. The coastal breeze broke through the trees and swarmed around them. Thomas was expecting to see the panoramic view of blue water when he was called to a stop. It was then he heard the shuffles and neighs of restless animals. He looked about and saw five exmoor ponies tied together to form a train and a young boy, his features hidden by a muffler and cap, seeing to their care.

"All righty, time to cover those eyes," said the man in charge.

Arabella's sudden pallor made Thomas ask in anger, "Why now?"

"Well, not that I have to tell you, but I'm guessing you will mind your manners better if I do. I can't let you see where we are taking you."

Thomas rolled his eyes, wanting to respond, "Obviously," but decided it best to keep quiet.

The man in charge ordered them to close their eyes which were then covered with a piece of cloth tied securely around their head. They were ordered to put their hands behind their back with their wrists together to be constrained with another piece of fabric.

Arabella was hoisted across one pony while Thomas struggled to mount his own ride. Their journey was slow and they swayed like a pendulum without sight or hands to steady themselves. Arabella gasped when she abruptly fell forward. She and Thomas instinctively tightened their thighs against their mounts and leaned back when their ponies carefully stepped down a steep incline. The assault of a harsh sea wind made them drop their chins to protect their faces from the assault.

Gusts of wind assailed them, making their jackets flap and echo like the sails of a ship. They only managed to stay mounted because they rode astride their ponies and were able to use their legs to hold themselves in place. Several times their ponies' hooves slipped against the rock they traversed. Not until they were led out of the wind and on level ground did their fears finally abate.

Thomas was told to dismount his pony and struggled with his hands bound behind him and his eyes covered. He barely straightened and pushed off against his pony with his head when he was grabbed by the arm and led away. His abductor pushed him to the cold hard ground.

Seconds later, Arabella screeched in alarm and joined him. He waited until she settled herself and then he leaned forward and bumped his shoulder against her own to assure her he was close. She quickly inched backward to sit shoulder to shoulder with him. She trembled and Thomas shifted so his bound hands could touch her own. He almost laughed when she tried to untie the strip binding his hands. He meant to comfort her and she rushed forward to initiate an escape.

Slaps reverberated as did the sound of ponies blowing out their noses and stomping their feet. It was a good guess, small barrels and other packages were being tied to the beasts for transport. Curses and grumbles exploded when someone dropped something or ran into someone, until one by one the loaded ponies tromped past them.

The silence was disconcerting. *Are we alone?* Not knowing the answer to his silent question Thomas asked to no one in particular, "Will you remove our blindfolds?"

The leader answered, "Not until the squire gets a look at you. He will decide whether they stay or go."

Thomas asked, "How long before he arrives?"

"Don't know," the man replied.

Thomas checked his oath. He took a cleansing breath and said, "Perhaps, you might offer the lady something to drink and ask if she has to see to her needs?"

"She already saw to her needs," their abductor replied. "I am not untying you, but if you are thirsty I will see what I can do."

"Do you want anything to drink, Miss Barrington?" asked Thomas.

Before Arabella could say "No, thank you," their abductor shouted, "What did you call her?" He came before them and kicked Thomas' foot when he did not answer and demanded, "What did you just call her?"

Thomas replied skeptically, "Miss Barrington."

"Crikey!" The man bent over and pulled Arabella forward.

Arabella cried out in fright.

Thomas instinctively leaned back on his bum and kicked out his legs to save Arabella from being assaulted. His feet made contact with his abductor's shoulders and the brute fell on his backside. Thomas rolled to get on his knees to use his head to push himself up to stand. He was hindered with his hands tied behind his back and his sight covered, but he made a valiant effort to gain his feet. Unfortunately, his abductor rallied faster and pushed him back on his bum. Thomas tried to butt his head against his assailant when the man yelled at his antics.

"Hold your blooming hide. I ain't gonna hurt the squire's *la petite-fille*. I am trying to release her. Why didn't you tell me she was a Barrington?"

Thomas stilled. Arabella gasped. Then he shouted, "Remove my blindfold, now!"

"All right, don't get all huffed up and out of sorts. How was I to know you actually knew the squire?"

The ruffian removed Thomas' blindfold and then Arabella's. She blinked her eyes into focus and then asked, "You know my *grand-père*?"

"Oh, aye and he's gonna peel my backside for manhandling you, though I expect not for your gent. Don't think he will be too happy seeing you with him dressed as a boy and unchaperoned."

"Well, regardless, you must untie him," reprimanded Arabella, "lest he be outraged more. You will have to make your apology to his lordship; else I doubt he will forgive you."

"Lordship, is it? Not sure an apology is gonna cut it. I am thinking I should just take you to your *grand-père* and leave his noble self here before he can get me hung."

Having her hands untied, she turned to Thomas to work on the knot securing his hands. He heard the man step back and she assured him, "He will do no such thing," and to Thomas, she wheedled, "You won't, will you, my lord?"

Thomas almost laughed. The one time Arabella showed him deference and it was to charm him into doing her will. The minx was testing out her wiles on him and while she lacked experience, she performed adequately to turn his anger into amusement. When all was settled, the important thing was they were unharmed and were about to meet her grandfather.

He jumped to his feet once he was untied and helped Arabella to her own. They each took a moment to stretch their limbs and rub their wrists, then Thomas imperiously ordered their abductor to reveal his face and introduce himself.

The man did as ordered; he pushed his hat back and his scarf down over his chin. "They call me Jake."

Arabella asked, "Jake or *Jacques?*"

Jake laughed. *"Tu parles français ?"*

Arabella answered, *"Oui."* And then a conversation in French erupted. Arabella exclaimed how her father and mother spoke to her and her siblings in both English and French so they would learn both languages. Since Thomas was fluent in the language, he did not take offense to their conversing in it.

After the niceties were settled, *Jacques* started a fire within the center of some rounded stones to make their stay more comfortable. He then opened an oak barrel to pull out a fine bottle of burgundy. When Thomas raised an eyebrow, *Jacques* remarked he did not think the vicar who awaited his supply would take offense to honor the squire's daughter.

Jacques continued his hospitality by pulling out a loaf of bread and a block of cheese from a saddlebag gone unnoticed until now. He handed the food over to Thomas with a knife and said, "I will leave you to await the squire while I go check on your friends. I will tell them to go to Helston and wait for you there."

Thomas pulled out a coin from a pocket inside his vest and gave it to *Jacques* who looked it over and saw it was a medallion. He raised his eyebrows in question and Thomas informed, "Give this to my men; otherwise, they might not believe you and assail you with more than questions."

Jacques tossed the coin, pocketed it and said, "They may try, *mon ami*, as many have, but none have bested me yet." He left with a gleam in his eye and chuckling.

Arabella took a swallow from the wine bottle she held in her hand, turned and handed the bottle to Thomas. She said, "I do not think Hugh will turn the cheek and forgive *Jacques* for hitting him from behind even when he sees the coin."

Thomas took his own swig of the wine, grinned and replied, "No, Hugh will want his own piece of flesh and I believe he and *Jacques* are well-matched. Bruises will be earned, but they will survive and most likely end up sharing a pint with each other and Timothy."

"They will wait for us in Helston?" she asked taking the bottle back for another sip. "The coin will satisfy them?"

"Yes," he answered. "Unknown to *Jacques*, I have more than one type of coin to communicate to my men.

The one I gave *Jacques* assures my men they can trust his word."

"*Très bien*," remarked Arabella taking another sip.

"I never heard you speak French Miss Barrington and now it seems you cannot stop."

Arabella eyes gleamed and laughed. "It is because speaking with *Jacques* brought it back and it is slipping out. Growing up *mon mère* and *père* would volley back and forth between the languages and speaking with *Jacques* reminded me of that time." She choked back a sob and explained, "I fear I am feeling a little emotional."

Thomas wrapped his arm around Arabella and brought her close to his side. "You have been through a lot this year, Miss Barrington. It is reasonable you feel sad; especially with your senses dulled with wine. I think you should eat something."

She turned her face towards him and said, "You are right, Bolton."

They looked into each other's eyes and Thomas felt a stirring of emotions. He released his arm around her before he did something unconscionable. Arabella herself looked startled at his abrupt separation and then she smiled.

She confessed, "You are a good man, Bolton, and deserving of an apology."

"For what?" he queried, concerned she guessed of the amorous feelings playing havoc with him.

"For all the terrible names I called you after *Jacques* coshed Hugh on his head. You see, I was sure if you gave me a pistol, I could have turned the table on the ruffian who came upon us. I am very grateful I was not able to do so, for I might have hurt *Jacques* and that would have been unpardonable. He has been most nice to us."

"Nice?" queried Thomas with surprise.

"Yes, 'nice,'" she retorted with a giggle. "Once he knew who I was he has been all hospitable. He made a fire for us, gave us food and drinks and do not forget," her voice escalating in anger, "he went to care for Hugh and Timothy!"

Thomas grinned at her outrage and gave her a mock apology. "Forgive me, Miss Barrington for not acknowledging *Jacques'* finer qualities."

Arabella returned his grin and went to reach for the bottle. Thomas held it away and up high before scolding, "Enough for you, Miss Barrington. I fear you are looking a bit foxed."

"I am more than capable of holding my wine, Bolton," she rebuked. "I am half French and imbibed since I was a baby."

"Well, perhaps you should eat something, Miss Barrington, so you have your wits about you when your grandfather arrives."

"Must you keep calling me Miss Barrington, Bolton? You make it sound like we are acquaintances and not friends." She cooed, "We are friends, are we not, Bolton?"

Her pouting lips made Thomas want to kiss them, but he knew better than to take advantage of an inebriated innocent. She was no experienced widow or doxy looking for some sport. No, anyone who took a liberty with Arabella would marry her. He would see to that resolution himself and that heated thought made him pause. She was not his concern; she was Harry's, and the sooner he remembered the better.

She was too tempting to call "friend," but he did not have the heart to tell her. Instead, he answered, "Yes, Arabella, but nothing more."

His reply surprised not only himself but Arabella. Her astonished expression swiftly changed to mischief and she replied, "What more could there be, Tommy?"

Thomas steeled his eyes at her for being impertinent and then before he could counter her movements she leapt for the bottle, forcing them both to the ground. Arabella laughed first and then Thomas joined in her mirth. There they lay, with her resting across him when a voice resounded, "What is this? Do not tell me our hidey-hole is now being used for trysts?"

Thomas quickly pushed Arabella off of him and scrambled to his feet. Arabella with glassy eyes looked at the man towering over her and then at the bottle she confiscated away from Thomas. Her victory made her giggle. Thomas looked down at her and exclaimed, "Miss Barrington! Mind yourself."

In a flash, Thomas was pushed against the wall of the cave, looking into some very angry eyes. His assailant's arm was pressed against his throat and a gun was pointed at his gut. Regardless, he recognized his attacker and greeted with surprising calm, "You are looking well, *Marquis du Benoît.*"

"You know me?" the marquis asked.

"Yes, we were introduced over a decade ago when I made my bow at St. James Palace. You have not changed much," replied Thomas.

"Good heavens," exclaimed Arabella who rose and ran to Thomas' aid the moment she saw her grandfather attack him. She asked, "Is this true?"

"*Oui,* c'est vrai," he answered while keeping a firm hold of Thomas.

Arabella pulled on her grandfather's unforgiving arm and shouted, "*Grand-père, Laisse-le partir !*"

The marquis looked at Arabella and asked, "*Il t'a violentée ?*"

"No! He did not assault me. I knocked him over trying to get the wine which he refused me because he said I am foxed. The bounder thinks he's my guardian, not *mon amoureux.*"

"*Très bien,*" replied the marquis before he released his hold on Thomas and removed the pistol from Thomas' side. He commanded, "You will make a proper greeting and explain how you are in the company of my granddaughter."

Thomas pushed away from the wall, straightened his clothing and transformed his persona into an arrogant aristocratic lord. He made his bow and informed, "I am Viscount Thomas Bolton, heir to the Earl of Belcrave."

"*Oui*," replied the marquis. "I remember you now. You are as toplofty now as you were then. Now explain how you are in the company of my granddaughter."

"We are looking for Nathaniel and hoped you would give us direction. Miss Barrington, on behalf of her sister, needs to ask Nathaniel some questions. I was not entrusted to ask them, so I was required to bring your granddaughter."

"I like how you speak of Arabella as being more burden than benefit. There is no need for me to kill you then, *n'est-ce pas* ?"

"I might strangle you, *grand-père*, if you do not explain to me this title of yours which none of your grand-children have knowledge. Did papa know?"

"Of course he knew. We did not emigrate until your father came of age and it is a long story that can wait another time. All you need to know is it is only a title and nothing more. Anything of significance was lost in the revolution. Now, explain yourself?"

"Do you know where Nathaniel is? I desperately need to speak with him."

"You cannot tell me why?"

"No," Arabella replied. "But it is of great importance to Rebecca's happiness."

The marquis frowned with worry and asked, "Where is your sister?"

"She is in London," replied Arabella. "Do you not know she is married and facing the *ton's* censure?"

"I have been busy trying to protect your brother, but I was assured before I left to take Nathaniel to France that you and Rebecca were well and living on the farm."

"Well, Rebecca is being judged poorly because of the duel that took papa's life. She married Bolton's brother Harry and their parents, the Earl and Countess of Belcrave are hosting a ball in Rebecca's honor. Rebecca is afraid she will be *cut* and thereby dishonor her husband and family."

"*Impossible !*" he exclaimed. "She is of noble blood."

"Well, she does not know it, nor does the *ton!*" she argued back.

"When is this ball?" he demanded.

Arabella looked to Thomas for the answer. He informed, "In four days."

The marquis announced, "I shall leave immediately to rectify this injustice regarding her suitability."

Arabella whined, "But what about Nathaniel?"

"I will ensure he knows you await him. He ships in tonight and then you may ask your questions."

Arabella begged, "But what of my questions for you?"

The marquis cupped Arabella's cheek with his hand and said, "They will keep, *ma petite-fille*." Then he kissed her forehead and left.

Thomas called out to him, "I suggest you wear your ceremonial attire if you still have it."

The marquis laughed.

Chapter Eight

Arabella looked at Thomas like a sulking puppy and confessed, "I have too many questions, Bolton. Why would papa lie about living in Cadgwith? Is our name even Barrington? Good heavens! Are we illegitimate?"

Before Thomas could respond, Arabella raced towards the cave's opening. Thomas caught her before she escaped and asked, "Where are you going?"

She gasped, "I need air, Bolton. I can't breathe."

Thomas walked her outside and the frigid wind immediately made their eyes sting, their hair fly about their heads, and their bodies shiver. The sky was covered with raging grey clouds, foreshadowing the coming rain.

He turned her around and said, "Come, I think you deserve that bottle of wine I took from you. It will settle your emotions and warm you."

When Arabella looked like she might argue with him, he counseled, "Do not speculate, especially on scenarios out of character for your father. You told me yourself he loved your mother and was a man of faith. I doubt a man with such values could deceive a lady he loved."

Arabella wrapped her arms around Thomas' waist and hugged him for pointing out her father's stellar characteristics. *Of course, he would not deceive his family.* She was so happy and enjoying Thomas' warmth it took her more than a moment to notice how his body grew taut. She quickly released him and almost chuckled at how her hug discomfited him.

With a grin, she admonished, "Bolton, is every lady who shows an iota of affection for you suspect? Did we not agree to be friends?"

Thomas relaxed and replied, "Yes, we did agree." He also remembered the reason why they could not be more than friends. An affair was out of the question since Arabella was a lady. A dalliance with an innocent required marriage and he was determined not to risk his heart again. He would only marry for convenience. He was learning very quickly Arabella was not convenient.

She vexed him as often as she amused him and while he was glad his brother Harry found love with Rebecca, he was not inclined to be at its mercy. He suffered the first time he was hit with cupid's arrow and never wanted to suffer the disappointment again.

Though in all honesty, his accelerated heartbeat whenever he drew close to Arabella gave evidence he was not immune to her. In those moments, he had to remind himself, as Harry's sister-by-marriage, she deserved his utmost respect. His clever intellect could persuade him differently, so the sooner he returned her to London and his brother the better.

He walked Arabella back inside the cave to their fire and left her to keep her own counsel while he considered how to see to their immediate needs. Leaving the cave was not an option since he doubted he could find it again. It was not called a hidey-hole because its location was easily spied. Besides, he did not know if a town was nearby to offer shelter, nor did he know in which way to travel to find the town. The last thing he needed was to get lost and caught in the rain with Arabella. Then, there was the question whether Nathaniel would wait for them to return.

The only clear option was to stay put and make Arabella as comfortable as he was able. He left her to take comfort in the wine. He took one of the lit lanterns *Jacques* left behind and ventured deeper into the cave to see if there were any hidden provisions. There were multiple cavities and he soon found a store of blankets, two lanterns, some dried fruits and meats.

He quickly gathered the items, stacking the blankets and placing what he could manage of the other items on the very top. He carried the heavy load, using the lit lantern to light his way. The awkwardness of his bulk made his lantern sway and cast shadows on the cave's walls, making it difficult to watch his step. By the time he reached Arabella he was glad to see her rise and grasp some of the items ready to fall from their perch.

The pattering rain reminded him how the cave would turn into an ice box if their fire diminished. He needed to feed it through the night with the dry wood stacked nearby and endure the night with little sleep to see to the task. Arabella's shiver, as if she was poked in the back, prompted him to drop his load and wrap her in one of the blankets.

She thanked him and then asked, "Will the rain keep Nathaniel from coming ashore?"

"Honestly," Thomas replied, "I do not know." She looked like she might cry, so he offered his most charming smile and said, "There are many who say they prefer my company over all others. Let us see if you agree, shall we? I have more blankets for us to get comfortable and bits of food to keep our hunger at bay."

Arabella returned his smile, grateful to him for trying to distract her from her worries. He was so full of consideration she eagerly agreed, "Yes, let us get comfortable, Bolton."

Thomas steeled his eyes at her double entendre and Arabella laughed, "Oh, my! Bolton, why must you look like I just compromised you? I know very well you are out of my league and even if you were not, I know you are too haughty and proud to think a stubborn, willful lady a suitable candidate for wife. However, I think you enjoy my company and don't raise your brows at me. I am not afraid to admit I like you, too. At least I do when you are relaxed and amiable. Can we just agree how sometimes we get on quite magnificently?"

Arabella bit her bottom lip and turned her attention to the fire, lest she break out into laughter again from leaving Thomas mute. She doubted the viscount ever associated with a lady as direct as herself. Even so, it would not surprise her if lightning struck her for the falsehood she told. Truthfully, she liked Bolton even when he wasn't relaxed and amiable. There wasn't anything she really didn't like about him, except when he tried to tell her what to do.

Who would not be attracted to him? He was handsome, titled, rich, fearless, strong, and capable, but even with all those stellar traits, it was how he made her feel that drew her to him. Her heart fluttered and her toes curled; especially when he drew close enough to suggest he would kiss her.

Just once, she wished he would press his lips to hers. Then, maybe her curiosity would be satisfied, *but what if I liked it?* Sober reasoning quickly burst any castles she was building in the air. She knew better than to reach above her station. A lord of Bolton's caliber would never offer for someone like herself, so it was better to be a friend than the pitiful lady who dared to admire him.

Her thoughts kept her quiet and gazing at the fire until Thomas dropped another blanket onto her lap, and said, "You look like you are ready to fall asleep. Why not stretch out and nap? I will wake you when Nathaniel arrives."

Thomas watched the fire and was ready to throw another log onto it whenever the flames waned. He was diligent in his duty and only took his focus away from the flickering fire when Arabella dislodged her blanket. More than once, he rose to tuck her back under her cover. Her peaceful features were a contrast to how she looked when she had made her bold speech before she fell into slumber.

She had been full of vigor and spirit in her profession and then, when he suggested she take a nap, she blinked and stretched out like a feline on the extra blanket he had given her. Between her weariness and the amount of wine she consumed she was asleep within minutes.

Her honesty never ceased to surprise him. She said nothing he would not have said regarding her ineligibility, yet he did not like hearing her discredit herself. Nor did he like seeing her aggrieved, so he kept vigil over her to make sure she was warm and safe during the night.

He gathered more wood from the side of the cave when he could no longer keep awake. He added a log to the fire and then placed the remaining pieces at a proper distance from Arabella where he would bunk down for the night. He did not want to leave his bed once he generated a modicum of heat in his blanket. He positioned himself to face Arabella as he stretched out on the hard and frigid floor. His teeth were ready to rattle and with no other recourse to get warmer he focused on the pattering rain rather than his discomfort. Whether from weariness or the lulling rain, he fell asleep until he was pricked awake.

He opened his eyes and brought his hand to his throat. He felt the knife and panicked before the sight of a person at his side registered. Before he could speak, the attacker asked, "Explain why the lady sleeps by your side with her leg upon your person?"

Thomas did not even have to guess the body snuggled by his side was Arabella's. She had rolled over to him during the night in either fright or cold. He replied glibly, "Do I have the pleasure of meeting the lady's brother Nathaniel?"

"Never mind me," Nathaniel replied angrily. "Who are you?"

"Viscount Bolton, Did your grandfather not send word how your sister and I await you?" he countered.

Nathaniel removed his knife from Bolton's throat and told the viscount to move away from his sister. Then, he explained, "I did not wait for dark. The rain was enough coverage for me to come ashore. I did not want to take the chance the weather would worsen and keep me aboard, so I came directly here for shelter knowing I could intercept anyone who came to collect me. Since I have satisfied your curiosity, explain yourself and preferably before Bella wakes and gets all sentimental about seeing me."

"You would be proud of how strong she has been since your father's passing," he mused with a grin.

"Start with how you know my sister?" Nathaniel queried.

"My brother Harry married Becca shortly after the duel. To hear Harry tell it, he fell in love with her at first sight."

"And my sister? Did Becca love your brother at first sight?"

Thomas replied, "Well, I cannot say what she felt when she married him, aside from gratitude for having him come to her and her sister's rescue, but since I have known them, I am hard-pressed to refute Becca and Harry love one another."

Shaking his head as if to remove the cobwebs clouding his mind, Nathaniel confessed, "I never thought she would ever find happiness with a man after what Damburten did to her."

Thomas queried, "And what did he do to her?"

"It is not for him to know, Nathaniel," interjected Arabella harshly. "Those answers are for Becca and I will not have you tell him what she herself does not know."

Astonished, Nathaniel asked, "What do you mean?"

Thomas excused himself and took a lamp to go to the back of the cave when Arabella hushed her brother and steeled her angry eyes at him. He left without being asked and the moment he was out of sight, Arabella rose and threw herself at her brother. She began to cry and Nathaniel was *non plus* on what to do. He hugged her and offered soft words of assurance until she began to hiccup and calm down.

Nathaniel soothed, "It's alright Bella, I am well, but tell me what you mean Becca does not know what happened to her?"

Arabella's mouth gaped and then she closed it in frustration before explaining, "Nathaniel, you brought me Becca unconscious, bloodied and bruised. Her clothes were ripped and soiled with dirt. Your only explanation was Damburten assaulted her and I needed to care for her while you and papa sought satisfaction. You did not explain the extent of Damburten's assault and Becca did not know. Did Damburten take her innocence?"

"He did not have the opportunity since I came upon him before he could." It took him a moment to understand his sister's distress and asked, "Are you telling me Becca thought she lost her virtue?"

"Yes," replied Arabella, "and the secret is making her sick with guilt; especially since she is *enceinte* and does not know if the baby is Harry's."

"But how could she not know?"

"Nathaniel," she replied with frustration, "she was unconscious and had no knowledge of such matters. How could she know?"

"Hell and damnation!" he cussed. "I am so bloody glad I removed that filth of a man from this earth." Nathaniel dropped his head and sobbed.

Arabella wrapped her arms around him and soothed, "Nothing is your fault, Nathaniel. Damburten deserved to die. I am only sorry it was by your hand, for the cost of his death took you and papa away from us."

"He shot papa, Bella. Damburten turned before he took the required dueling steps and shot our father at close range in the back. Papa never had a chance. I don't even remember running and picking up his gun to shoot Damburten, but I know I did it. I heard later he died."

"You did not know whether you killed him or not?"

"No, I shot him and then ran. Once I calmed down, I went and searched for a carter. I watched from afar and followed the wagon to make sure papa made it home. I even saw you when you came out to receive him. I wanted to come to you, but I was afraid to bring more trouble to your door. Afterwards, I didn't even know where to go or what to do. I slept in a field that night and dreamt of papa and the time our *grand-père* came to visit us in Truro. I thought it was a sign and left to ask him to help me."

"May I join you now," called out Thomas. "I expect you have more questions for your brother, but I would like to enjoy the fire and blankets with you." Thomas' voice grew louder as he approached and Arabella retorted, "You seem to do as you wish, Bolton."

"Bella," chastised Nathaniel. "I expect the viscount did you a great service and does not appreciate your sarcasm."

"Indeed," laughed Thomas before saying, "but Barrington her sarcasm is the least of my troubles with her."

Nathaniel laughed, grabbed the wine bottle and offered it to Thomas. "I shall change my wet clothes and then join you. We shall share whatever there is to eat and continue our conversation, *oui*?"

Thomas offered the wine to Arabella and she gave him a look that brooked understanding. She asked, "You heard our conversation?"

"Yes," he replied. "Your voices echoed and neither of you spoke softly. I thought it best to come forward before anything else you wanted to keep secret was revealed."

"You did not think to alert us sooner?"

Thomas grinned, "It was to my disadvantage to do so, besides, I did not want to interrupt or stifle a conversation that needed to be held at that moment."

He took the bottle from Arabella, drank from it, and lapped up the liquid left on his bottom lip, before saying, "Miss Barrington, I wish you and your sister entrusted me with your worries. I could have told you Harry did not doubt the baby's parentage. Becca might be naïve, but I assure you Harry is not. He knows the baby is his own."

"She needs to hear it from Nathaniel, Bolton, or else she will think Harry is being kind."

Nathaniel returned and having heard his sister, said, "Then, she will know by my hand. I will write to her and mail it to her post haste."

"Oh Nathaniel," cried Arabella. "She needs to know sooner. I fear her guilt may make her do something reckless."

"Write your letter, Barrington, and then tell me if there are horses nearby to get us to Helston. I have a rider there I can send off to deliver the letter to Becca in London. Once we see him off we can follow in my carriage."

"London," exclaimed Arabella. "No, Bolton, it is too dangerous!"

"I think not," Thomas assured. "Your brother's position is now elevated by his connection to the marquis and thereby grants him certain considerations. He will not be thrown in jail without a warrant and since there is none, nor is there a new baron acceding Damburten, I believe he is safe from prosecution for now. For those same reasons, I am beginning to believe the baron might not be dead. There was no news of his burial and none regarding his heir, who surely would be made known by now. While the *ton* will accept Barrington's guilt for a crime because he is not titled, I will not. Rest assured, the truth will be known."

"I shot him," reminded Nathaniel. "I saw blood."

"Yes," agreed Thomas, "but did you kill him? Remember, you were distressed and perhaps your mind saw more than your eyes. Did you check his pulse? Did the doctor say he was dead?"

Nathaniel replied, "I ran. I do not know what transpired after I left. The field was empty when I brought the carter to collect my father. I was angered they left him alone as if he was unworthy of any regard. Later, I was glad there was no one to stop us from collecting him or to arrest me."

"I shall visit the good doctor brought to the duel when we return to London and find out," offered Thomas. "I will see Damburten's corpse or have the doctor put before the magistrate for interfering with a murder investigation."

"Is it possible Bolton?" asked Nathaniel, "Might I put this sordid mess behind me. I wish the villain dead, but I would rather have him hung than gone by my hand. I do not like being exiled from my sisters."

"Nor do we like having you gone," cried Arabella who once again threw herself against her brother and sobbed into his chest.

Nathaniel patted her back and rolled his eyes. He said to Thomas, "This outburst is so unlike her, Bolton."

Thomas replied soberly, "She carried the burden of caring for Becca and the farm. She is in need of someone to shoulder her worries and to care for her. Allow her to release her pent-up emotions. She has withheld them for too long."

"You have much sympathy for my sister, Bolton. I hope you did not trespass on her weakened state? Should I have cut your throat when I had the chance?"

Thomas answered heatedly, "Have you become bloodthirsty, Barrington?"

Embarrassed, but not deterred, Nathaniel replied with equal anger, "I do not enjoy violence, but I am not afraid to protect what is mine. Do I need to call you out?"

"Only a fool would answer honestly, Barrington, or a gentleman with honor for which I am. Sheath your claws. I would never jeopardize your sister's good name or harm her."

Arabella's eyes grew wide and she dropped her mouth in concern watching her brother and Thomas engage in a battle of words. Before a fight ensued, she pushed herself away from Nathaniel and ordered, "Desist brother! You need have no fear for my good name. Bolton does not see me in any other light than as Harry's sister-by-marriage. He has higher aspirations than to develop a tendre for a lady with nothing to recommend her than a marquis for a grandfather." She blushed at how her emotional outrage revealed her hurt. She mumbled before she began to sob again, "Excuse me; I have to ...oh, never mind." She began to march towards the cave's entrance when she was halted by Nathaniel's words, "There is a chamber pot in the back of the cave for you to use, Bella."

Embarrassed to have her intentions publicized, she turned and angrily emoted, "And have the sound reverberate, no, thank you!"

Nathaniel retorted with a refrained chuckle, "But, Bella, it is raining outside!"

Arabella pressed her lips together, turned around and marched to the back of the cave. She prayed her brother and Thomas would give her the consideration of talking loudly or banging something about to give her some privacy.

Chapter Nine

Arabella returned to find Thomas and Nathaniel chuckling and when she asked what was funny they waved her off like a gnat. She was not amused, but before she could summon up a smarting response, Nathaniel pleaded, "It's late Bella and I am tired."

Contrite, she picked up one of her blankets and handed it to Nathaniel. Her brother took it and quickly tumbled over to the ground from his sitting position and fell asleep.

Thomas remarked, "Your brother is used to getting rest when the opportunity arises. I expect he had a difficult time these last months."

Arabella frowned and then nodded. She took her blanket and wrapped herself up like a cocoon and placed herself to lie down between her brother and Thomas. The dirt floor was hard and icy cold, more so, from the frigid weather quickly turning their cave into an icebox. They all shivered and endured the discomfort until exhaustion pulled them into a fitful and miserable sleep. They were too civilized to gather close to draw warmth from one another, except in their sleep. On more than one occasion, Thomas woke to Arabella snuggling into his side, much like a newborn puppy seeking its mother's warmth.

He was glad when the glow of dawn lit the sky, else the two of them might have circled the fire as they did their dance of escape and find. No sooner did Thomas move away from Arabella and settle into sleep than he was nudged awake and had to disentangle himself again from her attachment.

The fire was long extinguished by the time Thomas woke. The brutal cold brought him quickly to his feet. It made no sense to start another fire when they were leaving, so he slapped his arms and stomped his feet to warm his stiff and shivering body. He made enough noise to wake Nathaniel and Arabella.

The siblings soon joined his antics to get warm. Arabella was the first to admit she needed the cave's facilities and blushed when she demanded the men chant a ditty loud enough to mask the sound. Her obvious discomfiture brought assurances from Thomas and Nathaniel, rather than a tease. They informed she would have her privacy as they would leave the cave to answer their own call to nature.

The men returned and immediately set to distributing their dried goods to break their fast. The fare was sparse, but they were too cold to care. They ate quickly wasting no time with speech. They made sure to leave the cave as they found it. They covered the remains of their fire with sand, disposed of their waste, and returned the blankets, lanterns, and other items they took from the cave's storeroom.

Thankfully, the rain stopped and they only needed to deal with its aftermath of soggy ground and chilly air. Nathaniel was used to the stealth engaged by a smuggler and took great care to cover their tracks around the cave's opening, before leading them back to civilization. In less than an hour, they made their way over some rocky terrain and trekked through a cluster of woods leading to a pair of horses tied to a tree branch.

Nathaniel informed his party how *Jacques* left the horses for them, but Thomas recognized his sorrel. He quickly informed Nathaniel how *Jacques* simply returned the horse he took from him, lest Arabella praise their abductor for his kindness again. Nathaniel laughed.

Thomas almost guided Arabella to his horse, but left her to her brother's care when his better senses prevailed. Instead, he watched Nathaniel hoist her up to ride pillion. Satisfied, she was secure in her seat, he quickly sat his own horse. He waited for Nathaniel to mount in front of Arabella; then heeled his horse to follow Nathaniel's lead to Helston.

They rode in tandem until they reached the main road to the market town and then both men pressed their horses to gallop. Thomas stayed slightly behind and to the side of Nathaniel's horse, ready to catch Arabella should she tumble from her perch.

He didn't know how or when watching out for Arabella became his concern. He was not a fool to believe it was all done because he promised Harry to watch over the Barrington sisters. He had not thought of Harry since his brother left for London and if a promise was not the reason driving him to care for Arabella, then he was in serious trouble. He did not want a relationship founded on feelings that made him vulnerable to heartache. Unfortunately, he was pretty sure there was a beehive of feelings swarming, just waiting to be let out if he was not careful.

He determined long ago it was better to marry a lady knowing all she loved about him was his title and wealth, than to open his heart to discover it was all in vain. Even so, he would not deny he admired Arabella and wanted to see her happy; especially since he was in a position to help her. He planned to exonerate Nathaniel from the murder charge of Damburten and then, find Arabella a suitable husband. He was sure once he saw her settled he would be free of his overwhelming desire to watch over her.

They arrived in Helston and found Hugh and Timothy waiting for them at the same inn they had patronized the day before. Hugh sported a bruise on his chin, excessively proud he gave better than he had got. Thomas greeted his men, but did not let too much time pass before he handed Nathaniel's letter to Timothy with instructions to ride with great speed to London and give it to the *Marquis du Benoît*.

Thomas was sure Timothy would find the marquis at Carlton House, but if not, then he was instructed to proceed to Belcrave House and give the letter to Harry's wife. The letter was not to leave his hand aside to give it to one of those two recipients. Timothy assured his master he understood. Thomas inquired if he knew which inns provided the fresh mounts he kept for his couriers and when Timothy acknowledged he did, he turned to leave.

"Timothy," Thomas called after him. "You have less than three days."

Timothy tipped his wool cap and ran out of the inn. Thomas looked at Hugh and said, "Make ready the coach for travel, but first bring our bags in so we can change our clothes. Make sure there are hot bricks for Miss Barrington and ask the cook for a luncheon basket to take with us."

Both Nathaniel and Arabella stood silent, awed by the self-assured and decisive manner of Thomas. His lordly stature emerged immediately upon dismounting his horse and even the coarse woolen handmade clothes he wore could not disguise his nobility. Thomas looked at them and said, "Give me a moment to secure two rooms for our use and then you may go up, see to your needs and change. Hugh will bring up our bags." To Nathaniel he said, "You will have to wait until London before you are able to change. I do not think my clothes will fit you."

Nathaniel grinned, "You are too kind to worry about something insignificant, Bolton."

"Not so insignificant. You will have to bed down with Hugh in the stables when we stop for the night. Your sister travels incognito as my married sister, but without a better suit of clothes, you are delegated to sleep in the stable. Too many brows would be raised for me to get you a room. I already ran into one peer who imposed upon my privacy during this trip and until I investigate into what happened to Damburten, I do not want to bring undue attention to you."

"I wondered how you protected my sister's reputation from ruin," responded Nathaniel. "You continue to surprise me, Bolton."

Thomas ignored the backhanded compliment and asked, "What of the horse you rode? Is there someone you trust to return him to Cadgwith?"

"Someone will collect him from the stable not far from here. Even *Jacques'* little band has protocol. I will see to it, while you tend to your tasks."

"Well done, Nathaniel, we will meet in the private dining room after Arabella and I change our clothes."

Both Thomas and Nathaniel were seated when Arabella entered the private parlour after seeing to her ablutions and dressing. Her face glistened and her rich brown hair styled in a simple coif shone after being brushed thoroughly. She was dressed in a sapphire blue traveling ensemble that accentuated her striking figure.

Her eyes lit up and her lips broke into a wide smile when her brother and Thomas rose to greet her with clear admiration. She almost laughed at Nathaniel gawking at her. It was as if he never thought of her as a woman. The notion made her blush right when he complimented, "Bella, my goodness, you are amazingly pretty!"

"Thank you, brother," she replied, thinking her new wardrobe was the reason why he thought her so transformed. She explained, "You may thank Bolton for my new clothes. It was through his beneficence I came by them."

Thomas coughed and almost choked. Arabella made it sound like he was her protector and before he could explain himself Nathaniel laughed. He said, "I do not think my sister thought through her words before she said them."

Arabella looked at her brother, then at Thomas and when comprehension came, she crimsoned in embarrassment. Nathaniel laughed at her discomfiture and told his sister to sit down and eat. Arabella regained her composure by focusing on the questions she wanted to ask her brother, but before she could address one, Thomas announced they would leave as soon as she broke her fast.

He explained he did not want his team of horses to stand idle too long. Even more importantly, he wanted to take advantage of the daylight. He added for Arabella's benefit how there would be plenty of time for discourse in the carriage to pass the time. Arabella begrudgingly accepted the edict and turned to complete her meal with great haste.

Hugh tied down the bags on top of the coach and then settled himself on the driver's boxed seat. Nathaniel helped Arabella alight into the carriage and then to her surprise, he shut the carriage door without entering. She quickly lowered the pane window and complained, "I thought to finally have discourse with you and ask all my pressing questions."

"Later Bella," he replied. "I will ride until we get out of this town. I don't want my horse to be spooked being tied to the back of the carriage as we maneuver through the crowded streets."

Arabella pouted, pulled up the carriage window and sat back in her seat. She watched her brother mount and maneuver his horse over to where Thomas sat upon his own horse and wondered what they said.

Thomas, with all the arrogance his nobility allowed, looked down his nose at Nathanial to inquire, "There will be no hue and cry to the taking of this horse you ride, I hope?"

Nathaniel grinned and replied, "He is mine, Bolton, a gift from my father after he purchased the farm."

"Purchased?" asked a stunned Thomas. "Your sisters are under the impression it was an inheritance from a relative. Could there be more behind Damburtan's anger towards your family?"

"No doubt," replied Nathaniel. "I believe the farm was lost in a card game and Damburten's father, the baron at the time, was much displeased with his son. The locals often gossiped how the baron had a heavy hand in the raising of his son. I expect, Damburten suffered terribly for losing the property."

Nathaniel took a breath to settle the raging emotions that surfaced whenever he thought of Damburten. He continued, "I know more now than my sisters regarding our family history. It was not right for my parents to keep the knowledge from us, but I understand why they did it. Even *mon grand-père* at the time thought it wise to separate his name and his questionable activities from *mon père*; especially when he left Cadgwith to secure a different employment and life."

"You are generous in calling Free Trading questionable, Barrington," retorted Thomas sarcastically.

"His intentions were honorable, Bolton," he replied.

Nathaniel and Thomas heeled their horses forward to keep from blocking the traffic and their coach. Once they distanced themselves, so as not to be rundown by their coach, they slowed their horses to a walk to continue their speech. Thomas asked, "How were your father's intentions honorable?"

Nathaniel grinned at the viscount's curiosity and replied, "Bella would have my hide if I was to tell you first that which she is aching to learn of our family. You will have to wait, Bolton, and join the two of us in the carriage if you want to hear what I have to say."

Thomas gave a nod and heeled his horse into a canter the moment the traffic, from all of the carts and carriages either bringing goods to the market town or people to shop, were behind them. Nathaniel raced after him and soon their coach slapped its team of cattle into a faster gait to follow. Once they were a distance from the city and the road was clear, Thomas signaled Hugh to stop the coach. He and Nathaniel dismounted and brought their horses to the back of the coach to tie them up before entering it.

They took the back-facing seat and while they situated themselves, Arabella shifted to the center of her bench to place her knees between both men to be free of touching them. Nathaniel lost no time to be at ease. He unbuttoned his wool coat and rested his head with eyes closed against the seat's back, while Thomas watched in amusement at Nathaniel's easy manner.

They all jostled when the coach started and rolled forward. Thomas and Arabella waited for Nathaniel to speak which he did in the way of a prompt.

"Ask your questions, Bella"

Her cheeks blushed from her indiscreet thoughts and with embarrassment, asked, "Are we illegitimate, Nathaniel?"

Nathaniel quickly came forward in his seat with a succession of coughs. When it looked like Arabella was going to jump to his rescue he halted her with his open hand. "I am fine, Bella," he rasped, clearing his throat. "You just surprised me."

"Well," she pushed. "Do not make me ask you, again."

"I beg your pardon, Bella," responded Nathaniel. "It is just of all the questions for you to ask that one never occurred to me. For heaven's sake, why would you think so?"

In an emotional outburst, she exclaimed, "Our last name is Barrington and since our *grand-père* is a *du Benoît* it seems obvious to me why I would ask!"

"Well," drawled Nathaniel. "I suppose, but you may rest at ease. Our father changed his name legally before he married our mama thinking it would make our maternal grandfather think more kindly of him. According to our *grand-père*, the viscount loathed the French aristocracy for invading his country with nothing to recommend themselves but a title. He felt they were too arrogant and demanding, expecting the English nobility to host them as their equals. Our father thought presenting himself as an Englishman would eliminate one of the prejudices mama's father held against him."

Surprised, Arabella asked, "Mama's father was a viscount?"

"Yes, and before you ask why we did not know I will tell you. That blackguard disowned our mama when she married our father."

"I do not understand how anyone could take offense against papa or how anyone could disown our mama."

Nathaniel patted Arabella's knee to comfort her and said, "The aristocracy do not like to see their bloodlines tainted. They take great measures to contract mutually benefitting marriages."

Thomas could not disagree with Nathaniel's understanding, but he saw no point digressing into it. He said to return them to the topic at hand, "We could not find a Barrington cottage in Cadgwith."

"True," replied Nathaniel. "There is only one person who knows the connection of *du Benoît* with Barrington."

"His name is not *Jacques,* is it?" asked Thomas.

Nathaniel laughed, "You met *Jacques?*"

"Yes," replied Thomas, "but I did not mean to interrupt you, continue with your history."

Nathaniel responded with a smile, "I expect there is a tale behind your meeting with *Jacques* I shall be interested to hear." He took a moment to remember where he was in his story and then began. "As you can imagine I had many questions for *grand-père* when I discovered he was not a fisherman. Through our discourse, I learned of his nocturnal activities. Now I knew he participated in Free Trading, but I did not know he ran his own smuggling operation.

For that reason, he approved of our father changing his name legally, so as to separate him from being accused of smuggling through association. Father was eight and ten when he emigrated and had a more academic and theological mind than his brothers. He was close to our *grand-mère* who was devout in her faith. *Grand-père* told me he was glad his wife did not live to see the reign of terror they were forced to escape for she abhorred violence."

Thomas inquired, "You said *du Benoît's* intentions for his illegal activities were honorable, how?"

Arabella would have scolded Thomas for intruding upon her conversation with her brother, if she was not also interested in Nathaniel's answer. She held her tongue and listened attentively while her brother answered Thomas' question.

"Our father," began Nathaniel, "led us to believe our *grand-père* and *l'oncles* were fishermen who occasionally participated in the Free Trading activities rampant along the Cornwall coastline where numerous inlets, coves, and caves are used for smuggling. *Grand-père* might have continued the ruse with me if I did not wake in the middle of the night and find myself alone in the cottage. I ventured out and came upon a young boy who frantically explained how the men in the village were on the beach fighting the pirates. That in itself is another story."

Arabella began to press him and Nathaniel explained, "Bella, there is too much to tell and if I continue to veer off into story after story, your most pressing questions will never be answered. I was away from you for months. I cannot share what transpired in all that time in one breath."

"I am very sorry, Nathaniel," apologized Arabella. "Please continue. I will keep silent until you are done."

Nathaniel regrouped his thoughts and began, "*Grand-père* left France when the riots began. He spent most of his time in the country, but traveled to Paris on occasion to keep abreast of the politics. What he saw alarmed him. While he did not foresee the travesties to come, he did see enough to want to move his sons to safety. It was while he was there he came upon a young English aristocrat who was either abandoned or separated from his tutor. *Grand-père* saw the danger the nobleman was in and brought him home, not knowing at the time what he was to do with him. I think meeting him is what propelled *grand-père* to immigrate to England. He knew he had to see to the young man's safety having learnt of his identity and he would not leave his own sons behind to do it."

"Who was he?" asked Arabella in an excited voice.

"He was the Queen's godson making his grand tour with no clue to the mood of the country he entered. Either his tutor was a coward or somehow became a casualty of the riots."

"He never learned what happened to him?" asked Arabella.

"No," replied Nathaniel.

Thomas interjected, "He would be a fool to come forward if he was alive, Miss Barrington. He would suffer greatly for abandoning the Queen's godson."

"Oh!" she exclaimed.

Nathaniel continued, "*Grand-père* settled among his loyal servants as best he could, but kept his intentions from his serfs for he did not know if the hostility he witnessed in Paris had spread to his own lands. He only brought *Jacques* and his father with him to immigrate to England. However, by the time they reached Calais, the docks were swarming with aristocrats looking for passage. *Grand-père* was not the only nobleman concerned with what was transpiring in Paris."

"What did *grand-père* do? It is obvious he found passage, but how?" asked Arabella.

"Well," continued Nathaniel. "*Grand-père* is a decisive man and the moment he returned home from Paris his mind was made up. He sent *Jacques'* father ahead to purchase tickets in Calais for passage on a ship to England while *grand-père* settled his affairs and gathered whatever assets he could bring. He thought to access his money from his bank account once in England, but that proved futile, so like many emigres he came with his title but little wealth."

"*Du Benoît's* story is a familiar one, Barrington," interjected Thomas, "but I have yet to see how his intention to smuggle was honorable."

"Keep an open mind, Bolton," scolded Nathaniel. "My story is not complete."

Thomas waved him to continue with a scowl. He did not take kindly to being chastised by a commoner; regardless of his austere connection.

"*Jacques'* father, and forgive me for referring to him as such; it is just *Jacques* is named after his *père* and I thought it easier to keep my story straight to refer to him as so. Anyway, they met *Jacques'* father in Calais, but he was a passage short. You can imagine my *grand-père's* grief. He had known *Jacques'* father since he was a boy. *Jacques'* father said he was happy to see his son safe and would be forever indebted to *grand-père* for ensuring his welfare.

"*Grand-père* did not quibble with his loyal servant for the tide did not wait for any man, so instead he vowed to return for him in one month and any others seeking to flee France. As you have seen, *grand-père* is a passionate man and his vow was heard by many who stood witness to the emotional display, particularly an Englishman who recognized the young aristocrat in *grand-père's* party.

"By the time they reached England's shore, that man, an Intelligence Officer, approached *grand-père* and convinced him to work for England. *Grand-père* agreed to transport men and information for our government. In return, England provided the funds necessary to purchase a local boat and captain. The first trip retrieved *Jacques'* father and a number of other nobles and their trusted servants wanting to escape France, but the extraction turned violent when many local peasants learned of the escape and came armed to stop it.

"Our papa was nearly killed and it was then *grand-père* decided he and his sons were not being paid enough to take such risks. *Grand-père*, was recompensed and allotted additional funds for hiring a crew to replace his sons. *Grand-père*, convinced the government's liaison he needed to traffic goods between England and France as a

ruse to keep others from guessing he transported government spies. Of course, the French assuredly used *grand-
père's* ship the same as us, but the smuggled goods kept
anyone from guessing *grand-père* was a government
agent."

"The war is long over," said Thomas. "Are you
telling me our government continues to sponsor *du
Benoît's* smuggling activities?"

"No," replied Nathaniel. "*Grand-père* retired when
the war ended, having earned enough from the government to live comfortably. Jacques leads the Free Men to
bring in the duty-free goods. *Grand-père* came to Cadgwith
this time to meet me."

"He no longer lives in Cadgwith?" asked Thomas.

"No," replied Nathaniel. "He and my uncles live
elsewhere now. He keeps the cottage, but comes only
when he is needed. It was by chance he was there when I
searched him out after shooting Damburten."

Chapter Ten

Thomas nudged Nathaniel with his elbow when Arabella yawned. Her eyes were heavy and for the past few minutes her lids dropped closed and her head lolled back like a rag doll before blinking herself to come awake. Neither of them slept well during last night's frigid temperature, so they were being lulled to sleep by the rocking carriage.

Nathaniel easily discerned Thomas' nudge when Arabella blinked herself to alertness again. He suggested, "Bella, why don't you take a nap. I am getting near parched with all my speaking. There is plenty of time for us to talk later."

"Sleep will make the time pass quicker for us, since we travel until dusk," added Thomas.

Too tired to argue, Arabella rested her heavy head against the back of her seat and within minutes fell asleep. Nathaniel soon followed her into slumber. Thomas thought to keep guard over his sleeping companions, but lost the fight to stay awake.

The coach's jarring stop woke Thomas and the noises of neighing horses, clanking bridles, and people shouting for their servants alerted him they arrived at their destination. He announced to his companions, "We are here," and then leaned forward to prod Arabella awake when she did not stir.

He pushed open the carriage door and commanded Nathaniel, "Watch over your sister, Barrington, while I secure us rooms. There might be talk if they see a commoner debark, so wait until the coach is brought around to the stables."

"Will do," replied Nathaniel. "I'll help Hugh with the horses after you collect Bella and then follow his lead with what else I should do."

Thomas gave a nod of approval and then leapt out of the coach. He walked into the inn and demanded two of the publican's best rooms. Arabella was half awake, looking weary and crumpled in her dress by the time Thomas returned. He asked, "Would you like dinner sent to your room, Miss Barrington?"

Arabella's fatigue counseled her to agree. "I am sorry, Bolton, but yes I would like to eat in my room. I will surely fall asleep once my hunger is assuaged." Looking at Nathaniel, she said, "I am sorry we will not have our discourse, brother."

Nathaniel replied, "It is better you ask your questions when you are awake enough to remember the answers. We have time, Bella. Get some rest."

Thomas agreed and then helped her out of the coach and into the inn. He escorted her to her room and then went to command the goodwife to send someone to help her ready for bed. He ordered meals for him and Arabella to be sent to their rooms and meals to be sent to his servants in the stable. He sought out the publican and gave the man enough coin to reserve the private parlour for him and Arabella to break their fast in the morning.

Confident he did all that was necessary he headed for his room. On his way he checked Arabella's door to ensure it was locked and then feeling his own hunger and weariness, he continued to his room to eat and sleep. The night passed quickly and he woke feeling improved. Anxious to depart, he quickly saw to his ablutions, dressed, and went to collect Arabella from her room to escort her to the private dining parlour.

He felt a sense of urgency to return to London and not just because the solution to Nathaniel's problem was there. The issue nagging him was how much he enjoyed Arabella's company and how he was used to having her at hand. That notion did not bode well for him. It created a conundrum and begged the question of whether he would suffer from her absence. After all, he did not plan on keeping her company once he returned her to her family; *or do I?*

His bothersome thoughts kept him silent during their morning meal in the private parlour. Only the occasional scrape of the plate when Thomas cut his ham did any sound reverberate. Arabella focused on her meal but the tension kept her taking glances at Thomas. His deepening frown counseled her not to intrude upon him. He gave no indication for what bothered him, but his manner was not what she was used to from a man who displayed every social grace when in company. He looked too much like a man with a heavy decision to make and she would leave him to it. She did not want to be the spark to ignite whatever emotions were brewing inside him and finished her meal as quickly as possible.

Her whole body relaxed when she entered the coach and saw Nathaniel waiting and smiling. She quickly settled onto her seat and asked, "Did you sleep well, brother?"

Nathaniel shrugged his shoulders and replied, "I miss my own bed, Bella. I have slept on and in a number of different places, much with the same comfort of our dear cave. I will be happy to leave the nomadic life behind if I am able."

Arabella tapped his knee in sympathy and then was surprised to see Thomas open the coach door and enter. He sat across from her and she quickly scooted over on her seat, so their knees would not touch. Her mouth gaped in wonder at seeing him happy. *Where is his frown? Where is the ill temper that kept me quiet and chased me out of the dining parlour?*

Thomas tapped her mouth close with his knuckles when she failed to do so, and almost laughed at her surprise at seeing his good mood. He knew he was surly over breakfast and while he would not explain his reasons for it, he would offer why he was not riding his horse. He explained, "I thought to travel with you, so as to hear the answers to your many questions."

She was about to ring his ears for daring to close her mouth, until she was reminded of her questions. She turned to begin a long list of queries when Nathaniel preempted her with a question of his own, "Bella, did our father receive a proper burial? I followed the carter to our home and saw you receive him, but I left afraid I would not be able to keep myself from going to you. I have not returned home since then, and have worried about it."

"The vicar did a fine job," she replied. "He saw papa was laid to rest in sanctified ground behind the church and purchased a fine marker for him. I was too overcome to see to the arrangements."

"I am glad he was buried properly," responded Nathaniel. "I will visit his grave when I can return home. Tell me, aside from Becca's marriage, how have the two of you managed?"

"Not well, I fear," replied Arabella sadly as she recalled the hostility of the villagers. "The debt collectors came the moment they learned of papa's death. I found them quite belligerent and frightening and was only able to get rid of them when I remembered papa's savings box."

"What debtors, Bella?" asked Nathaniel enraged. "Our father paid cash for everything because the merchants wouldn't give us credit because of Damburten. Are you telling me the village merchants took advantage of you in your grief?"

"I suppose," replied Arabella looking like she was ready to cry. "But Nathaniel, they showed me the unpaid bills."

"Copies," returned Nathaniel. "I am sorry, Bella. I should not have left you to hide, but rest assured, once I am no longer a wanted man, I will see our monies returned."

Thomas did not like to see Arabella upset, nor did he like the idea how a bunch of heartless men took advantage of her in her time of grief. He queried, "Are there receipts of payment on the farm, Barrington?"

"Yes," replied Nathaniel. "Our father kept detailed accounts and the receipts would be in the bottom left drawer of his desk."

Thomas looked at Arabella and asked, "And your copies of payment, Miss Barrington?"

"Yes, I put them in the top drawer after I made sure the merchants marked the bills paid. I did not think to go through papa's papers. Becca and I were grieving. We could barely manage each day. I never thought to take inventory of what was in papa's desk."

"Do not be distressed, Miss Barrington," comforted Thomas. "I will send Mr. Higgins instructions to see the matter settled."

"Who is Higgins?" asked Nathaniel.

"Oh," gasped Arabella. "He is our steward, Nathaniel. Bolton has been extremely generous to Becca and me. He says it is his wedding gift to his brother and Becca, but he has exceeded most expectations for such a gift. You should see all the improvements being made to the farm."

"I see," replied Nathaniel angrily, steeling his eyes at Thomas. "I don't suppose, Bolton, you considered how the property belonged to me and therefore, your gift is to me and not your brother."

Arabella exclaimed, "Do not look at him as if he is trying to steal from you, Nathaniel! Of course, he knows the property belongs to you, but that did not keep him from seeing to your sisters' comfort. He did it for us as much as Harry. He even asked his brother if he wished to purchase the property from you, thinking you might need the money, but Harry has other aspirations."

"I suppose it was also due to his generous nature you are attired in such finery?" he asked pointedly reconsidering Thomas' interest in his sister.

Shocked, by her brother's unfair accusation Arabella looked to Thomas for help. The viscount had the audacity to grin and then break into an unrestrained laugh. It was then she saw the absurdity of Nathaniel's claim and laughed.

Nathaniel was not amused, so Thomas explained lightheartedly, "Your sister has a knack for getting her way, Barrington. You should have seen her press her case, telling me since I required her and her sister to travel to London, then the cost of a new wardrobe should be mine to bear. I was hard-pressed to dispute her logic, though I did contest when she took umbrage to my overriding her fashion choices; even the modiste's assurance of my exquisite taste did little to assuage her."

Arabella chuckled, "Oh, Bolton, I remember how I raged at you for changing my selections. I ranted at you and said you were lucky I did not dislike the dresses, for had I not liked them, I would not have worn them!"

Her recollection made Nathaniel smile. He could easily picture the scene described and asked her, "What did he say to that, Bella?"

"The rogue dared to grin at me! You can imagine, Nathaniel, how that raised my ire even more."

"I beg your pardon, Bolton," offered Nathaniel. "I had no idea my sister lacked manners."

"You have not heard all of it, Barrington. Your sister tried my patience on more than one occasion. She is a stubborn minx who does not know when to desist. Do you know she talked me into giving her and Becca defense lessons and actually used a technique on a peer of the realm?"

Arabella blushed and gave Thomas a beseeching look to say no more. Oh, how he looked like he wanted to share the rest of the story, but thankfully, he heeded her unspoken request. Nathaniel raised his brows to prompt him for more information, but Thomas diverted Nathaniel by saying, "I should warn you she wants to learn to shoot, too! She was quite vexed when *Jacques* captured us and she was not able to put a period to him."

"Bella," shouted Nathaniel with alarm, "Are you mad?"

"Well, I did not like being unprotected, but I am glad I did not shoot *Jacques*. Now enough about me, tell me about the farm and how we came to live there."

"It was *grand-père's* way of helping his grieving son after our mama died," informed Nathaniel. "*Grand-père* learned of a Barrington who inherited a farm he did not want, so *grand-père* purchased it. *Grand-père* did not know Damburten's harassment of the man's deceased relative was the reason the man wanted to sell. The man did not want to live next to a vicious neighbor as did his deceased relative and sold the farm to *grand-père* when he offered. Our father was too proud to accept it as a gift, so he made a number of payments to *grand-père* to purchase it."

Arabella asked, "Why would papa say he inherited the farm? Why not tell us the truth?"

"According to *grand-père,* he did not learn of the neighboring problems associated with the farm, until the man boasted of his good fortune to rid himself of it. *Grand-père* was then reluctant to sell the farm to his son, but our father was determined to become a gentleman of property. *Grand-père* relented and counseled our father to let Damburten believe he was the Barrington who inherited the property to explain his resistance to sell."

Arabella asked, "How did *grand-père* learn about the Barrington farm?"

"He was in London on occasion to see the queen," laughed Nathaniel. "She never forgot his good deed in helping her godson to safety and over the years tried to repay the debt. *Grand-père* always refused, explaining the time would come when she could repay in kind by providing a service to someone he loves."

Thomas was confident the queen would soon repay her debt. It was the only reason he could think for the laughter the marquis bellowed when he departed for London.

Nathaniel continued, "*Grand-père* was used to the posturing of court life, after all, he was an aristocrat, so he could easily tolerate the prince and his foibles when he stayed in London as his guest. It was during one of their evenings, while enjoying some fine food and enjoyable wit at the Beef-Steak Society Club that he overheard a man named Barrington mention an inheritance he did not want. *Grand-père* saw it as an opportunity for his son."

"Papa thought so too," Arabella agreed soberly. Her remark reminded everyone how their father's aspiration to elevate his children's society ended up causing his death. Arabella sniffed and Thomas quickly suggested he and Nathaniel take to their horses to give Arabella some privacy. Nathaniel heartily agreed and once the coach stopped, they both leapt out of the carriage and collected their horses.

Both men pushed their mounts into a racing gallop like boys seeking adventure. Nathaniel had no chance at winning against Thomas' thoroughbred, but both men taunted each other with good humor. Once they were far enough ahead of the coach not to be trampled, they brought their horses to a walk and Thomas asked, "What are your plans once you are vindicated?"

"You truly believe Damburten is alive?" asked Nathaniel.

"I do. The more I consider the matter it seems some news should have surfaced since the duel. In four months, the same gossip is regurgitated which is unusual. It is almost as if the old *on dit* is being flamed for a purpose and the only reason that comes to mind is Damburten wants to see you exiled or worse, dead."

"But why?" asked an astonished Nathaniel.

"You are the only one who would accuse him of murder. No other peer will bear witness against one of their own, unless honor requires them of it. Let me assure you, I will press them to do what is right. If my guess is correct and your grandfather seeks the queen's recognition for his grandchildren, then others will come forward to also bear witness against Damburten. Our challenge is to find the baron and bring him to justice before he takes steps to silence you."

"Bloody hell!" cursed Nathaniel. "You speak of murder?! Never in my wildest dreams did I think I could be murdered. Hung, yes; murdered, no."

"We will have much to achieve when we reach London. You must be outfitted and presented, much like your sisters. We need public opinion on our side and the best way to do that is to gain the *ton's* approval," remarked Thomas.

"Bloody hell," exclaimed Nathaniel again with distaste. "You would think I am making my *come-out* and seeking a wife to marry."

"Well," explained Thomas, "You are definitely being presented. Seeking a wife is yours to decide."

They heeled their horses into a gallop to gain some distance when they heard their coach rumbling behind them. They reached the village of Salt Hill just as the sun began to set and made their way into The Windmill Inn courtyard. They were surprised to find it crowded with carriages and to hear resounding bellows of gaiety. The inn was located on the north side of the Bath Road and was a favorite coaching inn amongst travelers for its fine dining and accommodations. Even the Prince Regent once hosted a breakfast for the Emperor of Russia, the King of Prussia and his sons, the Prince of Orange, and the Grand Duke of Oldenburg there. The proprietor was so favored for his hospitality he was often asked to sit and take a drink with his guests.

Thomas did not need to ask why the courtyard of the dark red brick inn was crowded. He could see a number of modified yellow-bodied two seat landaus with *dickies*, versus the four seated landaus offering a *vis-à-vis* view. The day was assuredly a Thursday for the Four in Hand Club routinely drove to Salt Hill village on the first and third Thursdays during the Season to dine.

He could not have ridden into a more volatile situation. He could hardly present Arabella as his sister to his peers when she would shortly be introduced to the *ton* as the marquis' granddaughter, nor could he bring propriety to their traveling together by availing the use of her brother, since most of the *ton* thought the man to be wanted for murdering a peer. He was hard-pressed to convince them otherwise with Nathaniel dressed more like a villainous peasant than a gentleman.

Retreat seemed their best option until he was sighted. "I say Bolton," asked a gentleman exiting the inn, "Are you coming or going?"

Nathaniel pulled his horse's head to make a run for it, but Thomas quickly checked him by leaning over and grabbing his reins. "Be still," he commanded, adding, "He is a friend. One I can trust."

Nathaniel relaxed his reins and took a deep breath to settle his rapidly beating heart. His horse quickly shook its head and shuffled its hooves in gratitude. Thomas' friend stepped off the inn's veranda and stumbled as he meandered towards them. He wore a long drab coat adorned with three tiers of pockets and mother of pearl buttons the size of five shilling pieces. He appeared foxed and whether that benefited them or not was yet to be seen.

As if to present himself properly, he parted his greatcoat and tugged on his vibrant blue and yellow one-inch striped waistcoat. Plush breeches with strings and rosettes at each knee were revealed. The ensemble, with a three and a half inch deep crowned hat, was the pre-scribed dress requirement for the Four-in-Hand Club members.

Thomas recognized Malcolm Sedgeworth imme-diately. He was one of his friends also dubbed a Dark Rogue. They attended the same schools and enjoyed many of the same pranks and adventures together since child-hood. Striking in appearance with emerald green eyes, Malcolm stood as tall and fit as his other rogue friends and like them, was greatly admired by the ladies. He had a habit of smoothing back his longer than fashionable wavy dark brown hair whenever it fell over his forehead.

Thomas dismounted to appropriately greet his friend and informed him, "I just arrived, Sedgeworth. I see the Four-in-Hand is gathered to dine and I expect the inn is booked full. Did you manage a room for yourself, or do you share?"

Sedgeworth rolled his eyes as if he was just asked something ridiculous. He shook his head at having to offer an explanation. "I have a standing reservation at the Windmill for these events, Bolton, and pay generously enough as the publican never disappoints."

"Then, I must impose on our friendship, Sedgeworth," stated Thomas.

"I am forever your friend Thomas, but I will not give up my bed, even for you," he retorted.

"How about for Harry's sister-by-marriage," he cajoled. "She is in the carriage and is in need of respite."

Malcolm raised his brows in astonishment and turned his attention to the darkened interior of Thomas' coach which he noted was not the viscount's. He inquired, "You have downgraded your ride to travel with the lady alone?"

"Not at all," responded Thomas. "Harry's wife took my coach to London while I travel with Miss Barrington and her brother. Allow me to make his introduction to you."

Malcolm did not flinch at hearing the Barrington name, or at the burly coachman whom he thought to be one of Thomas' ex-soldiers. He was astute to understand all was not as it seemed; especially if his friend had a hand in it. He asked, "I expect he is not in your custody and therefore, he is in need of a proper set of clothes."

Thomas smiled and patted his friend on his back, happy he was of a similar size with Nathaniel. He said, "Sedgeworth, I am in your debt. Villainy abounds and I assure you it is not by Barrington's hand. I will give you the details later, but for now, can you get him to your room through a back door and transform him into the gentleman he is. I know you always carry a change of clothes with you no matter how short the travel. Once dressed proper, return him to me so brother and sister can make their entrance. I will need you to be surprised when someone accuses him of Damburten's death and counter with questions to raise that old *on dit's* veracity. I will be at hand to help, but I would prefer you cry false first."

Malcolm removed his tall hat. His hair fell forward immediately and he swiped it back over his head. He looked up to Nathaniel on his horse, and said, "Come, before anyone else exits the inn and let us hope my clothes fit you." With another shake of his head he mumbled something about the trouble with having friends.

Nathaniel dismounted and handed his horse's reins to Thomas before following Malcom to the inn's back door. He tugged his wool cap low on his forehead and made no move to bring attention to himself.

Thomas watched until Nathaniel safely entered the inn's back door and then walked his and Nathaniel's horse to the back of the carriage. He tied the horse's reins to it, considered what he would tell Arabella and then entered the coach.

Chapter Eleven

Arabella moved to cower in the shadow of the carriage's corner when she saw all the vehicles in the courtyard and heard loud and bawdy laughter coming from the well-lit inn. She tried to make herself invisible and nearly choked on her own saliva when a gentleman called out to Thomas. *Is Nathaniel to be detained? Will this gentleman call out a hue and cry?*

The danger of Nathaniel being arrested increased, as did her anxiety, the closer they came to London where the murder occurred and where witnesses abounded. Clearly, this motley peerage making merry was a threat to her brother since no one came to let her out. She waited, afraid to do anything to jeopardize her brother's safety, until she saw her brother follow the man who had called out Thomas' name. At first, she froze in indecision, but when Thomas disappeared from her sight it made her believe they had left her. She quickly slid across the bench seat to follow after her brother when Thomas opened the carriage door and blocked her.

She exclaimed, "Who is that man and where is he taking Nathaniel?"

Thomas pushed her trembling body back into the carriage. Alarmed by her discomfiture, he sat next to her and drew her into his arms. He soothed, "Calm yourself, the man is a friend and is doing us a great service. Take a moment to settle yourself and I will explain what is to happen."

Arabella raised her pale face from his chest and looked at him. His expression was so fraught with concern her lips dropped in wonder which drew his attention to them. She froze and then almost gasped when his lips came down to meet hers. She did not know what to expect from a man who angered her more times than not, but soft warm lips were not it, nor were the sensations stirring within her.

Her eyelids immediately closed and she quickly returned the kisses making her feel all warm and dizzy. She loved the euphoric feeling and right when things began to get interesting, she found herself thrust away from him. The wonderful sensations kept her eyes heavy-lidded and dreamy well after the kiss ended, so it took her a few moments to fully open them to register Thomas' stern expression. She almost laughed, knowing he was castigating himself for kissing her and for putting her reputation at risk.

His amorous kiss was better than any elixir she could take for curing her fright. She no longer trembled with fear; and if not for his anxious fashion of inspecting the courtyard to see if anyone witnessed their peccadillo, she would think her inexperience was what caused him to break away from her. He came to his senses far quicker than she and now his agitation and frown told her, what he was about to do.

She quickly counseled before he could speak, "Do not look aghast, Bolton. I know you meant no insult and I will hold you to no apology. If anything, I want to thank you for making my first kiss quite enjoyable."

His head whipped around from looking through the coach's window to ask her, "First kiss?"

"Of course, did you think I was experienced?" Arabella clapped her hands in excitement. "Oh, thank you, Bolton. I did not know if I did it properly. Perhaps, if I had any practice I would not have been caught unawares. I think I might try it again."

"Not with me," exclaimed a startled Thomas.

"Of course not," retorted Arabella, hurt their kiss did not affect him in the least. She confessed, "I did not think to wed, Bolton, but you reminded me the benefits of marriage. Of course, I would not want to bind myself to a man I could not tolerate intimately, but I suppose a kiss is a good indication of whether we would suit. I could simply use it as a test with any man I might consider marrying."

Thomas dropped his jaw in surprise and then chastised, "You will do no such thing. I will not allow it.

Might I remind you how precious is a lady's virtue and acting like a strumpet is no way to ensure keeping it."

Arabella crimsoned and chastised, "For shame, Bolton. I thought us friends. I would never speak such with any other man and instead of being my confident, you became my accuser. Move aside, I have no wish to keep company with you."

Thomas immediately felt repentant. It was true theirs was a unique relationship based on various facets, and camaraderie was definitely one. He apologized, "Forgive me. I am angry with myself. I know what honor requires of me. Miss Barrington,..."

"Stop!" she exclaimed. "I would not accept, Bolton, if you think to make an offer for me. I will not marry a man who weds to satisfy honor. If I marry, it will be for love. Stop worrying over what amounted to an insignificant kiss."

Thomas did not think it insignificant, but he was wise enough to let it go; especially since it benefited him. Anyway, now was not the time to be at odds with Miss Barrington. They were about to engage in what must be their most convincing performance and anger with one another had no place in it.

Arabella broke the uncomfortable silence with her question. "How is your friend going to help Nathaniel?"

Thomas smiled. He appreciated Arabella's steely resolve. She constantly surprised him. Any other lady would cry outrage and demand an offer for no other reason than to become his viscountess. He was usually adept at protecting himself from such machinations, but he had little defense against Arabella who held that odd position of being and not being a family member. More often than not, he acted like a man with the authority to chastise her whenever she behaved impertinently or recklessly.

He convinced himself he was allowed to do so because she was Harry's sister-by-marriage. However, if he was honest, then he would admit her connection to Harry had nothing to do with it.

She could raise his ire in one breath and then in another make him laugh. She always managed to surprise him and more often than not, did things that made him marvel at her strength and courage. She was unlike any lady of his acquaintance, and his connection with her was unlike any he ever had with a lady. There was no artifice between them and so there was never a need to be on his guard. She always spoke her mind and he found he did the same with her. He would be hard-pressed, after their impetuous kiss, to say he was not attracted to her. The problem was, he was not sure he wanted to be.

Arabella's raised eyebrows reminded him she asked him a question and he had yet to answer. He quickly explained, "Baron Sedgeworth is going to transform your brother's looks by lending him a change of clothes that bespeak a gentleman. Then, we are going to enter the inn as if we have every right to be there and if anyone calls your brother a murderer, we are going to negate it with sound reason. The gentlemen are here to party not to bring a man to justice."

"It sounds very risky for Nathaniel. Are you sure they will not take him into custody?" she asked.

"I will stand his guard if necessary, but I think our reasons will convince them Nathaniel is not wanted for murder."

"What reasons?"

"Have you forgotten there is no warrant for his arrest? Damburten was not buried. Who is to say he is not alive; especially since no one acceded to his baronship?"

Arabella argued, "They will want to know why Nathaniel ran away from the field."

"Ah," replied Thomas smugly. "He ran for the carter to transport his father home, nothing more."

"They will leave it at that?" she asked.

"For now they will. Once you are settled in your room, Sedgeworth and I will direct the conversation to other amusements."

"My room?"

"Yes, Sedgeworth graciously relinquished it for your use."

They were so focused on their discussion they did not see Nathaniel and the baron approach. The carriage door opened surprising both her and Thomas. Her eyes widened and then her features beamed in approval at seeing Nathaniel outfitted brilliantly. He wore a double-breasted bottle green tailcoat squared over his waist to reveal the longer brocaded green waistcoat with silver embroidery underneath. A white pristine cambric shirt and cravat with riding breeches and shiny black boots finished his ensemble. Sparkling in the folds of his cravat was Malcolm's emerald stick pin to give Nathaniel's stature credence.

"Oh brother," Arabella exclaimed, "how fine you look!"

Nathaniel laughed and offered his hand to help his sister debark. The moment her feet touched the ground she smoothed out her skirt and straightened her jacket, patting her coif to see if any pins needed to be pushed in. Her hands ran into another set which startled her. She started to turn to see who dared to take such a liberty with her person, but stopped when she heard Thomas say, "Allow me."

If her brother or the baron took notice how she responded to Thomas' touch she dared not look at them and reveal even more. She stood still and focused on keeping her equanimity; lest her cheeks blush from the feelings swarming inside her. The viscount vexed her to distraction. In one moment he was outraged he kissed her and in the next, he was running his fingers through her hair—with witnesses of all things! She was angry enough to demand satisfaction.

"There," he remarked. "Now you are fit to be introduced." Their laughter made it clear neither Sedgeworth, nor Nathaniel thought Thomas acted improper. She fumed at their mockery.

"Allow me to present Miss Arabella Barrington," he said to Sedgeworth, "sister to Mr. Barrington and Harry's recently wedded wife Rebecca." To Arabella he introduced, "Miss Barrington, I present Baron Malcolm Sedgeworth, a loyal friend of countless years."

Arabella made her curtsy and as she rose the baron took her hand. He looked deep into her eyes and said, "Your servant, Miss Barrington."

Arabella blushed at his blatant admiration and when he did not release her hand she flustered. She did not know what protocol demanded in such a situation. If it was anyone else, other than a friend of Thomas', she would jerk her hand back, but she did not want to embarrass Thomas or appear gauche.

His titled friends were handsome, charming, and used all of their assets to discombobulate her. Their flirtatious manner was both daunting and pleasing. Of course, they were probably trifling with her for amuse-ment or to set up the viscount's hackles. Regardless, the attention was novel, entertaining, and made her feel admired for more than being a sister or friend. *Why, I feel pretty!* She almost laughed when Thomas cleared his throat, more than once, to prompt Malcolm to release her hand.

The baron looked as if he forgot he held Arabella's hand and quickly released it, though reluctantly. He recovered his sheepishness by jutting out his elbow and asking, "May I have the honor of escorting you inside, lass?"

"I am no lass, my lord," she replied mischievously in retaliation to Thomas' earlier insult of treating her like a child. "I am a woman full grown should your eyes deceive you."

Malcolm gaped at her bold statement and replied, "Most assuredly, Miss Barrington."

He covered her hand on his arm and noted Thomas' scowl. He gave his friend a pointed grin and received a steely eye for his boasting. Thomas took his friend's teasing hit with forbearance and sighed. He was having trouble reconciling his first sight of Arabella, a dreary looking maid, with the coquette on Malcolm's arm. He had mistook Arabella for a maid when he first called on his brother at the Barrington Farm, but that opinion of her soon faded when he came to know her better.

Thomas did not expect others to see the beauty, strength, and grace he admired, nor did he expect to be irked by it. He and Nathaniel followed the grinning couple and stopped when Arabella pulled on Malcolm's arm. He watched her inspect and smell the beautiful sweet purple wisteria covering the front of the inn and witnessed Arabella's bright smile when Malcolm remarked, "It is considered to be one of England's finest."

They entered the inn and a gentleman, wearing the same attire as the baron, called out, "What's this, Sedgeworth? Are you dallying when you should be keeping our company?"

"Mind your manners, Peterson," chastised Malcolm.

Another gentleman exclaimed, "Well, do tell, Sedgeworth, who have you brought us?"

Before matters could take a vulgar turn, Thomas stepped in front of Arabella and into the inn. He proclaimed, "Careful. Miss Barrington and her brother travel with me to London. The queen awaits them." Thomas may have overdone the royal summons, but he felt these men, full with drink, needed a hard reason to remember their manners. The silence was astounding and then another voice called out to him, "Bolton, Is that you?"

The Four-in-Hand Club members were already drinking port and so were imbibing for a while. Their reasoning and reflexes were dull and it took them awhile to comprehend who stood before them. Before long, another peer exclaimed, "Barrington, did you say? Hell's bells, Bolton, did you capture the villain who killed Damburten?"

"Watch your tongue," chastised Malcolm who followed Thomas with the others into the inn, "lest you be called to account. Mr. Barrington is not wanted for any crime. He is a gentleman."

"I thought he killed Damburten," slurred another peer as he waved his tumbler around the room looking for affirmation. "Seems I still hear it tossed around in the clubs."

"Most likely by Damburten himself," suggested Thomas. "I don't suppose any of you saw the devil lately?"

Malcolm looked at Arabella when she tightened her hand on his arm and his obvious inspection alerted

Thomas to her distress. He suggested to Nathaniel, "Why don't you escort your sister to her room so she might rest."

Arabella looked at Thomas with grateful eyes and said, "Thank you and if you please, I shall dine in my room."

Thomas said he would see her meal delivered and then waited until she was out of sight before he probed the group for an answer to his question. Before long, speculation erupted of possible sightings. Malcolm initiated the guessing by saying he thought he spied Damburten at Newmarket. Then, as if they were in a game, every possible suggestion was made to where he might be. By the time Nathaniel returned, most of the group was under the impression Damburten was idling away somewhere too afraid to be brought to justice for killing Barrington. The tragic death was revisited and someone remarked how Nathaniel should have shot the baron when he had the chance.

Thomas shook his head at Nathaniel when it looked like he was about to confess he did and then before anyone could press him, Thomas introduced a sporting topic to veer the conversation away from the Barrington saga. By the end of the evening, Nathaniel was laughing and joking with the Four-in-Hand Club members, fascinated how they accepted his alleged murder of Damburten as nothing but a *bit of gammon.*

Those gentlemen with rooms left for their beds when they could no longer keep their eyes open. Others simply took to sleep where they sat. Nathaniel went to take a pallet on the floor in Arabella's room stating he felt safer to stay by her side with the inn full of drunken men. Thomas agreed it prudent to do so and then, along with a begrudging Malcolm, took to sleeping outside Arabella's room in the hall just in case Arabella was not the only one at risk. Drink made men foolish and it was possible one man might not believe Nathaniel guilt-free and decide as a lark to bring Nathaniel to a magistrate in the name of justice.

The next day, Arabella followed Thomas through the haphazard bodies of the club members still sleeping off the effects of their heavy drinking on the inn's floor. Thomas had let Arabella sleep well past dawn knowing even with a later departure they could arrive in London by nightfall. They were confident Timothy would deliver Nathaniel's missive before the marquis left for Rebecca's ball. After all, a horse traveled faster than a carriage bound by roads. However, as an extra assurance, they wanted Nathaniel at hand in case Timothy failed his task.

They exited the inn and saw Baron Sedgeworth give his *tiger* instructions to drive his landau back to Town before he joined them. Malcolm explained he wished to travel with Thomas and his party. He gallantly opened the door to Thomas' coach, assisted Arabella into it, and then offered her his company. Thomas frowned when it looked like Arabella was about to accept and quickly rebuked his friend for the impropriety of his offer. His voice was heated. Malcolm immediately took affront and retorted, "By jove, Bolton! While I cannot argue your reasoning, I do take affront to your tone and manner. Stand down man. You would think she was under your authority and not her brother's!"

Nathaniel quickly intervened and ameliorated, "My sister oftentimes acts without thought. I expect Bolton got into the habit of checking her manner in my absence, but you are right, Sedgeworth. The duty of her protection is mine and mine alone. She shall ride without company until which time I choose to keep it. Then, either of you may join us."

"Are you not being harsh, brother," interjected Arabella who would have liked the company. "They are no threat to me."

"You prove my point, Bella," explained Nathaniel. "As we near London we will come across many more carriages and be seen. You place your reputation at risk by riding unchaperoned in a closed carriage. Mama taught you better. Tis well you remember her teachings."

Duly chastised, Arabella quietly entered the carriage, but not before Malcolm extended his apology, "I meant no offense, Miss Barrington. Do forgive me."

To her surprise, he brought her hand up and placed a kiss on it. Her spirits were immediately lifted and she beamed a smile so bright Malcolm responded in kind. He shut the door for her and hurried off to catch his *tiger* who was readying to depart. Without a mount, the baron had little recourse but to return to London in his own landau.

The coach started, but not before Arabella caught sight through the window of Thomas frowning at her.

Chapter Twelve

Arabella's eyes shot wide from slumber when a heavy weight fell on her body and held her captive. Fear prompted her to fight until her barely cognizant brain recognized her sister's voice. Strings of words floated like bubbles around her. Some were distinct and clear; others were smothered by the cover in which her sister's head nestled and broke into nothingness. Annoyed at her confinement and the scare to which her sister inflicted, she scolded, "Desist!"

Rebecca quickly released Arabella and sat up, all the while laughing. She responded to her sister's reprimand with mirth, "Do not begrudge me, Bella. I am just so happy to see you. Have you missed me?"

Rebecca's cheerful nature had Arabella responding in kind with sparkling eyes and a grin, but then her brows drew together with worry. Rebecca looked overly fatigued.

"Do not frown, Bella," Rebecca replied in response to her sister's concern. She smoothed her gown over her rounded stomach and said, "My baby and I are fine." Unaware of what her sister knew, she asked, "Bella, you know the baby is Harry's?"

"Yes," she answered.

Rebecca laughed again, so full of merriment she could not sit still. She shifted on the bed from one spot to another in excitement as she informed smugly, "*Grand-père* gave me a letter from Nathaniel at my ball. Can you believe our *grand-père* is a marquis? We are quite connected dear sister. Did you know mama's papa was a viscount?"

Arabella immediately sat up, wrapped her arms around her knees and looked at her sister with sadness when she replied, "Nathaniel told me." She still could not believe how highly her family was connected. "Where were they when we needed them, Becca?"

Rebecca explained, "Our uncle, the new Viscount Ketterling, saw me at Almack's and thought I was mama having a striking resemblance to her. He has been kind to me and wants very much to meet you and Nathaniel."

"Nathaniel told me mama's father disinherited her when she married papa, but why have we never met this uncle, Becca?"

"He was restrained by filial duty. Apparently, the old viscount wanted mama to marry a duke and when she refused, he disinherited her and demanded her name never be mentioned again."

"What of mama's mother? She obeyed her husband's dictate?"

"It is a sad story, Bella," Rebecca continued. "Apparently, she stayed in contact with mama and came for each of our births. She actually died in a carriage crash on the way to my birth."

"Mama never told me anything," Arabella expressed sorrowfully. "I was only four when you were born, Becca, but I do remember Nathaniel shushing me to be quiet, saying we must not upset mama further. I did not know the reason for her sadness."

"She named me after her mama, Bella."

Arabella's stomach growled, forcing her to redirect her attention. The news of her mama being born into a family of nobility did not move her as much as her hunger. She did not have an emotional connection to this new uncle whom unlike her *grand-père* she knew existed. At least, her grandfather showed a modicum of care for her family over the years, even if from a distance. Her stomach called out again prompting her to get out of bed and find some food. She flipped her covers back and turned to maneuver her legs off the side of the bed until Rebecca stopped her and said. "You cannot race downstairs to eat. There are house rules we must abide."

"What do you mean, Becca?"

"Consider all the rooms on the first floor open for public display, meaning guests may come upon you at any time. Besides, the house is full of servants who would wag their tongues, if you left your room before you were properly dressed and coifed, spreading the news through the servant grapevine within the hour. The servants would tell their masters and by the end of the day every parlour in Mayfair would be discussing you and your peasant manners. Harry's mama would be mortified. Trust me, I learned the hard way how one does not remove downstairs until properly dressed. Charlotte, that's Harry's sister, actually shoved me into a closet, so her mama's guest would not see me. There are no runs to the kitchen here, Bella."

"Good heavens!" exclaimed Arabella. "Do you tell me I cannot eat until I am properly groomed? I will starve."

"Don't be dramatic. I'll ring for a maid to help you dress and to bring a tray of food to satisfy your appetite. You will get used to all the rules a lady must adhere."

Arabella asked Rebecca as her sister went to pull the bell cord, "How did you know I arrived?"

"Harry went riding with Bolton earlier this morning who told him all that happened. Of course, I pressed him for details and once dressed I came to see you."

Arabella inspected her surroundings. Last night, Thomas brought her to Belcrave House and snuck her up the servant staircase. Neither of them wanted to be seen by anyone attending Rebecca's debut ball, until they were ready to be seen. She was weary when they arrived and did not give any notice to the townhome or to the room Thomas deposited her in, other than to find the bed.

The four poster Jacobean bed frame was a heavy, elaborately carved piece of furniture. Arabella could attest the bed with its downy mattress and quilted satiny cover offered her a warm and luxurious sleep, until she had been rudely awakened. Two small matching tables were placed on each side of the bed. A highboy stood against one wall and a writing desk and chair were near the window. A small sofa of the lyre form was against another wall. The floor was covered with an Aubusson rug boasting of gold medallion motifs to compliment the gold marbled silk wallpaper and rich crimson curtains.

"Where am I, Becca? Whose room did I take and where are you staying?"

"Harry and I are right across the hall. This was Bolton's old room. Harry told me his brother did not want you alone in the guest wing, so he situated you close to me. Do you mind using his old room?"

Arabella shook her head side to side. No, she didn't mind being in his room. If anything, she wondered if the room held any secrets to tell about him, but after a cursory look she reconsidered. The room with its heavy and archaic furniture did not match the elegance of the man she knew. More than likely, the countess repapered the room and used furniture previously stored in the attic to decorate it.

Rebecca called "enter" in response to a knock at the door. A maid entered carrying a tray of food in response to her pull on a bell cord that rang in the kitchen. The young servant placed the tray on the desk and removed the sterling silver cover for Arabella's inspection of the food she brought. She asked the "miss" if there was anything else she needed. Arabella assured the servant there was not and dismissed her. The maid made her curtsey and left.

"You should have let her stay and help you dress, Bella," chastised Becca.

"I want to eat and do not want to do so with an audience. I will manage, Becca. Do not worry."

"Very well," Rebecca responded. "Then, I will leave you to it and return in one hour to take you to make your curtsey to Harry's mama and extend your gratitude for her hospitality. Do not dawdle, Bella. The house will be filled with callers soon to compliment the countess on her successful ball. Harry says I do not have to keep his mama company since he will not tolerate any man showing me remarked attention. He argues I am married now and have no need for callers other than those I wish to see."

"I never knew Harry to be possessive," remarked an astonished Arabella. "Are you concerned?"

Rebecca laughed and said, "Oh, no. My husband is not possessive as protective. He knows I am uncomfortable with flirts and courtiers and uses his husbandly right to keep their attentions away from me. He will be our protector and accompany us to Mademoiselle Lavigne's, although I do not know why she does not come to us as she did before at Bolton's manor home. Harry says it is not an option, but I do not understand why."

Arabella quickly deduced neither Bolton nor Harry thought it proper to have Bolton's former mistress in his parent's home, even if she was now earning a respectable living. The fallout of such knowledge coming to light would produce more drama than either brother wished to suffer. It wasn't until those thoughts were processed did her sister's words set in. She asked in astonishment, "I have to visit Mademoiselle Lavigne?"

"Oh, yes," replied Rebecca. "We are to be formally presented to the queen. Mademoiselle Lavigne is working on our presentation gowns. It wasn't necessary for me to be presented to the queen when I was just Mrs. Harry Bolton, but as a favor to *grand-père* Queen Charlotte met me to acknowledge me as *good ton*. She wanted news of our meeting and her favor to spread through Mayfair to make sure my ball was attended. It was then she commanded I be formally presented, along with my siblings. If I had not already met her informally and learn she was quite nice, then I would be completely petrified of making my royal curtsey. I am at ease knowing I will be doing it with you. The countess is sponsoring us."

"Becca, I am not sure I should. I am practically on the shelf. What need is there for me to be presented?"

"It is *grand-père's* wish," replied Becca. "Besides, the queen's acknowledgment will make us all respectable in the eyes of the *ton*. Nathaniel will be presented at a royal levee and make his bow to the Prince Regent while we will be presented in the Queen's Drawing Room. Both Viscount Ketterling and *grand-père* will sponsor Nathaniel. You have no choice, Bella; especially since *grand-père* told the queen it will satisfy her debt to him. Do you know of the service he did for her?"

"Yes," Arabella answered remembering her *grand-père's* story of how he came to the aid of the queen's godson. She did not have a choice but to comply, lest she anger her queen, and who knew the penalty for disobeying a royal summons. Besides, she did not want to disappoint her *grand-père* or jeopardize her brother's safety.

She did not tell Rebecca what else their *grand-père* did for England. She did not want to endanger him by speaking of his clandestine affairs. After all, it was not long ago the war ended with France and he could inform Rebecca if he so chose.

She asked, "Will Bolton also accompany us to Madame Lavigne's? He was rather particular in our dress selections before."

"Not us Bella," laughed Rebecca. "His highhandedness was for you alone. Besides, Harry would never tolerate Bolton telling me what to wear."

"Well, I did not tolerate it either, but I had little power to do anything about it. I still get angry thinking how he overrode my dress selections and how the modiste inferred his fashion sense was better than mine!"

Rebecca laughed and remarked, "No wonder Harry said his brother was done with you. Were you a terrible trial for him, Bella?"

Surprised, Arabella asked, "Did Bolton say I was a hardship?"

"No," answered Becca. "Of course not, he is too much a gentleman to say something rude, but he did say he feels free to return to his life now you are safely returned to the bosom of your family. He also told Harry he was considering finding himself a wife." Becca clasped her hands in glee and remarked, "Do you suppose my marriage to Harry inspired him to wed?"

"No doubt," replied Arabella sadly at discovering Thomas was relieved to be rid of her.

Misinterpreting her sister's downturned lips, Rebecca said, "Oh, you must still be tired, Bella. I am sorry I woke you, but I wanted to see you and ask you how Nathaniel looks. I do not think it is fair I do not get to see him until he can be properly attired. Nor will Harry let me visit him at Bolton's townhome. He says it is improper for me to spend time in a bachelor's home and how his brother would never allow it. I do not like it! Can you imagine the audacity of Bolton?"

She could easily imagine it, remembering how Bolton governed her throughout their journey to Cornwall. His most recent impertinence made her crimson in anger and she complained to her sister, "You should try being under his authority, Becca. He had the nerve to scold his friend Baron Sedgeworth for offering to keep me company in the coach!"

Arabella's emotional outburst sobered Rebecca; especially when the propriety of the situation was clear to her. She asked her sister, "Unchaperoned? The baron asked to sit in a closed carriage with no one else, but you?"

"Well, yes," responded Arabella guiltily, "but" she emphasized by raising her index finger into the air, "with Nathaniel there Bolton had no right!"

"Well, he was wrong to usurp Nathaniel's authority as head of our family, but Bella, lest you forget, Harry put us under Bolton's protection and thereby his authority, until we were returned to Harry's care. You must forgive Bolton's impertinence, as I am sure he forgot he did not need to concern himself over you anymore. He must have been mortified if his manner was called to account. Perhaps, that is why we will not see much of him."

"What do you mean?"

"I told you. He no longer needs to watch over you because he has fulfilled his promise to Harry and returned you safely to your family. He will undoubtedly resume his bachelor lifestyle now he is unencumbered. Her answer silenced Arabella which prompted Rebecca to take her leave.

Arabella conceded she needed help and pulled on the bell cord to summon a maid when she was unable to style her hair into anything considered fashionable. The servant who brought her meal returned and thankfully, did not look smug when Arabella asked for assistance.

The maid directed Arabella to sit on the chair next to the desk where a small cheval mirror allowed her to watch as the servant's nimble fingers expertly twisted and pinned her hair into a becoming coif. The maid used some tongs she heated to add some wisps of curl. Arabella instantly saw a remarked difference in the styling of her hair by an expert hand and was pleased. She looked far better than she ever had before.

"There you go, miss," stated the maid after placing the last pin in Arabella's brown hair.

Arabella thanked the maid who looked surprised. Among the aristocracy, servants were not recognized by their employers for doing their job. That distinction fell to the housekeeper or whoever had authority over them. If anything, servants were expected to be invisible and not intrude upon their employer's household and guests. Arabella never subscribed to the doctrine.

A knock resounded shortly after the maid left and Arabella called out for her visitor to enter. She expected to see her sister return to collect her to meet the countess. The maid had not finished styling her hair when Rebecca first called, so she had sent Rebecca away to return later. Now, embarrassment quickly marred her facial features with a blush when not only Rebecca, but Harry and an older woman whom Harry favored entered her room. Quickly ascertaining the lady's identity, she stood and curtsied. Her tardiness had made her host come to her.

Emily, the Countess of Belcrave, grinned at Arabella's display of reverence, and offered her hand to help her rise. "Very pretty," she complimented, but then quickly criticized, "but too deep a curtsey for a countess. I will instruct you later on the proper depths to greet our elevated society."

After a quick inspection of Arabella, Emily remarked, "You will do, Miss Barrington. Unfortunately, I have no time to exchange pleasantries. My parlour is bursting with callers, ready to revisit the imbroglio committed by Lady Caroline at last night's ball. I must leave you to play hostess, but rest assured, I shall welcome you properly at dinner."

The countess turned and left, but not before giving a curt command to her son, "Take the service stairs, Harry. I do not want any of you waylaid by the curious, so do take care not to be seen. The *ton* will learn soon enough of Miss Barrington's arrival."

Harry grinned at his mother and then kissed her cheek with affection. The countess blushed at the uncommon display and then hurried out the door.

"My," gasped Arabella before looking at Harry and saying, "I do believe I like your whirlwind of a mama." Turning to her sister she asked, "You get along well with her, Becca?"

Rebecca looked at Harry and laughed. She answered, "Yes, though we stumbled in the beginning as she was not sure if I had hoodwinked Harry into marriage. It is understandable she greeted me cautiously after all the speculation regarding me and our family. Last night's success, and the knowledge I carry Harry's babe, redeemed me."

Arabella asked, "What did Lady Caroline do at your ball last night to create all the excitement? I am beginning to regret I did not attend, regardless of the late hour."

Harry intervened and said, "Come, you can tell all in the carriage, Becca. We must go or you both shall be late for your appointments with Mademoiselle Lavigne."

A coachman perched on his outside seat of the countess' barouche was ready to drive them. Harry helped his wife and Arabella into the open carriage and gave them the forward facing seats. He sat across from them and then waited for his wife, who was ready to burst, to tell all her news.

"Oh, do begin, Becca," commanded Arabella. "You are fidgeting with excitement. What happened last night?"

"Well, last night, there were so many revelations I do not know where to begin," Rebecca started.

"Start with Lady Caroline," prompted Arabella.

Rebecca chuckled and said, "Well, I am happy to say I defeated my nemesis. Isn't that right, Harry?"

Harry grinned and agreed.

"Heavens!" exclaimed Arabella wide-eyed and open-mouthed. "How could you possibly have a nemesis?"

"Well," replied Rebecca. "I don't rightly know or maybe I do. You see, this year's *diamond of the first water* is Lady Caroline Southwaite. She is very beautiful and talented. Unfortunately, she is also arrogant and vain. Her mother hosted a *musicale* designed to showcase Caroline's talent. The other debutante's performing did not have half of her skill, most likely her mama conspired for Caroline to outshine them, but they drew accolades for their shy and sincere performances.

"I found their mucking through their challenging pieces heartwarming and amusing, so when Lady Caroline appeared and demanded quiet for her performance, I listened with a critical ear. I was hard-pressed to explain why the piece did not move me. Lady Caroline did not miss a note and trying to figure out why I was not impressed made me miss the end of the lady's sonata. She noticed I was the last person to lend my applause to the already effusive approbation and she took affront.

"She thought to shame me and Harry's family. I think she believed a person of my station was not trained in the finer accomplishments, so she was more than pleased when I said I never learned to play the piano. She taunted me and said in a very loud voice I could leave if I was not used to being in esteemed Society.

"Her insult rallied me into offering to sing. She could not refuse my offer since her guests shouted out encouragements for me to do it. I suggested Beethoven's *To the Distant Beloved* and discovered Lady Caroline did not know the music. She might have suggested I sing something else, but the countess intervened and offered to accompany me. I think Harry's mama saw it as an opportunity to remove Caroline from the center of attention and spare me anymore of the lady's hostility. Needless to say, I surprised them with my voice."

"Well, they would be foolish not to recognize your talent, Becca," Arabella stated. "You have a beautiful voice our mama helped you to develop. I doubt there are many ladies of the realm raised by mamas as attentive and talented as was ours. But surely, there must be more for you to call her an enemy?"

Harry intervened and explained, "I was at the club this morning and the *on dit* to why Caroline dislikes Becca is because she drew some of Caroline's admirers away from her and Caroline did not like it. She thought to put Becca in her place. She never expected my wife to take her on and come out the victor."

"Now my curiosity is truly peaked. What happened, Becca?" asked Arabella.

"Well," she explained, "last night as uncle and I were leaving the dance floor, I heard Caroline announce to all and sundry that the only reason Harry married me was because I was with child. Can you imagine the audacity of the lady at my own ball to slur me and my baby's good name? I could not let it pass and faced her. She gave me the *cut-direct*, but I did not let it deter me. I told her she was not welcomed and told her to leave."

Harry laughed and said, "You are leaving out the best parts, Becca. Allow me. You told her she was rude and vulgar, and while you turned a blind eye to her ill manner the last time you were in her company, you would not tolerate any viciousness towards your family in your home. Then you told her to return to the nursery to relearn the manners that behoove a lady for she clearly forgot how to behave as one."

"Oh my goodness, did she leave?" Arabella asked smiling.

"Not immediately," grinned Rebecca, looking mischievously at Harry.

"Well, the lady did protest," chuckled Harry, "but my wife showed her backbone when Lady Caroline asked what right she had to order her to leave. Becca in a voice for all to hear proclaimed she was Mrs. Harry Bolton. She gave Lady Caroline the option of leaving on her own accord or being escorted out by my father's footmen. Becca told her and everyone listening she did not take kindly to anyone disparaging her or her family."

"My goodness, Becca," stated Arabella. "Pending motherhood made you a lioness. I wish I was there to witness it all. How did it end? Did the lady choose wisely?"

Harry answered, "Her parents the Earl and Countess of Southwaite came to her aid and shouted their outrage. I do not think they expected my father to side with Becca. He ordered them to leave and told them they were *persona non grata* in his home. After that the Prince Regent and your grandfather, the *Marquis du Benoît*, arrived. No one paid much attention to the departing Southwaites. However, there is much chatter in the clubs today."

"Oh, dear," gasped Rebecca. "Have I shamed you and your family again, Harry?"

Harry reached over and clasped his wife's hand. He smiled and said, "Becca, you never did anything to shame me or our family. I am sorry you suffered at Damburten's hands, but he is the one who trespassed, not you. Last night, the lady who behaved badly and put her character into question was Lady Caroline, not you.

"Unfortunately, she was not sent home to rusticate. You will see her on occasion as we will attend some of the same events. Her parents will be putting their own twist of what happened last night and while they are not welcomed at Belcrave House they will most assuredly be received by many others who sympathize with their plight. Remember, Southwaite is a wealthy man with his own set of cronies to do his bidding. I doubt Caroline will repent. She is too vain to believe she was in the wrong. More than likely, she blames you for her embarrassment. I would not put it past her to take revenge in some sensational way, though she would be a fool to target a Bolton, again."

Chapter Thirteen

Arabella sat as stiffly as her uncle in his curricle. She was so tense she almost jumped off her seat when Viscount William Ketterling slapped his leather reins to start his cattle forward. Without a glance to her, he remarked, "I am sorry your sister could not join us."

His tentative voice put Arabella at ease. She was glad to know she was not the only one feeling awkward with their first meeting. She turned her focus from the road to look at him and immediately recognized the same classical features as her mama. He had the same prominent cheekbones and narrow bridged nose that was slightly rounded at the end. His hair was sprinkled with grey, but in his youth it was probably the same dark rich brown color as her mama's. His almond-shaped brown eyes were as kind as her mother's and when somber, reminded her of when her mama worried.

She blinked to attention realizing those somber eyes were focused on her and not the lane because she had not answered him. She quickly offered an explanation, "The modiste wore Becca out. She not only had to try on her presentation dress, but a number of additional ensembles recently commissioned for her. She is growing prodigiously round with child."

"I am happy she met and married a good man," he remarked. "I have no concern regarding her future happiness. It boggles my mind I am to become a great-uncle which makes me feel particularly ancient."

Arabella laughed at his absurd comment. "I think not, my lord. I think you will have to fend off the marriage mart mamas with a stout cudgel if you wish to remain single."

"Do call me uncle, Arabella," he asked soberly, "and if you are uncomfortable to do so, then address me as William. I regret not knowing you in your infancy, but hope you will allow me to know and help you now. I loved your mama very much and wish we had the chance to renew our bond before her death."

"She never spoke of you," whispered Arabella.

"Perhaps, it was too painful, or maybe she did not want her children to be as disappointed in our father as was she. I did not know your father, aside from an initial introduction, but I often thought it magnanimous of him to change his name to appease my father's prejudices against the French."

"My papa was a loving husband and father," she praised. "I miss him terribly, as do my siblings. My sister especially suffers guilt for being the reason behind his death."

"She must not harbor such thoughts," counseled William. "The culprit is Damburten and we will see justice done regarding his villainy. Did I tell you I met Nathaniel before coming for you? He was just fitted for his own court dress when he learned a ceremonial sword was required. He professed he was proficient in the art and Bolton sent his footman off for two foils to ascertain his skill.

"I was directed to the nursery on the top floor when I arrived. Imagine my surprise to hear steel strike steel. I ran in with no thought to how I was to intervene, but immediately calmed when I saw them wearing protective gear. Their skill and agility captured my attention and I stood transfixed watching them. They are well-matched in the art."

"My *grand-père*," explained Arabella, "instructed my papa and he in turn taught my brother. I confess I picked up the foil to try my mettle, but not under my papa's watchful eye. Nathaniel knew I was envious of him being tutored by papa, and so he offered to teach me. He is a very accommodating brother."

William chuckled. "So, how do you fare?"

Arabella laughed and replied, "My rudimentary knowledge of fencing would surprise you, but I do not have the arm strength to see me victorious."

"Well," replied William. "You will never be put to the task. You have a number of champions you may call upon if needed. I expect Bolton will apply to your grandfather, the marquis, for a lesson."

Arabella smiled and then her lips flattened in thought. William looked at her when silence replaced their nimble chatter and asked what was on her mind. She revealed, "Had the duel been swords instead of pistols, my papa would be alive. Damburten would not prevail over a fencing master."

"The baron was the one challenged and therefore entitled to choose the weapons," explained William.

"Yes," responded Arabella sadly.

William slapped the reins to get his cattle to pick up their pace. He and his niece were in such a heavy discourse they gave no notice to Mayfair's multi-storied grey stone mansions or to the green park squares they passed. However, the crossing traffic at Park Lane drew William's attention. He stopped his curricle and waited for a carriage to pass; then, he jostled his horse's reins to move the team across the road to enter Hyde Park through the Grosvenor Gate.

Arabella was surprised at the number of carriages entering the park and exclaimed, "Good heavens! Look at all the people!"

William grinned at her excitement and maneuvered his cattle to follow the line of slow moving carriages before them, much like the carters waiting their turn to bring their wares to market. Curricles, barouches, landaus and phaetons congested the lane leading to Rotten Row.

"Shall we take another route," inquired Arabella.

"Not at all," replied William with a grin. "It is the social hour and the traffic is expected. You see, during the Season, it is *de rigueur* to drive along Rotten Row to see and be seen. Noblemen get to show off their cattle and carriages. Ladies get to show off their finery and most important of all, marriage mart mothers get to assess the eligible bachelors to which they may market their daughters. How else is anyone to know who is in town and available for matrimony? Besides, there is no way for me to turn my team around. Look behind you, we are no longer last in line."

"I never saw such a sight," marveled Arabella turning her head all around to see what was on show.

"Oh you must not look so eager, Arabella," informed her uncle. "Ennui is all the rage. You must look bored as if you have seen it before and everything has grown tedious."

Arabella chuckled with delight and responded, "Oh, don't be a goose, uncle. I could never behave falsely. Do not forget this is my first time to London and I am not the type to dissemble. I shall do as I please and enjoy everything while I am here. I do not look to wed and so shall not worry about offending the sensibilities of any eligible man too supercilious to think beyond what society thinks."

Even so, William noticed how quickly Arabella checked her excitement. She pushed her wayward hairs into her bonnet, sat straighter in her seat, and smoothed out her skirts to look the picture of decorum. Aside from her gleaming eyes, she looked as demure as any other debutante making an appearance.

"The park is bigger than I expected," she remarked.

"Indeed," replied her uncle. "There are multiple crossroads and areas considered both public and private, where picnics and duels, as you know, take place. It is not a place a young lady should venture without escort; especially at night where footpads are known to commit crimes."

He steered his cattle into the heavily congested lane known as Rotten Row following the queue of carriages before him. The *route du roi*, "the king's highway," was engineered to improve the road from St. James Palace to Kensington Palace in the mid-seventeen hundreds.

He explained, "The old lane was once the site of many robberies before it was lit with lamp posts. Some say the twist on the once rutted road's name came from the bumpy ride, or from the "rotten" ride travelers suffered; others claim it was a Celtic derivation from *rattanreigh* meaning good mountain path."

Arabella nodded in understanding, but her eyes darted, looking at all the aristocratic splendor around her. She leaned forward in her excitement a number of times and then jerked back to sit demurely. William chuckled at how poorly she acted for someone who did not give a whit what society thought.

He directed, "Look to your right, Arabella. The Serpentine draws many a visitor and painter."

Arabella inspected the S-curved shaped lake and marveled at its pristine beauty. An expansive green lawn preceded the blue water and was dotted with plane trees. In the distance spanned the lake's bridge. Ducks quacked and glided across the glistening blue surface.

Returning her focus forward, Arabella asked, "Why is it stop and go, uncle? Surely we should be moving steady now we are merged onto the lane?"

"Look there," he replied, jutting his chin in the direction where a rider was conversing with a lady in a stately barouche. "We are at a standstill until that carriage or others who stopped for their owners to engage in discourse decide to move forward. Usually, the culprits do not stay idle too long as they do not wish to be the brunt of any parlour talk later."

"She is quite pretty," remarked Arabella noticing a young auburn-haired lady with a narrow forehead, high cheekbones, and tapered chin. The beauty's slate blue eyes sparkled while she flirted with a gentleman seated on a horse. William looked at the lady whom his niece called pretty and gasped, "Oh."

"What is it uncle?" asked Arabella.

"Well, the beauty is Lady Caroline Southwaite," he answered. "She is the vixen behind all your sister's troubles."

"The viper!" snarled Arabella, deciding Rebecca's nemesis was not pretty, after all. She silently criticized everything about the lady and began to slur the man flirting with her until she recognized him. She bit her bottom lip, rather than shout out the expletive that came to mind when she saw Bolton's friend speaking with her family's enemy.

Edward Constantine Fairowe, the Earl of Fairgrove, noticed Arabella's scrutiny and gave leave to Lady Caroline to make his way to her. The traffic moved and William jostled his leather reins to move his cattle forward in the queue of carriages. They rolled a few feet before William pulled his team to a stop again.

Arabella's temper fumed. A number of sharp rebukes flitted through her mind. She was ready to give Edward a sound scolding, until the grin and wave Lady Caroline directed at her as if they were bosom buddies distracted her. The exhibit, no doubt, was conspired to question the veracity of what happened at Becca's ball, for surely if Lady Caroline was *persona non grata* with the Boltons, then she would not dare to greet the sister of one. The lady's nerve of villainy made Arabella's temper flash, and like the Greek god Zeus with his lightning bolt, she was ready to wield justice upon Edward for his disloyalty.

Edward was unaware of Arabella's outrage and cheerfully tipped his hat when he brought his horse next to her uncle's curricle. He greeted, "Miss Barrington, this is a wonderful surprise."

Arabella gaped her mouth, astonished the man could greet her as if he did nothing wrong. She quickly closed her mouth and scolded, "How can you call Bolton your friend and speak with that...that person who did my sister harm?"

Edward's brows shot up and then he laughed loudly enough to draw attention. He leaned over to speak softly to her, so others might not hear. He explained, "Machiavelli councils to keep your friends close and your enemies closer. Do not think ill of me. I know what transpired between Lady Caroline and your sister. Trust me, as Bolton's friend I can be more useful to him if I am in the lady's camp."

"Oh, you speak of Sun Tzu's *Art of War*," marveled Arabella impressing the earl with her literary knowledge.

Edward inquired, "You have knowledge of his teachings? I would not think it worthy of a lady's interest."

"Many things interest me, my lord," she replied with a grin. "My brother was enthralled with the book and so without his consent and I might add, before he was done with it, I absconded away with his copy and read it."

Her uncle watching the intercourse cleared his throat when it seemed he was invisible. "Oh," Arabella gasped again. "Do forgive me, uncle. My lord Fairgrove, allow me to present my uncle William Keane, Viscount Ketterling. Uncle, this is Edward Constantine Fairowe, the Earl of Fairgrove. He is a friend of Lord Bolton's and an acquaintance of mine."

William's eyebrows scrunched at her declaration and he asked sternly, "And how is he an acquaintance of yours?"

Arabella widened her eyes at the underlying innuendo. She opened and closed her mouth rethinking her explanation. The last thing she wanted was to confess how the earl thought her a doxy upon their first meeting.

Seeing her struggle, Edward intervened. "I came upon Bolton while traveling and he introduced me to Harry's sister-by-marriage. I confess I was disappointed when Miss Barrington retired early to take her meal in her room and therefore, denied me her company."

"Is this when you searched for Nathaniel?" William asked.

"Indeed, uncle," she answered. "There was little time spent for amusement; such as entertaining a friend of Bolton's. I retired early to bed for Bolton wished to depart early the next morning. I did not see his lordship again until now."

"Very true, I hope I may enjoy your company this Season. Have you committed to any engagements, yet?"

"I only arrived last night and since then have been in a whirlwind of appointments. My drive with my uncle is my first of its sort," she laughed. "I do not know what invitations my sister accepted on my behalf. I do attend tonight's performance at Drury Lane. Is that not correct, uncle?"

"Indeed," William replied. "I have the honor of escorting you, since Belcrave was kind enough to lend me his box."

"Then, if you permit, I shall attend you during the intermission. I also am engaged to attend the opera this evening, as I escort my mama and my sister to tonight's performance. Perhaps, Bolton will join me and also make his salutation to you."

Surprised, Arabella inquired, "He accompanies you?"

"Yes," replied Edward. "He is doing the pretty with my sister and so I stand as chaperone, even though my mama is there."

Confused, Arabella asked, "The pretty?"

"Ah," grinned the earl. "Did you not know Bolton seeks a wife? My sister dropped her handkerchief and Bolton was foolish to pick it up to use the analogy." Upon seeing her eyes sadden and her bottom lip pout, he apologized. "Forgive me, Miss Barrington, I did not know you held expectations for Bolton."

Arabella brows rose in surprise, collecting herself she rebutted, "I do not have any, my lord. Besides, Bolton is far above my touch for an alliance which he would be the first to acknowledge."

"Then, why the sad face?" he prompted, quickly astonished by her honesty.

"I am used to his company. It seems strange we could attend the same event, but not with each other. I am used to having him at hand."

"Will you allow me to be at hand for you?"

William coughed again to put a stop to the improper conversation. He said, "I think we held up the line enough, Fairgrove," he said curtly as he slapped the reins to move his cattle forward. Arabella turned her head, afraid her uncle's abrupt departure insulted the earl. To her surprise, the earl tipped his hat to her. The acknowl-edgement made her grin and she blushed when he smiled back. She quickly turned forward.

Her uncle frowned and scolded, "You are doing a fine job of playing the coquette, for a lady not interested in marriage. Be careful Arabella or you might catch a fish you do not want."

Arabella laughed.

"Do you suppose Rebecca will be rested enough to attend the theatre?"

"I am thinking to discourage her uncle?"

"Why?"

"She is quite emotional being with child. I do not want the play to upset her. I doubt "The Distressed Mother" is uplifting.

William chuckled, "No, you are right. However, it is no sadder than a Shakespearean Tragedy."

"Well, that decides it," Arabella replied. "Becca is tenderhearted and cries buckets over Shakespeare's works. I take them away from her whenever I see her reading one. She is a voracious reader and feels she is lacking having not read all of the master's works."

"Well, I will keep my eye out for something amena-ble to her sensibilities," he said. "Are you comfortable with only me for company?"

"Indeed, I am looking forward to getting to know you better."

They made the loop and then headed to Belcrave House. He informed on the drive, "I am having my townhome refurbished, Arabella. It is my hope you and your brother will reside with me during the Season. I appreciate how Belcrave and Bolton extended their hospitality to you and your brother, but I feel very strong the honor of caring for the two of you is mine. I hope you and Nathaniel will indulge me in this."

"Indeed," replied Arabella, "but I see no need for you to put out an expense for us. We would be quite happy to live at your home with no improvements."

William chuckled and replied, "My townhome needs refurbishment. My father did not reside there during the Season after my mama died. He stayed at his club when he came to do his duty in Parliament. He said the house was too full of memories of his wife to live in it. I also preferred to stay with my friends, rather than rattle about alone, but with my need to marry I am setting the house to rights. I hope to complete the improvements within a week's time and move you and your brother in to live. I want to host a ball shortly after to introduce the two of you to Society."

"Heavens be, why?"

"It is *de rigueur* after making your curtsey. Besides, it would please me very much to acknowledge you publicly as my sister's children."

Arabella released a sob before proclaiming, "Mama would have loved to see her children partake of the Season."

William returned Arabella to Belcrave House and saw her up the steps. The door opened and Arabella walked inside. No sooner did the door shut behind her than the stoic butler informed, "The Earl and Countess request your presence in the drawing room."

Alarmed, Arabella asked the butler to lead her. The servant raised his eyebrows and Arabella waved him forward. She did not want her hosts to think her ungrateful by not being prompt. She followed closely, taking in the splendor of Belcrave House.

Since her arrival, she gave little attention to the ostentation of Belcrave's home. Her first entry was by stealth and she arrived through a back entrance and the servant stairs. This morning, after returning from Madame LaVigne's, she rushed through the ornate entry and stairs with little thought of her surroundings to change into a promenade dress for her drive through Hyde Park.

She followed the butler to a set of closed pinewood doors painted in egg-shell and bordered with gilded mouldings sculpted with laurel leaves. The butler, with a practiced flair, grasped, turned the gilded knobs, and opened the double doors wide. He strutted forward with all the pomp and circumstances his position afforded him and announced in a stentorian voice, "Miss Arabella Barrington."

The glitter and decorative richness of the room completely captivated Arabella. Everywhere she looked she saw gilded furniture with satiny green brocade upholstery. Laurel leaves and fans were sculpted into the furniture's wooden frames; lion heads were carved into their arms and legs.

The walls were silk papered in cream and each wall was decorated with the same narrow gilded moulding as the entry's double doors into an enormous square. At the center of each square was either a gilded framed painting or a gilded framed mirror. The room's large paned windows were covered with heavy green velveteen curtains and were topped with matching swag valances. An Aubusson carpet made of blue, green, and gold threads bearing the Belcrave crest at its center covered the expansive floor.

Arabella, much as her sister did before her, looked up as if the angels called to her. She saw a glorious heaven painted on the ceiling, bordered with a moulding of gilded medallions. She might have stood there with her head back entranced, if Lady Belcrave's remark did not penetrate her dizzying thoughts.

"My goodness,'" Emily exclaimed, "Have you not seen to your ablutions, Miss Barrington?"

Arabella looked at the butler and then returned her attention to Bolton's mother. She informed, "Dawson said you wished to see me."

The earl huffed drawing Arabella's attention. She made a meager curtsey and then looked back at the countess who was reprimanding, "Well, yes, Miss Barrington, but it is expected one does not present oneself until one's looks are improved."

Arabella blushed. The countess, either because she did not want to annoy the earl, or took pity upon her, said, "Well, never mind, Miss Barrington." She turned to the earl and introduced, "My lord, allow me to present Miss Arabella Barrington, Rebecca's sister, Viscount Ketterling's niece and the *Marquis du Benoît's* grand..."

Before she could finish the earl barked, "Oh, all right Emily. I don't need her family tree. We know well-enough who is her family." He steeled his eyes and judged Arabella and when she did not drop her eyes from his inspection, he chuckled and remarked, "Looks like Barrington raised a bunch of cheeky girls. Well, it bode well for your sister; mayhap, it will for you, too." Without another word he left.

"Do not mind him, Miss Barrington," informed the countess. "Last night's ball reminded him how we have our own daughter to present next year and thereby another ball to host. He is off to his club to moan to his peers the burden of having daughters. He will not join us for dinner. Harry and Rebecca opted to eat in their room."

The countess rolled her eyes as she continued, "Rebecca actually sent word, via a servant, mind you, to inform her ankles were too swollen to leave her bed. I do not know who was more uncomfortable, the servant for relaying the message, or me for hearing it."

Arabella laughed and the countess grinned in return. Emily continued, "I know you attend the theatre tonight and if you are of a similar mind, we may do the same and eat in our rooms."

"Oh, yes, my lady," she answered. "I would love to rest before the play."

"Very good," Emily replied. "I will alert Cook and see you tomorrow morning. Remember we are to practice your deep curtsey wearing the hoop for your presentation dress." She handed Arabella a letter before she took her leave.

Chapter Fourteen

Arabella looked down at the note in her hand and in the process was able to see her less than pristine state. Her gloves were soiled from perspiration. She had clutched her hands in her excitement more than once while driving through Hyde Park and had even wiped their dampness against her coat. The mark of that wipe was evident and noteworthy upon the earl's inspection. Who knew what else was amiss? She had not bothered to tidy herself, nor check her appearance in a looking glass.

It was no wonder the earl looked at her with distaste and the countess with astonishment. Embarrassment flooded her senses when she recalled how she had waved Belcrave's well-trained butler forward when he hesitated to present her. Never before had she suffered an inspection that made her feel gauche.

She shook off her humiliation and hurried to her room. She was too curious to read the letter the countess handed her to remove her coat or bonnet. The letter bore her grandfather's mark on the outside and with apprehension she sat at her desk and opened it.

> *My petite-fille,*
> *I cannot attend the Season's amusements without causing speculation to abound regarding my circumstances. After all, how many times can I appear in state dress? Your uncle, Lord Ketterling, assured me he will be close at hand to watch over you. I will see you and Nathaniel make your curtsey and bow respectively, and then attend the ball your uncle hosts in your honor. Be assured my most magnanimous appearance will add consequence to your stature and like Becca, silence anyone who dares to call you common. Our proper reunion will have to wait until after the Season ends when I can visit you as your grand-père and not the marquis.*
> *Your brother knows how to contact me if the need arises.*
> *Your loving grand-père*

She had yet to attend any of the *ton's* events and already she felt overwhelmed by the prejudices of her betters; the censure regarding her manner; the etiquette and rules she was required to abide by; and the undeserving viciousness against her family. How else to describe Lady Caroline's behavior to her sister or the number of judging looks and speculation she spied on her drive today? She had no idea how her warmhearted and kind sister managed on her own.

She folded her *grand-père's* missive, placed it in the top drawer of the highboy dresser, and then pulled the bell cord to summon a maid to help her undress. She would bathe and take a nap before it was time to eat and dress for the evening.

Arabella crossed the hall and opened the door to her sister's room when Harry answered "enter" to her knock. Her uncle was to arrive any minute to escort her to the opera and she wanted to wish her sister goodnight before she left.

The moment she entered, Harry exclaimed, "My goodness Bella, you look awfully fine. You will have the other debs scowling at you and whispering behind their fans unkindly."

"Hush!" chastised Rebecca to her husband when she saw Arabella pale, "You are frightening her!"

Duly chastised, Harry rushed to help his wife sit up from her prone position in bed where she was resting with her feet propped on a pillow. Once situated, she concurred with her husband's findings, "Harry is right, Bella. You look remarkably elegant. I am glad there was an evening dress in the lot Mademoiselle Lavigne sent over this afternoon while you were out with uncle. How do you feel?"

Arabella grinned and twirled. She wore a round dress made of midnight blue gauze over a dark blue satin slip. The round neck of the high-waist gown was cut low over her bosom and was edged of the same material with a soft falling ruffle. Layers of the same colored midnight blue gauze with tiny crystal beads sewn into the trim comprised her short puffy sleeves. A dark blue satin ribbon was wrapped under her bosom with its ends falling down the back of her skirt. Two rows of wreaths made of matching gauze decorated the bottom of her skirt with more tiny crystal beads sewn into their centers to complete a most elegant look. She wore dark blue long gloves to finish an ensemble that reminded one of a brilliant blue sapphire.

The maid styled her hair up into a full tuft on the crown of her head and decorated it with two simple short dark blue plumes and a crystal pin. A few soft curls framed her face. Her neck was bare, but she wore silver dangling earrings. At four and twenty, she did not look the ingénue she was, but a sophisticate.

She completed her full turn and then replied, "It is nice to have new clothes and I was excited to attend the opera, until Harry reminded me I am likely to be as much on display as the actors. Do you really think people will take me in dislike and speak about me?"

"Only the envious, Bella," replied Rebecca, "and they are not worthy of your notice or friendship. Uncle will champion you and I daresay Bolton, no matter what he said about washing his hands of you, will also see you protected. He attends the play with a friend."

"Yes," replied Arabella. "Bolton is attending with the Earl of Fairgrove and his family. I was told Bolton is courting the earl's sister, so I very much doubt he will have time to notice me."

Both Harry and Rebecca noted Arabella's frown and laughed.

Harry rebutted, "There is little chance you will go unnoticed, Bella. I expect more eyes will be on you than the stage."

Arabella blushed and shook her head in denial.

Rebecca looked at her husband and asked, "Have you informed Dawson, Bella is to wear my fur cloak? It is cold this evening and I want her warm."

Harry grinned and said, "Yes, Becca. Do not worry. Dawson knows to give Bella your cloak to wear."

Viscount Ketterling led Arabella into the Earl of Belcrave's private box. The heavy crimson curtain, used to block the hall light from disturbing the performance, was pulled to the side and secured with a wall tie. It would be released when the performance began.

William urged Arabella forward to take a seat near the rail. The box was located on the second tier on the side of the theatre, to the right of the His Majesty's box, and gave a prominent view of the stage. More importantly, the close vantage point made it easy to hear what the actors said. Those that sat in the upper balcony and farther out were hard-pressed to hear all the dialogue. Only the privileged with their costly and elegant private boxes were afforded the luxury of hearing the performance.

Drury Lane held over 3,000 seats and relied on its elaborate scenery, flamboyant costumes and production effects to enthrall its audience, unlike the smaller theatres of Queen Elizabeth's reign, where a Shakespearean actor only needed to belt out his verse for his audience to be entertained.

Arabella was amazed at the elegance of the theatre with its decor of gilt motifs and railings; crimson velveteen curtains and upholstery. The theatre was engulfed with shimmering bright light. A massive crystal chandelier, numerous wall sconces, and multiple stage lights were all aflame while the audience took their seats. William explained the theatre was gas lit when he caught Arabella looking at the chandelier.

"Gas lighting was introduced a couple of years ago, Arabella, and to my knowledge Drury Lane was the first theatre to install it. The trend to pipe gas into homes is on the rise, but there are many who hesitate to use it, remembering the first installations where many townhomes exploded because of a gas leakage."

"Is your home gas lit, uncle?"

"No," he answered with a grin. "I am one of the hesitant ones."

Noise from the pit caused Arabella to peer over her balustrade. A number of young men wearing clothes in gaudy colors were making jests and laughing wholeheartedly. She looked at her uncle for an explanation.

"They are nothing, but a bunch of rascals looking for sport," he explained. "They buy fruit from the orange girl and peel the skins to throw at the performers if the play is bad. Sometimes, they throw the whole orange. They can become quite boisterous even in their praise."

Arabella caught the eye of one young man who had the audacity to wink at her. Her uncle laughed and said, "They are also known to have no shame in inspecting and commenting on the ladies in the balconies."

"Indeed," chuckled Arabella, her cheeks flaming with embarrassment.

"You look a trifle warm, niece," commented her uncle with a grin. "Would you like to remove your cloak?"

"Thank you uncle," she replied and stood. William removed Rebecca's borrowed fur cloak from her shoulders and placed it on a vacant chair before returning to his seat.

Arabella looked out at the expansive theatre with its three rows of tiered boxes on each side of the stage. Their balconies were all beautifully appointed with gilt emblems and sconces. The stage itself was humongous, boasting eighty feet wide by ninety-two feet deep; and from its height, hung two enormous velveteen crimson curtains.

"Is the theatre unpopular, or perhaps, the play?"

Surprised by her inquiry, William turned his attention to the empty boxes where Arabella looked. It took him a moment to understand her question. "Oh," he explained, "It is *de rigueur* during the Season to arrive late to the theatre. It makes for a grander entrance, but the gesture turns flat when more and more peers are of the same mind. Drury Lane, like Hyde Park, is another venue where the crème of society come to see and be seen."

"I do not see Bolton," she remarked.

It was on the wings of her words when their attention was drawn by a trill of laughter. "Ah," remarked her uncle, "The viscount and his lady."

And indeed Bolton finally came. He was dressed exquisitely in a formal black tailcoat and pantaloons. Even across the theatre she saw he wore the customary black and white evening ensemble and top hat for gentlemen. He was assisting an animated young lady to her seat with one hand, while his other hand rested against his chest to keep his glistening black satin cape, lined in brilliant red and draped over his arm, from falling to the floor. His friend, the Earl of Fairgrove, was busy assisting an elder lady with white ostrich plumes in her hair, onto a front row seat next to the young lady whose laughter had drawn their attention. Both gentlemen sat behind the ladies, and as if to ascertain if the ladies were comfortable, leaned forward to speak to them.

William stood and released the curtain to keep the hallway light from entering their box when the theatre lights began to dim. Arabella welcomed the darkness so she would not have to witness the burgeoning romance of the viscount and the lady who might become his wife. The possibility was anathema to her. She forced herself to turn her head and look at the stage.

As the paneled curtains began to part, William whispered, "*The Distressed Mother* is a tragedy comprised in five acts, Arabella. Ambrose Phillips translated Racine's *Andromache.* It is about how a mother is compelled to marry her husband's murderer in order to save her son's life."

Arabella's mouth opened in astonishment. She quickly shut it when the stage scene was revealed. The men's long hair and flowing gowns were disarming. *Is this how the Greeks looked?* The character Orestes entered the stage. With great animation, he showed his surprise at learning his old friend had not died at sea.

The minute the curtains closed at the end of the third act, gas was fueled into the stage lights, the overhead chandelier, and the wall sconces to make their flames grow. The theatre became brightly illuminated and Arabella quickly brushed away the tears glistening on her cheeks. She was embarrassed to be seen as a *watering pot* and laughed when her uncle offered his square piece of linen.

He remarked, "And you were worried your sister would find the play too distressing."

Arabella sheepishly grinned and retorted, "Is that meant to be a pun, uncle?"

William looked puzzled, but reasoned out the pun on the word distressing and the play's title. "No," he replied, "but I will take credit for being witty if it removes your sadness."

Neither of them heard the Earl of Fairgrove enter, but immediately turned when he exclaimed, "My dear Miss Barrington, what grieves you?"

William rose and greeted, "Fairgrove."

Fairgrove returned the salutation as he approached Arabella and asked her again, "Are you ill?"

"No, my lord," she answered waving off his inspection of her. "I am not ill. You may give all credit of my sorrow to the outstanding performance of the actors."

Fairgrove rebutted, "You are being too generous. I think there is more behind your tears, but I will not press you. Aside, from your emotional downturn, are you enjoying yourself and your popularity? You acquired a bevy of admirers in the pit based on their avid inspection of you."

Arabella looked at the dandies in the pit and was surprised to see many of them smiling and nodding to her. Uncomfortable with their shouts of praise, she instinctively sought out Bolton in Fairgrove's box. She thought to find comfort in knowing he was watching out for her, but instead, she was reminded his attention was now directed elsewhere.

Fairgrove saw where she looked and informed, "My mama and my sister Adelaide. Bolton would have accompanied me, but my sister begged him to stay. Adelaide complained she would look a sorry sight to be without any gentleman in attendance."

"She makes her debut into Society, my lord?"

"Technically, no," replied Edward. "She made her curtsey three years ago, but it was the year our father passed away and her Season was cut short. My father's death left my mama heartbroken and my sister dutifully stayed by her side, using her stubborn personality to keep our mama from falling into melancholy. I owe her a great debt of gratitude for remaining at home until our mama was ready to participate in the Season again. That said, my sister is wasting no time in using her wiles to bring a gentleman *up to scratch*, Bolton to be specific."

"She is one and twenty then. Younger than me," remarked Arabella as if that was the only information she recalled from the earl's confession.

"Indeed," responded Edward looking as if he was walking on eggshells until he thought of a clever retort. "Of course, I would not dare ask your age, but rest assured you look as lovely as any lady making her debut."

Arabella laughed and replied, "Well done, my lord." Turning to her uncle she asked, "What say you uncle? Is it time for me to wear a cap and place myself on the shelf?"

William shook his head, "Arabella, do not be absurd. Every man in this theatre took their inspection of you when we arrived and have yet to stop mooning over you. I do not think you have to worry you are past your prime."

"Indeed not!" exclaimed Edward. "And if it pleases you Miss Barrington, will you do me the honor of driving to Hyde Park with me and my sister tomorrow afternoon? Adelaide hopes to press Bolton to come, so we will make a fine party if you join us."

"The honor would be mine, my lord," Arabella replied adding with a mischievous smile "with or without Bolton."

Edward grinned and explained he must take his leave to order the refreshments he promised for his party. He offered to send them drinks and then assured he would pick her up tomorrow at half past three o'clock in the afternoon.

Arabella was in a sound sleep when she heard her name whispered and her shoulder shrugged. It took her a moment to wake, but once she did, she was surprised to see Bolton hovering over her, still in his evening clothes. The idea of him partying while she slept angered her into frowning and crossing her arms on top of her blankets. She hissed, "What do you want?"

He pulled the bed covers back and threw her robe at her, commanding her to follow him. To her surprise, she did. She followed him down the servant staircase and into the library. The house was silent with everyone abed. The impropriety of the moment did not occur to Arabella until she found herself alone, standing toe to toe with Bolton. She had no idea why he came, but his seriousness made her tremble.

"You are cold," he observed and removed his cape to place around her shoulders.

"You are frightening me, Bolton. Tell me what is wrong. Is it Nathaniel?"

He quickly assured her, "No, not Nathaniel. I came to learn what troubles you. Fairgrove said he found you crying. Why Bella? What happened?"

She turned away from him and went to sit on the winged leather sofa. The cold leather seeped through her clothes and made her tremble. To minimize the contact of her body on the frigid surface, she quickly pulled her knees up under her night dress and wrapped her arms around her legs. Bolton came and sat by her side. He drew her close and wrapped his arm around her shoulder. She sighed and dropped her head against his chest. She did not hesitate to accept his comfort, nor confess her fright.

"I did not want Becca to attend the play because I feared she would get emotional," Arabella began. "Instead, I cried over the premise of a mother faced with having to marry her husband's murderer in order to save her son. The idea of giving yourself to a man who killed your loved one resonated and scared me. I am so glad Becca is married to Harry, but even I do not know if that will stay Damburten. What if he demands Becca submit to him to keep Nathaniel from the hangman's noose? What if he demands something of me? The baron's wickedness scares me and knowing he is alive and capable of hurting my family frightens me even more. I am sorry my tears worried you."

"You seem better?"

"Yes. I shared my concerns with my uncle in the carriage ride home and he assured me Damburten could never hurt us again. He said we are too well-protected and connected for him to dare."

"You will leave Damburten to me, Arabella," he commanded. "I will settle the matter one way or another with him."

"Now, you are frightening me, Bolton. This is not your concern and I would not have you put yourself in jeopardy. Have you forgotten how you washed your hands of me?"

"I never said anything of the sort," he replied angrily.

"But I was told you wish to return to your life and now that I am in the bosom of my family, you have no need to see me."

"I am here, am I not? And I shall see you tomorrow, or more precisely, later this afternoon with Fairgrove and his sister," he replied. "Do not presume to know my mind, Arabella." He kissed her forehead like one does a child and pulled her to her feet, announcing, "I shall take my leave and not worry you know the way back to your room."

Arabella watched him leave before making her own exit. She walked up the main staircase to her room in a daze, her mind on the tender kiss he bestowed upon her head. *Is it the act of a guardian or lover? Do I desire one over the other? Of course I do.*

She could no longer deny the feelings Bolton stirred within her, even when reason told her she was far from eligible to be anything but his friend. The Earl of Belcrave expected his heir to marry a lady of title and wealth. She had neither. She was not groomed to take on the mantle of a countess and that ultimately was what Bolton needed.

She reached her room and it was then she realized she was still wearing Bolton's black cape. She removed it and was ready to fling it on a chair when she realized the brouhaha its sighting would make when the maid spied it in the morning. *Heavens be!* Chatter would begin immediately how she entertained a midnight caller. The maid could attest the cape was not there when she helped Arabella dress for bed. That tidbit would travel through the servant's grapevine and then through every Mayfair mansion, until every member of the *ton* heard the lascivious tale. Heaven forbid if someone recognized it was Bolton's cape.

A nervous fluster made her race around the room to look for a hidey-hole and when none appeared, her temper piqued. She cursed and began a tirade regarding arrogant viscounts. *Who does he think he is to sneak into my room in the dead of the night and risk my reputation? He will not be the one accused of impropriety. No, I will be the one tainted.* In her angry rant she forgot how Bolton listened to her fears and comforted her.

She thrust the cape under her bed covers seeing no other alternative to keep the item out of view from the maid, who in the morning would bring her warm water for her ablutions. Once she dismissed the servant, she would retrieve the cape, and take it to her sister's room to have Harry return it to his brother. *Ugh! What a trial it is to be above reproach.* She got under the bed covers and snuggled into the downy mattress. Her toes touched the cape and she maneuvered the vexing item up with her feet to bring the cape against her chest. She hugged it close, burying her face into its folds and breathed in the musky bergamot scent. The smell reminded her of Bolton and surprisingly, she fell into slumber.

Chapter Fifteen

Bolton waited with Fairgrove's sister Adelaide in the earl's barouche while his friend bounded up his family's townhome to retrieve Arabella. He could not fault Adelaide's enthusiasm. She chatted and flirted with all the effervescence of a determined lady wanting to marry. After three years of being a dutiful daughter, she was eager to ply her wares and ensnare a gentleman. Thomas could do nothing but let her, since Edward asked him to pay her court.

Edward feared Adelaide was too green to enter the marriage mart, even though she made her debut three years ago. Edward hoped to polish her sensibilities by providing a safe suitor, and who else could he ask, but one of the Dark Rogues, men he trusted and called friend. They each knew how to charm a lady and guard themselves from the parson's noose, if they chose.

After all, they eventually needed to marry to continue their line and who better to wed than a lady tutored since infancy to marry a nobleman, to manage a household, and to know her duty of breeding the next heir. At the very least, Thomas would give his sister cachet in the competitive marriage mart known as the Season.

Edward dropped the bronzed lion's head door knocker and was taken aback to see Arabella at the door's threshold. Belcrave's butler did not look pleased, no doubt thinking the lady made his job of announcing guests superfluous, but Edward's eyes gleamed. He could not keep his lips from widening into a smile by her punctual appearance. He stepped back to allow her to exit the manor and then complimented, "Miss Barrington, how clever of you to be ready. I thought to kick up my heels for at least fifteen minutes awaiting your arrival. Yet, here you are without need for me to help you into your redingote or to hold your purse. Your punctuality makes me speechless."

"And yet," she retorted, "you managed to deliver one. Perhaps, you are the clever one, my lord."

Edward laughed and proffered his arm. Arabella hesitated when she saw Bolton steel his eyes at her.

"Shall I deliver my monologue on the advantages of taking a gentleman's arm?" Edward suggested when she did not avail herself of his escort.

Arabella shook her concern for Bolton away and gave Edward a beaming smile. She placed her hand on his arm and replied, "There is no need, my lord. I am happy to avail myself of your escort."

They walked down the front steps side by side with her arm entwined with his before Edward released her and proffered his hand to help her step into the open carriage. Arabella took the seat facing forward next to Adelaide. Edward followed her in and sat with his back to his team of horses across from her and next to Thomas. He introduced his sister Adelaide. His sister's enthusiastic greeting followed by her hearty discourse kept Thomas from making his own salutation.

Adelaide quickly explained why she could not meet Arabella last night, "I could not leave my mama. Memories of dear papa assault her at the oddest times. Last night, she remembered how he often fell asleep during a play. He did not enjoy them, you see, but suffered going to the theatre because he knew mama took great joy in attending. The memory would have sent her into melancholia if I was not there to turn it into a comedic recollection."

"I hope she is in better spirits today," remarked Arabella.

"Oh, indeed," replied Adelaide. "She is having tea with her intimate friends. They will keep her in fine fettle until I return. Did you enjoy the play? Have you read the reviews?"

"Yes," answered Arabella. "The reviewer proclaimed Mr. Macready is the best tragic actor with the exception of Kean. I agree Macready gave an admirable performance, but I am no expert. It was the first time I attended the theatre and I must admit everything enthralled me."

"I thought the reviews a bit harsh on the play-wright," remarked Adelaide. "What think you, Bolton?"

Bolton smiled. Fairgrove's little sister would do well. She managed to introduce a genteel topic and bring her company into the conversation. In short order, she managed to express familial devotion, project social graces and display a witty mind.

He answered, "No doubt, the reviewer dislikes all things French. After all, it was not that many years ago we were at war with the country, but the man insults his own by writing how we Englishmen are puzzled by a French play."

"No doubt," interjected Edward. "He wrote that contretemps just to rile up his readers and get them, as we are doing, to talk about him. However, I do think he made a valid point regarding the costumes and hair. I had a devil of a time identifying the men from the women. I don't think any of the Greek men carved into the Elgin marbles sported long hair as did the men on stage."

Everyone laughed when Adelaide recalled the one frustrated actor who kept replacing the wig falling from his head. "I thought he was going to throw the blasted thing into the audience."

"Adelaide," corrected Edward, "your language."

Arabella was hard-pressed not to like Adelaide, even when she swore. She put everyone at ease and kept the conversation moving along, encouraging each person to participate by asking questions on various topics. Arabella quickly relaxed in her company, especially when

Thomas was equally as attentive to her as he was to Adelaide. She did not have to watch him woo her, as she expected, which pleased her.

They entered Hyde Park and Adelaide was still laughing over Arabella's recollection of her morning's curtseying practice. "I must be at it again later this afternoon."

"Do not be too concerned," remarked Adelaide. "Every debutant experiences the same trials the first time they put on hoops. Without the weight of the dress to hold the apparatus steady, the hoops can quickly gain momentum and cause any number of calamities. You should not blame yourself for the trifle."

Arabella's guilt over destroying one of the countess' ceramic figures and turning it into a ridiculous story made her somberly confess, "I do not think the porcelain figurine my hoop knocked over onto the floor and shattered into a million pieces was considered a trifle."

Silence ensued until Thomas grinned and told his own story of destroying a cherished family vase. Then, Adelaide and Edward confessed their own mishaps, along with the ridiculous stories they told to keep from being punished. Each confession made their small party laugh.

They were so deep in their festive banter they did not notice the spectacle they were making of themselves with their smiling faces and good cheer. Only a shout from a mounted gentleman or a greeting from a nearby carriage drew their attention momentarily away. They were all too busy having a merry time to complain about all the stops and starts the carriage was making as it meandered through Rotten Row.

Another stop placed their barouche parallel to a lady's carriage traveling in the opposite direction having made her turn at the end of the lane. Thomas immediately turned his eyes away from the interloper and Arabella wished she thought to do the same. She did not want to greet Rebecca's enemy.

"Is this your sister, my lord," asked Lady Caroline of Edward.

"Indeed," replied Edward. He said to his sister, "Adelaide, allow me to introduce to you Lady Caroline Southwaite."

The carriages were beginning to move forward so Caroline hastily said to Adelaide, "I hope to see you at Almack's, Lady Adelaide. I am sure you, at least, have your vouchers in hand." Caroline steeled her eyes at Arabella to make sure her insult was perceived before her carriage moved away.

Adelaide hissed, "Why that witch!"

Arabella was confused and asked, "What did she do?"

"I may have arrived late to the Season, Miss Barrington, but trust me, I am well-informed of what Lady Caroline did to your sister. Her little remark regarding vouchers has nothing to do with me, but to bring to light how you may not have them. Attendance at Almack's is governed by its Patronesses and they are very high sticklers in granting them. Not everyone who requests vouchers gets them and those young debutantes denied are treated badly. To be blunt, the *ton* is vicious in calling them common and lacking. Lady Caroline is extremely ill-mannered to question your possession of them, and so I will not call her friend."

Adelaide's rant made Arabella open her eyes wide in astonishment before her lips began to tremble and tilt up into a quivering smile. The idea Adelaide was slaying the incomparable Lady Caroline for her, made her laugh so hard her eyes teared. She could not speak, so to show her appreciation she leaned over and hugged Adelaide, causing both of their leghorn straw bonnets to fall off the crown of their heads. Once disengaged, Arabella saw Thomas grinning at her.

He asked, "Do you want to attend Almack's, Miss Barrington?"

"Do you attend?" she countered.

"I will not," he replied soberly.

"Then, why would I attend when I know no one and have no one to escort me?"

"I would escort you along with my sister, Miss Barrington, should you acquire the necessary vouchers," interjected Edward.

"Oh, please try," begged Adelaide. "It would be so much fun to attend in your company and I would love to snub my nose at that mean-spirited Caroline."

"I would love to see you do it," grinned Arabella.

"Then you shall," stated Thomas.

Arabella looked at Thomas to discern his truthfulness. He looked back at her with a self-assurance she could not discredit.

Edward laughed and offered, "Adelaide and I shall pick you up tomorrow night, shall we?"

Thomas made his way to the Cowper's mansion. Of all the Almack's Patronesses, Emily Cowper was the one who would grant him vouchers for Arabella. She had a generous nature and was not a high stickler like the other Patronesses. She was known to favor the newly presented debutantes with a warm smile and Thomas was determined for Arabella to receive it.

He was not about to let the ill-mannered Lady Caroline gossip about Arabella's lack of vouchers and taint her stature. The lady's snide remark made him rise to Arabella's rescue like a knight in shining armor. He was determined to slay Lady Caroline by getting Arabella her vouchers, but even he wondered what made him think he could do so as if it was no great feat.

He was a capable and powerful man in his own right, but the Almack Patronesses were not a group of ladies with whom to trifle. If the ladies took offense to his request he could do more harm than good. The Patronesses owned enough clout to ruin a lady and her chances of making a good marriage if they wanted. Of course, he would never let it happen, just like he would never let anyone hurt one of his family members and that was how he justified his compelling reason for asking Emily Cowper for a voucher. He was protecting his own.

He rushed up the Cowper townhome and when he reached the landing, he pulled a calling card from his tailcoat pocket. He folded the corner of the card to inform the lady he came in person and then dropped the door knocker. The door opened and Thomas handed his card to the butler who fell mute when he boldly stepped inside as if he had every right. Thomas announced with all the arrogance he owned, "I shall await Lady Cowper in her drawing room."

He removed and handed his gloves, hat and greatcoat to the astonished butler. The befuddled servant had the temerity to blush at his failure to stop the lord from entering, but drew on his courage as gatekeeper to the Cowper's townhome to inform, "My lord, my lady has a guest."

Thomas only paused a second before replying, "Announce me. She will wish to see me." He had no choice but to intrude since he needed the vouchers for tomorrow's assembly.

The butler handed Thomas' belongings to an underling and strode forward to lead the way to the drawing room. Thomas followed and without waiting to see if he was to be received, entered hard on the butler's heels. He almost grimaced when he saw Emily's guest.

He did not expect Lady Jersey to be visiting. He sought out Lady Cowper because they made their debuts together and held a modicum of teasing affection for one another. She liked to profess all men were in need of a wife and how she was ready to help him find one.

Emily beamed upon seeing him and extended her hand as he approached. Thomas took and placed a soft kiss on the back of it, "Lady Cowper, as always, a delight." He turned to Sarah Jersey, the highest stickler of all the Almack Patronesses and was stayed by her reproof, "None of that foolishness, Bolton."

Emily asked, "What brings you to my home, Bolton?"

"Vouchers," answered Sarah.

"Nonsense," remarked Emily, "unless cupid's arrow finally struck him?"

Thomas raised his brows and quickly disabused the countess. "You misunderstand, my lady. I am on an errand of mercy for my brother's-sister-by-marriage."

"Harry's wife has a sister?" asked Sarah.

"For heaven's sake, Sarah," scolded Emily. "You would think he came to call on you!"

"Well," countered Sarah, "am I not the one who granted Harry's wife vouchers? And that was before we knew her connections. I know good *ton* when I see it and I recognized the chit had it."

"Not a chit, my lady, but Mrs. Harry Bolton," corrected Thomas.

"Why are you requesting vouchers on the lady's behalf?" asked Emily. "I understood her grandfather is the *Marquis du Benoît* and her uncle Viscount Ketterling. Surely, the request should come from them?"

"Indeed," answered Thomas, "but I assigned myself the task when the need arose for her to attend tomorrow's assembly. Time is of the essence, so I must beg upon your generosity."

"Beg?" giggled Emily "on hand and knee?"

"If you wish," replied Thomas, "but my valet will have an apoplexy to see the knee of my pantaloons scuffed."

"Don't be absurd, Bolton," chastised Sarah. "Of course, Miss Barrington will have vouchers. The queen recognizes the family and is in anticipation of their debut. Why the urgency for tomorrow's assembly. Does it have anything to do with Southwaite's daughter?"

"There is talk?" he queried.

"The girl is foolish to continue her slanderous quips. She hurts no one but herself, even though she claims she is misunderstood. Envy is not a desirable quality for a young lady to display on the marriage mart," counseled Sarah.

Emily nodded her agreement and then left her seat to go to her gilded writing desk. She pulled from the top drawer a lady's voucher, bent over to inscribe the name of Miss Arabella Barrington, then signed and pressed her seal onto it.

Thomas asked, "Only one, my lady?"

"The only one that counts," she mused.

Thomas looked at the card and saw it was an annual pass granting Arabella permission to attend all the Almack's balls during the Season if she wished. He took and kissed Emily's hand. Lady Cowper laughed as if she deciphered his secret and then laughed again when a startled look crossed his features. She reminded him to pay her man of business ten guineas for the voucher before waving him off.

"Most assuredly," he replied and made his bow to the ladies before he left.

He headed straight to Belcrave House as he was anxious to put Arabella at ease about the voucher. He hastily removed his tall hat and gave it to Dawson the moment the butler opened the door.

Thomas asked, "Where might I find Miss Barrington?"

"In the drawing room, my lord," answered the butler, while waiting for the viscount to hand him his gloves, and greatcoat.

Thomas divested himself quickly of his outerwear and inquired, "And my mother? Has she visitors?"

Dawson answered, "She is not receiving, my lord. She just left the drawing room to assist Mrs. Bolton to her room?"

Concerned, he asked, "Becca is ill?"

Noting the viscount's concern, the family butler assured, "No, my lord; however, the countess feared Mrs. Bolton's fits of hilarity might do the baby harm and ordered her to bed."

Thomas's curiosity quickly moved him to the drawing room to see what was causing all the laughter. He arrived in time to see Arabella scold his younger sister.

"Oh, do control yourself, Charlotte. I have no wish to explain to your mama how I broke another one of her treasures."

"If mama treasured that ordinary piece of bisque it would not be in the drawing room," responded Charlotte. "Now try again, you almost did it properly. Extend your right foot behind your left to rest on the ball of your foot. Keep your back straight and your head lowered. Bend your knee and keep lowering yourself down until your right knee almost touches the ground. Hold for a second or two and then slowly raise yourself back to an upright position." Charlotte watched and applauded, "Oh well done, Arabella. You remembered to gracefully round your arms as you dropped. You must show mama!"

Charlotte turned and gave her brother a cursory grin as she passed him to find their mama. He did not notice. His eyes were on Arabella and her odd ensemble. She stood wearing the armature of a hoop skirt over her sprigged muslin dress. He strode forward to congratulate and tease her, but her bright-eyed and flushed expression sparked emotions in him that quickly sobered his playful mood.

He drew close enough to bell back her hoop before he stopped. He looked into the depth of her light brown eyes and heard her breath hitch. If he was in another frame of mind, he would have applauded her nerve of not backing an inch, nor saying a word. It was a game of wills, one he had played with her before, yet never to this degree. Energy that was far from playful pulsed between them. He had thought he held the advantage when she gasped, but then she had closed her eyes, tilted her head back, and gave him access to her lips. His resolve almost crumbled.

As a gentleman, he had no other choice but to refuse her gift. He gently took her face in his hands, turned down her head and kissed her forehead, discovering more emotion in that chaste kiss than in any he ever experienced with another woman. He regretfully released her head and turned to leave, only to find his mother and sister watching. Charlotte, the minx, giggled. He ignored his mother's unspoken censure and strode past them. Not until he stood on the pavement outside Belcrave House did he realize he forgot to give Arabella the voucher for Almack's.

Chapter Sixteen

Arabella stared up into the blackness of her room. Sleep failed her. Every time her eyes closed she recalled the embarrassment she suffered at Thomas' hands. She had practiced all afternoon to make a royal curtsey and her spirits had soared when she saw Thomas had witnessed it. He had looked as cheerful as Charlotte did when she ran out of the room to inform the countess of her accomplishment, but then his expression sobered, and like a lion on the hunt, he came at her, one step at a time, ready to pounce if she sought escape.

In anyone else, his manner would have frightened her, but Thomas' serious attention only made her pulse quicken in anticipation. He was not looking at her like a guardian. The fluttering of her insides, her rapid heartbeat and short breath reminded her of their first kiss at Salt Hill. He had stopped within inches of her body and in that moment, she desperately wanted him to kiss her.

She wanted to know if his kiss would be as glorious as their first. Part of her hoped it was not for she knew he would never marry her and the last thing she wanted was to pine for a man she could not have. In his eyes, as well as the *ton's,* she was completely ineligible, lacking the proper qualifications to be a future countess. Granted, she had talents thanks to her dear mama, but she was far from the aristocratic lady someone of Thomas' stature required.

Even so, she could not deny she wanted to be the one he called his own. She wanted all the intimacy marriage provided; especially the kissing. Their kiss at Salt Hill still assailed her memory and triggered questions. *Were the sensations he stirred in me an anomaly? Would a second kiss confirm my feelings are true or disabuse them as fanciful?*

She had closed her eyes in anticipation of his kiss, but unfortunately, his lips did not meet hers. He had kissed her forehead, and to her mortification, when she opened her eyes she saw his sister and mother standing witness to the whole scene. The warm sensations flooding her quickly dissolved and were replaced with embarrassment and then anger. She wanted to curse Thomas for leaving her alone with the countess and Charlotte to explain what just happened. *Good heavens! I don't know what happened!*

Charlotte had giggled and the countess had shushed her. To Arabella, she said, "Be assured, I will speak with my son. He has no right to behave in such a manner with you."

Arabella was so mortified she barely got the words out, "I beg, do not, my lady. He meant no offense, merely rewarding me as might my brother for a job well done."

"Yes," agreed the countess. "But he is not your brother, Arabella."

"No," she concurred. "He is not."

Both Charlotte and the countess looked at her as if she had grown a second head. Then, the countess waved her off to rest before dinner. Arabella was more than happy to take her leave.

A slight creak alerted Arabella someone was in her room. She was about to reach for the silver candlestick on her bedside table to defend herself when the glowing remnants of her fire illuminated him as he walked towards it. She watched her intruder add a scoop of coals to her dying fire. His consideration for her comfort smoothed her growing temper from seeing him enter her room as if he was entitled. She quickly closed her eyes and decided to feign sleep rather than rant at Thomas as she wished.

She waited and when he did not nudge her awake she tightened her lips in frustration. *Is he just going to stare at me?*

Thomas looked down at Arabella with her plaited dark brown hair lying by the side of her face. He came to deliver the voucher he forgot to give her earlier. He should have left it with Dawson, but he wanted to see her face when she received it. He could have returned after dinner to do the deed, but he did not want to suffer his mother's inquisition. He could have waited until morning, but he did not want her to worry to whether he secured the voucher or not. He could think of a number of reasons to justify why he snuck back into her room, but he was no fool. He wanted to see her and see her alone.

His mouth twitched in amusement at seeing her pretend to sleep. Apparently, he was not as quiet as he thought upon entering her room. He watched her and saw the tell-tale signs she was awake. Her eyes moved behind her lids and based by her still chest, she was holding her breath. He smiled, knowing how her temper was rising to be under his inspection. He gently ran his finger down her cheek to put her out of her misery, and said, "You might as well open your eyes, Arabella. I know you are awake."

She shot her eyes open and settled them into a glare. She scolded, "Have you no decency, Bolton! Why are you here?"

"To see you, of course," he replied glibly.

She sat up and quickly pulled her covers up to her neck remembering she wore only a thin cotton night dress. She chastised, "And you were compelled to see me before dawn broke? Do you not realize how you put my reputation at risk?"

Thomas frowned. No, he did not consider her reputation. His feelings drove him, as they did last night, to see her. He did not consider visiting his family's home, albeit in the middle of the night, an egregious action. After all, he still had a room designated for his use, her room to be exact.

Last night his concern for why she cried at the theatre compelled him to see her. Tonight was different. Tonight was about seeing her expression when he presented her with the Almack's voucher and if he was being honest, receiving her gratitude without a witness to check her manner. The enormity of visiting her in her bedroom in the middle of the night reminded him of the bachelorhood he put in jeopardy.

He scowled at Arabella as if she was at fault for his misconduct. He could not accuse her of seduction, that label could only apply to him since he was the one to enter her bedroom. Angry beyond belief, he turned, grabbed her dressing robe and threw it at her. He ordered her to meet him in the library and then left, leaving the door wide open with every expectation she would obediently follow on his heels.

She ranted, "Arrogant, demanding, scoundrel! How dare he order me to do his bidding!"

She was ready to ignore his command and stubbornly snuggled down into her bed when her instinct prodded her to comply. Undoubtedly, he would return to collect her like a recalcitrant child if she did not join him and then wouldn't that be putting a kettle to boil. Quickly donning her robe, she raced downstairs to the library.

He stood with his hands clasped behind his back pacing. "You took your time, Miss Barrington," he accused.

Gone was his teasing and warm manner and in its place he looked severely vexed. She returned his glare and retaliated with equal vigor. "It is indeed my time, Bolton, and you are lucky I gave it to you. Who are you to be angry with me? I did not seek you out and if you find me so disagreeable, then why are here instead of finding company to your liking?!"

Duly chastised, Thomas' features softened. He pulled the voucher from his pocket and offered it to her. Arabella looked at the heavy-papered card for a moment dumbfounded, then with understanding of what the card meant, took it into her hand and turned her eyes to him with appreciation.

He said, "I did not want you to worry over the voucher. I meant to give it to you earlier, but was distracted by your stellar royal curtsey."

Arabella knew the curtsey was not the distraction, but his flushed face gratified her more than any apology he could offer regarding his ill manner. She gave him a brilliant smile that drew him like a magnet. He cupped her face in his hands. This time, she did not close her eyes, but watched what he would do. He sighed when his eyes fell to her lips. He brought her head down to kiss her forehead again. Her brows drew together in frustration and she remarked, "I am not your sister, Bolton."

He let her go and brusquely said as he left, "I am well aware, Miss Barrington," while silently castigating himself for why that was a issue. It was easy to forget he did not want a love-match when he was in her company, and that was more a problem than his desire to be in her company.

"I wish Bolton came with us," remarked Adelaide sitting with her brother and Arabella in the earl's black lacquered town carriage emblazoned with their family's crest. They were waiting to alight at Almack's and had to wait in a queue of carriages on King Street until theirs made its way to the assembly hall's entrance. "It is quite disheartening to think I will only have my brother with which to dance."

"Nonsense," retorted Edward. "You will have plenty of suitors. Did I not tell you how lovely you look this evening?"

"Yes," she replied, "and I thank you for your filial adoration, but really Edward, even I know I am not a *diamond of the first water.*"

"You demean yourself for no reason," argued Edward, "and if Lady Caroline sets the bar for such an accomplishment, then you would do well to remember how gentlemen looking to marry, aspire for more than a pretty face."

Adelaide's lack of confidence surprised Arabella. She could not keep silent. "Lady Adelaide, unlike me, you have all the accomplishments a nobleman looks for in a wife, but more than that your generosity of spirit is what will draw you suitors. I enjoy every moment we spend together and I can tell Bolton feels the same way."

"But I have the family nose," she informed. "It looks quite distinctive on Edward and every male member of my family, but it does me little credit."

"Your nose," Arabella explained, "is not what brings attention to your face. Your eyes gleam in amusement. Your whole face lights up no matter what the topic or with whom you speak. You are charm and gracefulness personified and I can think of no one who will not want to make your acquaintance."

Adelaide grinned and then laughed. Her face blushed in embarrassment to be under Arabella's inspection and when she saw her brother grin, she replied, "Dear me, you make me sound like a beauty which I never considered myself to be. Thank you, Miss Barrington."

"Oh, do call me Bella," she replied.

"I thank you as well, Miss Barrington," interjected Edward. "She needed to hear from someone other than a family member she is a gem."

They made themselves into the largest of the three assembly rooms where everyone converged to socialize and dance. Two smaller rooms were set aside; one for refreshments, the other for card playing. A small orchestra in an upper balcony played and filled the room with music. Ladies and lords alike preened along the border of the walls and around the room's supporting Roman pillars, leaving the central floor vacant for dancing. The Countesses of Jersey and Cowper, acting as the evening's hostesses, stood at the end of the dance floor. Edward escorted his party to them. He made his bow and then presented his sister and Arabella.

The Countess of Jersey remarked to Arabella "I know your sister, Miss Barrington."

"As do I," replied Arabella with a grin. She heard all about Lady Jersey from Rebecca. Lady Sarah, with all the arrogance of her rank and power as a Patroness, once tried to intimidate her sister in Hyde Park. She snubbed her nose at Rebecca and then informed the Countess of Belcrave she did not have the time to consider the request of vouchers for Harry's wife.

Sarah was astonished when Rebecca did not cower under her condescending manner, but responded to her arrogance with grace and spirit. Rebecca's pluck quickly changed the Patroness' opinion of her from condescending to admiring, and Rebecca was told she would receive her vouchers.

The tale of their first meeting became a parlour *on dit* for weeks following their meeting. It was one of the stories Arabella first heard from her sister when she arrived in London, along with the advice Arabella should respond to Sarah with equal, but respectful vigor should they ever meet.

"She has backbone," countered Sarah.

"A family trait," volleyed Arabella with amusement.

"Your lineage is impeccable, Miss Barrington, but as a commoner you should not aspire too high," she taunted.

Arabella smiled and offered, "I like to think myself uncommon, my lady."

"How so," pressed Sarah with gleeful anticipation of sparring words with a skilled wit.

"I like to think myself equal in worth to any lady," she replied. "I assure you I do not aspire to marry for anything other than love. I look not to elevate my station in life, but to secure it with a loving husband."

"In that matter you are entirely uncommon," Sarah finished sternly, disappointed in Arabella's romantic notion.

Lady Cowper held a different view and proclaimed gleefully with her hands clasped at her breast, "Oh, how perfectly romantic." She looked around and asked mischievously, "Where is Viscount Bolton?"

"He does not attend, my lady," answered Arabella.

"Tis a shame; Bolton always provides me much amusement." She turned her eyes upon Edward and remarked, "At least we have one of our Dark Rogues attending. Perhaps Fairgrove, you will provide our amusement this evening."

"Heaven forbid!" he laughed. "You forget I will be too busy watching over these two ladies to do anything worthy of speech."

"How disappointing," chuckled Emily.

As they walked away Adelaide turned to Arabella and asked, "Do you really mean to marry only for love?"

"It is my fondest wish," she replied.

Adelaide inquired, "But what of my brother?"

The question stopped Arabella in her tracks and without consideration of Edward's presence, or to the propriety of such a discussion in a public place she exclaimed, "What?!"

"Will you marry my brother if you fall in love with him?"

Edward chuckled having listened to the conversation with amusement. He counseled Arabella, "Do not let your courage slip now, Miss Barrington; especially not after successfully sparring words with Lady Jersey."

She was relieved the earl did not put much credence into his sister's inquiry or put her to the blush for the idea, *but is it possible? Can I fall in love with Fairgrove? Can I be misreading my feelings for Bolton? Perhaps, it is not love, but admiration for a man of stellar character, intelligence and charm, and oh, so much more. Can I simply be starstruck, having never been in the company of a man to whom I admire?*

She knew nothing of love other than familial love. Her parents were a shining example of what she wanted in a marriage, *but do I really know what they felt for one another? Could their happiness been born from friendship, rather than fanciful feelings?* She took Edward's inspection and admitted he was indeed a handsome, charming, and amusing man. *Is it possible to feel for him as I do for Bolton? Is Fairgrove, as high in the instep as Bolton regarding who he will marry?* Adelaide did not think so, but what did Edward think? And if not him, *is there someone else who can fulfill my wish to marry for love? Shall I participate earnestly in the marriage mart to discover the possibility?*

Edward raised his brows after suffering Arabella's lengthy inspection and almost laughed when Arabella's eyes rounded in embarrassment. Adelaide laughed having witnessed the scene and suggested, "Come you two. We are beginning to draw attention." She quickly wrapped her hand around Arabella's arm and pulled her to the side of the room.

Fairgrove's expression grew anxious as lords collected their dancing partners and began to line up for the first dance. Arabella quickly surmised the reason behind his intense search of the ballroom, and counseled, "Do take your sister to the floor, my lord. I am no shy miss afraid to stand alone while the two of you dance. If I become too anxious I shall walk over and fence with Lady Jersey again."

Adelaide scolded, "Do not jest, Arabella. Lady Jersey has the clout to ruin any young lady's reputation if she so chooses. Do not trifle with her even in jest."

"I am well-reprimanded and will heed your wisdom," replied Arabella. "Rest assured I only meant to put you both at ease. Please take the floor."

Edward knew the importance of the first dance. His sister could be marked an undesirable if she was left standing behind as a spectator, while the Season's beauties pranced about. He would not have others find her lacking when he was at hand to promote her worth. He replied,

"Thank you for your consideration, Miss Barrington. I do hope you will save the second set for me."

Arabella chuckled, "Indeed or any other that meets your interests."

Edward raised his brows and grinned. Arabella blushed and quickly replied, "I did not mean to imply I seek more than one dance with you."

"The idea honors me, Miss Barrington," and with that last remark, Edward escorted his sister to the dance floor.

A chorus of giggles turned Arabella's head to the amusing party not far from her. She was not surprised to see Lady Caroline at the center of a group of young ladies whose eyes were turned on her. No doubt, Caroline was behaving badly, making indiscreet remarks centered on her. *Heavens be! Does the lady have no conscious, or perhaps it is the ton whose amusement in gossip is the true culprit?*

Arabella would have looked away except curiosity over the lady's changing features intrigued her. The glacial eyes shooting darts at Arabella turned soft and gleeful as the lady looked past Arabella. Caroline turned coy and flirtatious with the bat of her eyelashes. Arabella marveled at the lady's change in manner and turned to see which gentleman caused Caroline's transformation. It was not until the man drew closer did she recognize Bolton's friend, Baron Sedgeworth. His aid to her and her brother made her smile at him which caught his attention. A flash of recognition widened his eyes and with alacrity, he redirected his steps to her.

"Miss Barrington! How fortuitous to find you here. I do hope you are not engaged and will join me in this dance. We are not too late to join the line."

"I am not engaged, my lord, and would be honored to partner with you." Malcolm offered his arm and escorted her to the dance floor. The minx in her could not resist turning her head towards Lady Caroline and grinning at her as they passed. Caroline bristled and glared which made Arabella's grin widen and draw Malcolm's attention. He reciprocated with a generous smile and suddenly his admiration lifted the weight of being judged by others from her shoulders.

They took up their positions and Arabella caught sight of Edward and Adelaide down the line. Adelaide gave her a beaming smile and Edward nodded to Malcolm. Arabella was flush and exhilarated by the end of the set, and no sooner did they return to the sidelines than they switched partners.

Arabella was back on the floor with Edward and Adelaide was partnered with Malcolm. The evening proceeded with introductions to friends of Edward and Malcolm who graciously requested dances of them. Both ladies might have wondered how the evening passed so quickly, if not for their sheer exhaustion at the end of the evening.

Edward shook his head at his companions when they settled into his town coach and sighed in relief. He was far from sympathetic to their complaints of weariness and said, "The fault is yours to own for being so pretty and charming."

Adelaide giggled, before shouting an "Oh, no!"

"What?" Edward and Arabella asked in unison.

She quickly explained, "I forgot to snub Lady Caroline, so she may know I will not call her friend."

Edward counseled, "There is no need, Adelaide. I believe Miss Barrington's popularity tonight negates anything Lady Caroline said or could say about her. The lady cannot continue her vicious innuendos without maligning her own name, or insulting all those who gave Miss Barrington marked attention tonight, including me."

Chapter Seventeen

Thomas was in no mood for social discourse. After hearing an earful from his brother and Nathaniel during their morning ride in Hyde Park he wanted to be left alone to sulk. He lifted the pages of the London Times in front of his face to keep his fellow club members from approaching him, but that did not keep him from hearing the young bucks chattering about Arabella's beauty, grace, and wit. Many expressed their disappointment to find her dance card full, while others boasted of the pleasure of her company. It was more than a reasonable man could tolerate.

He lifted his newspaper higher anytime someone sought to greet him and pretended he was so absorbed in what he read he did not hear their salutation. The ruse worked to discourage anyone from joining him, except the person who plopped down in the seat across from him and laughed.

Thomas was not amused, nor was he about to listen to the man who had the privilege of Arabella's company last night. He suffered enough. His brother and Nathaniel regaled in Arabella's success. Nathaniel exclaimed he was happy someone finally noticed his sister's worth. Harry said his wife expected to see Arabella married before the end of the Season.

Thomas fumed while they spoke of Arabella's triumph and prospects, silently scolding them for only wanting to see Arabella married. *Where is the scrutiny to ensure these gentlemen are worthy of her? After all, who are they and what are their intentions?*

Some sounded as if they just burst onto the London scene and were too young to make an offer. Others were too worldly and experienced to be dancing attendance on an ingénue. *Did Edward not vet them? Was he too busy looking after his sister to care about Arabella?*

Thomas worried his judgmental peers might misconstrue Arabella as a flirt with her bright-eyed and cheerful manner, versus being the naïve young lady experiencing Almack's for the first time. If only Harry and Rebecca offered Arabella the protection she needed at these events, but Rebecca was done attending the Season's balls and routs where gossip still abounded regarding the duel causing her father's death. Besides, she was growing heavy with child. The only reason she and Harry remained in Town was for her to make her royal curtsey, and to attend her siblings' Presentation Ball.

They intended to leave the day after the ball to search out an estate to purchase with Harry's trust fund. Barrington Farm belonged to Nathaniel and with a child on the way they wanted to settle into their own new home as quickly as possible. Thomas wished them well. But, where did that leave Arabella? Once removed to her uncle's home, what lady would guard and guide her in society?

He would speak to Ketterling and inquire. While he was compelled to intervene, he knew he had no right to do so. His thoughts made him ill-tempered. He was in no mood to listen to his friend gloat over his evening with Arabella. Apparently, it did not matter. Edward was not going away. Using all the hauteur he could muster, he dropped and succinctly folded his newspaper, before giving his friend a scathing look. Edward laughed again.

Last night, Thomas struggled whether or not to attend Almack's, but he knew Lady Cowper would draw the wrong conclusion for him being there, as would others. The last thing he wanted was to stir gossip or to mislead Arabella regarding his intentions. He had none. Therefore, he had no business attending Almack's, known as the hub for gathering the most eligible of bachelors and debutantes on a weekly basis.

Even the Dark Rogues, with their reputations for abhorring marriage, were not safe from the schemes and flirtations enacted by mothers and their daughters. Thomas had no need to look at the latest pool of debutantes, so he never attended the assemblies. When the time came to start his nursery, he would contract a marriage, like any other business deal he negotiated. His disillusionment as a young man was a constant reminder why he wanted a marriage of convenience. He knew better than to trust a young lady's admiring eyes or her enthralled attention. After all, gently bred ladies were all tutored at a young age to simper and dote on prospective suitors, as his experience proved. He had no desire to engage in the marriage mart; especially after seeing firsthand how a lady's attention could quickly be redirected from her present suitor to another gentleman of higher title and wealth.

He would rather enter into an honest marriage of convenience than to discover he was played a fool. Love-matches were rare. His brother and elder sister were lucky to have found one, but then they were not pursued for their title. Their spouses desired only them, and unfortunately, Thomas had no way to know if a lady truly cared for him.

He was content to enjoy the company of widows, opera singers and the occasional mistress where terms were negotiated upfront and affairs ended amicably until he met Arabella. Never in his wildest dreams did he believe securing the happiness and welfare of a common girl could give him more enjoyment than the bachelor activities of a Dark Rogue. The partying, drinking, gambling and company of ladybirds all paled compared to spending time with her. Life was richer. He found amusement in banter, in arguments, and astonishingly just being with her.

"I just missed you at Hyde Park," remarked Edward, breaking Thomas' sudden revelation. "I went riding with Sedgeworth this morning and met up with your brother and Barrington. They said you left having remembered a business meeting. You are finished?"

Thomas' features hardened at his friend's joviality. Edward was too close a friend not to ascertain his present mood and the reason for it. He would not suffer his friend's provoking jests and intended to put a stop to it with his wit, "Harry and Barrington were gossiping like a couple of matrons. I tired of their discourse and decided to see to my morning meal. Do you wish coffee?"

Edward raised his arm to hail a servant. When the man appeared he ordered a cup of the black brew favored by Americans and a plate of food to break his fast. Then, he returned his attention back to Thomas and informed, "Sedgeworth was quite taken with Miss Barrington. He wished to know if he trespasses on your interests should he pursue her."

Surprised, Thomas rebutted with anger tinging his voice, "I have no understanding with Miss Barrington."

"And yet, you acquired the Almack's voucher for her and are assisting her brother." Edward pressed, "I would say you have a marked interest in the lady."

Embarrassed, Thomas denied the accusation, "Nonsense, for a time I was charged to care for her, but her brother owns the responsibility now, and even if he was absent, she has a grandfather and uncle to watch over her."

"You seemed rather possessive of Arabella when I first met her," challenged Edward. "I think you were ready to call me out for manhandling her. You wish me now to believe you do not hold a tendre for the lady? Consider before speaking, Bolton, for I will take you at your word."

"You sound as if you wish to pursue her yourself," accused Thomas heatedly. "Surely, she is ineligible to be your countess?"

"Under normal circumstances I would agree, but last night Miss Barrington revealed she was only interested in marrying for love. I like her frankness and the idea of marrying someone who does not covet my title, property, and wealth is tempting; especially when the lady is like-able and has already won the admiration of my sister. I would not discount Miss Barrington simply because she was not trained to be a countess. She is smart and can learn. Plus, there is the added benefit of how mama would be distracted from her megrims by tutoring Miss Barrington to be her successor."

Thomas' features tightened in anger. He did not like the notion Edward would use Arabella, rather than cherish her. He asked, sarcasm marking his words, "Are you seeking a wife or companion for your mother?"

"I see no harm in having both," answered Edward, unaware of Thomas' growing hostility. "I like Miss Barrington and am open to seeing what may come of getting to know her better."

Thomas asked, "You have no guilt trespassing upon Sedgeworth's interest?"

"We stand equal in her esteem. I trespass on no one's claim, unless you have one, Bolton. So, do you?"

Out of habit, Thomas was ready to proclaim he did not, but when he opened his mouth no words came out. At his friend's grin, he quickly shut his trap and steeled his eyes. He did not like being the brunt of anyone's amusement.

Edward pressed his lips together to keep from grinning again and counseled, "Do not hurt yourself to answer, Bolton. You are warned of my interest, so proceed as you will; but I suggest you make up your mind sooner rather than later. Or else, you might be congratulating either Sedgeworth or me on our good fortune."

Thomas heard enough and stood to take his leave before he lost his temper. He announced "You must excuse me, Fairgrove, but I have business to attend."

"You have more business, Bolton? I applaud your industry, but if you wait until I break my fast you may accompany me to Tattersall's; then afterwards, we can call at Belcrave House."

Thomas asked, "You have business with the earl?"

"No. I pay my respects to Miss Barrington and to thank her for her felicitous company last night. If I am lucky, I will beat Sedgeworth in asking her to drive with me for the social hour. It will be my last chance before her time is constrained. She is moving to Ketterling House and then will make her curtsey to our queen. Do you attend her debut ball?"

"I received my invitation and will make an appearance," replied Thomas without expression. "I must take my leave, Fairgrove, but I will see you later."

"As you wish, Bolton, have a good day."

Thomas took satisfaction in knowing he did not lie. He had a pile of correspondence demanding his attention at home. There were proposals for new investments, updates on his current business affairs and of his manor, as well as parliamentary initiatives to review and decide upon. He could spend hours dictating orders to his secretary on business and responses to social invitations. All these matters could easily keep his mind busy. Instead, his thoughts whirled singularly on Arabella, who undoubtedly would marry this Season, perhaps to one of his best friends.

He told the White's *maître d'* he would send a groom to collect his mount as he chose to walk home. His mind was too distracted to maneuver his horse through the busy streets of Mayfair, and he hoped his stroll would banish the notions filling his head. Edward said Arabella would only marry for love. *Does she love Fairgrove? Sedgeworth? Have I missed a spark igniting between either one of them?*

Perhaps, but he could not remember anything, except how he felt at seeing his friends trespass upon her attentions. He hated to admit to a flare of jealousy, but what else could it be? *My friends, nor I for that matter,* would ever press a lady for more than she wanted to give, nor would we take advantage of an innocent. Hadn't I denied myself the luxury of kissing Arabella's lips again?

Thomas was determined not to mislead Arabella and though he wished her happy, he was not sure he wanted her happily married to one of his friends. She constantly tested his resolution regarding what marriage could be. Unfortunately, he was hardened into believing a marriage of convenience was his only option to safeguard his heart. *After all, women are fickle, aren't they? How many of my lovers professed to want only me, then took another lover the minute our relationship ended?*

The business side of marriage was even more calculated than an affair of the heart. His own father negotiated the settlements for his eldest sister. Thomas applauded him for financially securing her future, but then there was no doubt his sister loved her husband. *What assurances do I have the woman who proclaims her affections for me are true? Especially when the settlements spell out in black and white what is important to her in marriage. Can I trust she wants me more than the coronet she would claim upon our marriage? I am not sure I can, so why set myself up for heartbreak?*

It was easy to admit he liked Arabella, more than liked her, and to admit how he did not like how other gentlemen found her attractive. He especially did not like the notion of being displaced as the man who saw to her safety and happiness. He reasoned he had some hard thinking to do.

He was not surprised his feet took him to Belcrave House instead of his own townhome; especially when his thoughts were on Arabella. He considered Providence guided him, so he did not bother to deliberate further on the matter. He rushed up the steps to rap on the brass lion's head door knocker which Dawson opened. He strode inside and hastily removed his hat, gloves, and greatcoat and gave them to the butler, all the while inquiring to Arabella's location.

"She is in the drawing room with Lady Charlotte, my lord," he replied with a sniff as if he disapproved of whatever they were doing.

Curious, Thomas went to see what put Dawson out of sorts. He opened the drawing room doors and saw the furniture was moved aside to provide an unobstructed area for Arabella and Charlotte to frolic. *Frolic?* He almost chuckled aloud. *Heavens be! My sister is instructing Arabella how to waltz!*

He strutted forward, much like a rooster ready to avail himself. Here was something he could lend knowledge and he was a far more suitable tutor than his sister. Arabella blushed at seeing him and Charlotte burst out in exclamation, "Thomas! You are just who we need!"

Thomas teased, "And what, pray tell, do you need of me?"

Charlotte swatted him on the arm and rebuked, "Don't be a goose. I am teaching Bella to waltz, but since I have not yet been formally instructed, we are having a dickens of a time. Can you help?"

"Charlotte," scolded Thomas sternly, "I do not think mama would approve of your language. I doubt very much the devil cares whether you can dance the waltz or not."

"I beg your pardon, Thomas. Please do not tell our mama. I shall do better."

Thomas grinned and looked at Arabella who looked like she was ready to burst with laughter. He asked, "You have an opinion to share, Miss Barrington?"

"Only in that I am of the same mind as your sister. I saw Harry and Becca dance the waltz and marshalled out the steps, but I cannot seem to replicate them to dance with a partner."

"You have not danced the waltz before?"

"Harry introduced it to Becca and while they danced I provided the music on the piano. Becca cannot play and I did not want to take Harry away from her to learn. They were newly married, you see, and only had eyes for each other. I would have greatly disappointed them if I insisted on dancing with Harry."

"Well, Harry is not newly married now. Why is he not here helping?"

"Do not scold him, Bolton. Becca was not feeling well this morning. He is seeing to her comfort. Besides, Charlotte and I are managing fine."

"Has a doctor been sent for Rebecca?"

"No, it is not necessary. She just needs rest. I think she is worrying over her changing figure and how Harry might find her..." Arabella did not know how to finish. Her sister was afraid Harry might think her undesirable and she did not know how to say the word without sounding gauche.

"More beautiful," completed Thomas with a grin.

Arabella chuckled and replied, "Yes, 'more beautiful.'"

Charlotte rolled her eyes and complained. "You two are ridiculous and now that you are here, brother, I think my time could be put to better use."

She left without a by-your-leave, shutting the drawing room doors behind her. If Thomas did not know better he would think his sister was playing matchmaker. But then he remembered the doors were shut when he arrived; no doubt, keeping the spectacle of their lesson from the servants.

Thomas asked as he drew close to Arabella, "Do you wish my help?"

He did not want to chance her saying "no," so he offered up his arms into the waltz position and was pleased when she stepped forward into his frame. She placed one of her hands in his and the other on his shoulder.

Goose bumps coursed throughout her body from the contact and she felt the invariable ninny, silently remonstrating, *you would think I never danced before.* Then, she remembered she never danced the waltz, a type of dance where a couple practically embraced one another, nor had she danced with a man she found more than attractive.

Thomas used his thumb to massage and loosen her tight grip on his hand and then used his other thumb to massage her stiff back. He hoped to break whatever notion was making her rigid. He was so focused on her distress he did not notice his own heartrate accelerate at having her close. Relying on his unfailing charm to break the taut tension, he asked as he led her into the first step, "You play the piano?"

The question surprised her and quickly brought her mother to mind, "My mama was most proficient at playing and wished for Becca and me to learn. Unfortunately, Becca had no desire. She always said her left hand would not cooperate with her right. Instead, mama tutored her in voice. My sister sings as beautifully as did my mama."

"Your mother must have been very talented to teach her daughters," opined Thomas.

"Indeed. My grandfather had mama professionally trained when she displayed a natural ability for both voice and playing the piano. I think he thought to increase her worth in the marriage mart. After all, he aspired for her to marry a duke, but mama loved and chose my papa. She used her talents to benefit her children and to earn money for her household."

"An industrious lady," he praised. "Do you aspire to teach your children one day?"

"I do not know if I shall marry or have children, but if I did, then nothing would please me more than to pass down my mama's legacy. If not my own, then if Becca and Harry permit, I shall instruct their children."

Their conversation distracted Arabella from thinking about her steps, so they were able to complete a turn around the drawing room without a hitch. Thomas marveled at how well they danced together. How much she trusted him to lead her.

He remarked, "After all the reports I heard regarding your Almack's debut, I expect you will marry by the end of the Season."

Arabella laughed and turned her attention to a table sporting a number of bouquets. Thomas followed her line of vision and tensed at the sight of the flowers, causing him to misstep and make Arabella fall against him. She laughed and her gleaming eyes quickly chased away his anger.

He spun her to hear her laugh again and then asked, "Has one of your admirers caught your fancy?"

Sobering, Arabella confessed, "I have no wish to marry for convenience, no matter how much I want a family to call my own."

"Fairgrove said you want to marry for love."

Arabella smiled and said, "It is my greatest wish to be loved as Harry loves my sister. You know of what I speak, Bolton. You witnessed their affection for one another. Can you imagine being united with someone who wishes your company above all others; someone who will share their hopes and dreams with you; someone you can count on to stay by your side and help carry your burdens, as you will help carry theirs; someone who will take joy in seeing you happy, as you relish in their happiness; someone who wants to build a family and life with you, and will never regret marrying you. Finding someone who loves you as much as you love them sounds like heaven to me."

It was as if she echoed his own wishes, and then fear settled as he wondered aloud, "Have you found someone to love?"

"Perhaps, reluctantly," she grinned.

Thomas wanted to ask who, but feared the answer. He abruptly stopped their dancing and left the room without issuing a word.

Arabella stood with her mouth agape at seeing him walk away. *Did I speak too freely? Did he guess he is the man of my dreams and made a hasty exit before I could embarrass us both?* Her pride kept her from being hurt; her reason reminded her to not be surprised by his silent rejection. After all, he was a viscount.

If anything, she should thank him for not humiliating her. She looked at her flower bouquets. *Might there be another who might cherish me as I wish and for whom I might fall in love?*

Miracles were known to happen. Look at her parents. Who would think her papa could win the hand of a viscount's daughter. Perhaps, even without a dowry or title, she could win the hand of a nobleman? She grinned and then laughed at the absurdity of the idea. *I am on the shelf at the ripe age of four and twenty; am I not?*

She decided she would not worry about seeing Thomas again, since her time in London was marked by her presentation ball. Once it was over, she could leave, thereby eliminating any chance meetings with him in the future. She would never burden her family with the cost of another Season and any other place she might meet him would be at Harry's home. She could easily make sure he was not a guest whenever she planned to visit her sister. Indeed, she need not worry about him; she only needed to worry about Damburten being alive.

The baron once turned the villagers against her and her family, making their life miserable. Who knew what pound of flesh he craved in retaliation for the bullet he suffered at Nathaniel's hand or for the duel that embroiled him in scandal. Damburten was too dangerous for them to live near, so if they could not return to their farm, where were she and Nathaniel to go?

Chapter Eighteen

Bloody hell! What does she mean by reluctantly in love? Maybe, "perhaps," means she does not know if she is in love. Now that makes sense. How does anyone know if they are in love? And with whom does she think she is reluctantly in love?

Thomas' head hurt trying to puzzle out her response to his question. *Is she or is she not in love with someone?* He was glad when he finally arrived home and could avail himself of a stiff drink even if it was too early to indulge. Baxter opened the door and greeted him. He remembered his horse while he divested himself of his greatcoat and ordered Baxter to send a groom to the stable near White's to retrieve it.

His loyal servant said he would see it done and then informed, "Viscount Ketterling awaits an audience with you, my lord."

Thomas asked, "Where did you put him?"

"When he learned you were not at home he asked for his nephew. Mr. Barrington and the viscount are in the library."

"Tell them I arrived and will see them shortly."

"Immediately, my lord."

Thomas rushed up the stairs wondering why the viscount was here. His valet was in his room and ready to shave and help him into a clean set of clothes. He impatiently resigned to his servant's ministrations and then hurried to greet the viscount. He relaxed finding William and Nathaniel in comfortable repose, each with a book in hand, which they immediately set aside upon his entry.

Nathaniel was the first to speak, "I am glad you are home, Bolton. My uncle insisted upon it before he revealed his news."

Thomas raised his eyebrows at William. The viscount crimsoned and said, "I did not think you would be long and had no wish to repeat myself."

Thomas asked, "You were offered refreshments?"

"Yes," replied William. "And unless you are in need of substance, please take a seat, Bolton. I have two things I wish to discuss with you. One is Damburten and the second is Arabella's wardrobe expenses. I understand you took the costs on yourself and I would like to reimburse you for the expenses."

Surprised, Thomas replied, "There is no need to recompense, Ketterling. The honor was mine to attire her."

"It well may have been, Bolton," retorted William heatedly, "but I will not taint my niece for receiving such a generous gift. I can easily hear the gossipmongers hissing how she has *carte blanche* under your protection."

Thomas' nostrils flared in anger. He practically shouted, "I would not tolerate anyone speaking such slander against Miss Barrington and would see the offender on a field of honor if such a man dared."

"And if it was a lady, a gaggle of them, wishing Arabella ill, such as the like of Lady Caroline," argued William. "I think not; especially when I am more than able to bear the cost. Besides, the honor of attiring Arabella belongs to me, not you, Bolton."

"Actually," intervened Nathaniel, "the honor is mine, but unfortunately I do not have the funds. I agree with my uncle. We must repay you for your generosity to protect Arabella's reputation, but do not think us ungrateful, Bolton. It is time we release you from the promise you made to Harry. Arabella is no longer alone or unprotected."

"As you wish, Barrington," replied Thomas begrudgingly, before turning to William to inform, "I will make an accounting of the expenses and have it delivered to you, Ketterling."

"Thank you, Bolton."

"Now," pressed Thomas, "let's discuss what undoubtedly you want to learn of my investigation of Damburten and the duel. My men found no witnesses to attest the baron deliberately turned early to shoot Mr. Barrington in the back. At least, there are none willing to come forward and accuse a peer of murder. Your nephew informed me the speculation regarding the crowd reported to be on the field of honor is false. Nathaniel said he and his father demanded satisfaction of Damburten the night they arrived in London. The duel was held early the next morning. Aside from Damburten's cohort, who acted as his second, and the doctor who remained in his carriage, he could not recall any other witnesses. In hindsight, I believe Damburten planned to kill Mr. Barrington before he even arrived on the field."

William asked, "Do you know the name of Damburten's second?"

"No," answered Nathaniel. "I am not even sure I would recognize him. My focus was on the duel. Damburten's second did not even try to settle the grievance between the duelists before they took their positions on the field as he ought. Since Damburten was challenged, the weapons were his to choose and he provided them."

Thomas added, "I personally spoke with the doctor and I believe he speaks the truth in saying he saw nothing as he did not take the field until he was needed." Thomas looked directly at Nathaniel to say, "You left after you shot Damburten which you believed was fatal. As you know, he survived and recovered. My guess is he hid out in his townhome until he was able to travel. He must have thanked his lucky stars to learn you were accused of murdering him. He probably thought if he could hide away until you were convicted of his murder, then he would be free to return to Town and his life."

"Well," informed William, "he is not worried Nathaniel will accuse him. I overheard a gentleman at Tattersall's say Damburten was to attend Whitacker's Ball. The young deb making her come-out has a fifty thousand pound dowry and Damburten has his eyes on it."

"I shall charge him with my father's murder and demand justice," declared Nathaniel.

"It is what we all wish, Barrington, but without a witness to corroborate your story and with no proof of a crime committed, we cannot bring Damburten to trial."

Nathaniel asked incredulously, "Do you mean to tell me he will be accepted in Society? He will attend balls and routs without censure for taking my father's life? He will be allowed to court young ladies and receive their hand in marriage without a taint to his character?"

"Rest assured, Barrington," calmed Thomas. "No father would give his daughter and fortune to a man of Damburten's character. I will see to it Whitacker and any other family seeking a suitor know of the baron's villainy."

William counseled, "Damburten will not stand for your interference, Bolton. You best watch your back."

"Crikey!" exclaimed Nathaniel. "Do my sisters know they might come face to face with Damburten?"

"No," replied William, "but the Whitacker Ball takes place after your presentation ball. Becca and Harry plan to leave the next day, so they will not be around, but Bella must be told."

"She will need protection," announced Thomas. "I know Miss Barrington also harbors a fear of the baron, and I would not put it past the man to harm her."

"I will see it done," replied William.

"Allow me, Ketterling," offered Thomas. "I have men in my employ trained for this type of work. Miss Barrington will not even know they watch her."

"Very well," replied William, "but I shall cover the cost."

"As you wish," responded Thomas disappointedly. "Which reminds me, do you have a lady to act as hostess for your ball and to guide Miss Barrington for the rest of the Season?"

"Indeed, Bolton. My aunt, Lady Crosse, arrives tomorrow. She was a favorite of my sister's and is not lofty. She married a Captain in His Majesty's Navy, but maintains her title as a Lady and can easily navigate Bella through the Season."

"I am glad." Thomas looked at Nathaniel and inquired, "Do you move to your uncle's tomorrow Barrington? I think I will miss you for I am used to your company."

"Do not cut me loose, yet, Bolton," teased Nathaniel. "I am in need of friends and companionship as much of the next fellow."

"Then," he said, "let us continue our morning rides and break our fasts at my club."

"Thank you, Bolton," replied Nathaniel.

"Yes, thank you, Bolton," echoed William. "Thank you very much for taking care of my nieces and nephew. I am forever in your debt. You may seek my aid should you ever need it and I will not fail you."

Thomas gave his own thanks and then saw William out. He should be relieved to unburden himself from the Barrington brood; instead he felt a pang of remorse for not being the man they sought if they were in trouble. With that thought, he went to his study to tally up the expenses of Arabella's attire, forgetting his need for a restorative.

Arabella was at first alarmed the baron was in Town and then her ire rose at how Damburten, the man who murdered her father, was resuming his life as if nothing happened. She found it incredulous he claimed it was her father who fired first. Damburten said he reacted in defense to a shot reporting and was mortified to see his opponent bleeding in the back. Before he could investigate the circumstances, he was shot. He professed he suffered greatly at having the bullet in his chest removed and exclaimed great appreciation for being able to recuperate at his friend's manor home. He explained he did not know he was thought dead until recently, when he returned to Town.

Arabella wanted to scratch Damburten's eyes out for his false tale, but she was counseled on the danger to Nathaniel should she do it. Nathaniel's freedom was at stake. Damburten could charge Nathaniel with attempted murder. The only thing holding the baron back was the praise his peers were bestowing on him. Damburten was being hailed for his forgiving and generous spirit towards the Barrington siblings. *After all, haven't the Barringtons suffered enough?* His peers called him a jolly good sport for not only accepting Mr. Barrington's challenge to duel, but for suffering a wound from it.

Thomas was not fooled by the baron's conciliatory manner. Damburten was a threat and Thomas was quick to put in place a protection detail to watch over Arabella. He sent investigators to look into Damburten's finances and to discover if there was a way to neutralize the baron without actually killing him. Thomas was prepared to hog tie the villain and ship him off to the Americas, but there was always the possibility Damburten would simply return more vengeful than ever.

In the days that followed, Thomas made schedules for his best soldiers to watch over Arabella. He met with his business associates and friends to learn more of Damburten and his activities. He kept his word to meet with Nathaniel for their early morning rides in Hyde Park and listened with pride when Nathaniel described his and his siblings' royal presentations to Queen Charlotte and the Prince Regent.

Thomas was glad the queen showed the Barrington sisters particular favor by kissing their foreheads when they dropped into their deep curtseys at St. James Palace. The affectation recognized both sisters as ladies of noble blood. Nathaniel laughed recalling how Arabella, more so than Rebecca, feared she would trip on her long train and then he went on to describe his own concerns of stumbling or poking someone with his ceremonial sword when he was presented to the Prince Regent.

News of their royal distinction spread like wildfire through the *ton* grapevine and anyone who thought to snub the Ketterling ball quickly changed their mind. The *ton* knew better than to shun a royal favorite.

Their ball was a success. The *Marquis du Benoît* accompanied by the Regent himself made an appearance and chatter abounded to whether the marquis or the viscount would dower Arabella. By the time Thomas arrived Arabella was surrounded by a bevy of suitors and he thought he missed his opportunity to request a dance.

He felt a modicum of pleasure to know she penciled him in for the first waltz and then crimsoned when she smiled, appearing to read his mind. Usually, he was the one to bring on a blush with his charm and smile. The irony of how he was the one blushing did not amuse him.

At least, she was not mad at him for taking his abrupt leave when she confessed she was reluctantly in love. In reflection, she had every right to be angry with him. After all, he was her champion and confident, so why shouldn't she confess to him when she fell in love.

He took a position near a colonnade to watch over her until it was time to collect her for their waltz. His stomach churned at all the gentlemen dancing attendance on her. He did not like it and glared at her as if she was purposely drawing them to her to upset him. Her response in the form of a wink surprised him. He almost chuckled aloud when one of her suitors quizzed her about it and she feigned, by poking her eye, something was in it.

However, his amusement died the moment her suitor drew close to blow into her eye. Thomas was ready to throttle the self-serving man, until he remembered Arabella had a brother and uncle to watch and protect her.

He decided he would not last the evening watching men fawn over her, nor could he continue to stare at every gentleman who drew too close to her, without drawing notice. For his own sanity, he would leave after their dance. He grabbed a flute of champagne from the tray of a passing footman and gulped it down to mollify his temper. He was ready to call back the footman for another flute when he heard his name.

"Bolton!" He turned at the overly sweet salutation and saw the buxom Lady Penelope Selby at his side offering a flirtatious grin. The widow made overtures to him before he left to fetch Harry and Rebecca to London. At the time, he considered accepting her offer for a dalliance, but now, the invitation did not appeal.

He offered only a modicum of civility, "Lady Selby."

"My goodness, Bolton," she cooed, "such an abrupt greeting from someone who once charmed me beyond distraction. I have not seen you in Town. Were you away?"

"Indeed, I visited my brother and then business kept me occupied. You are well?"

"My, you do dissemble. All of Mayfair knows you went to collect Harry and his new wife. She and her siblings made quite a splash. I understand the royals favor them."

Thomas hardened his features to let her know he would not encourage gossip on the Barringtons.

Lady Selby laughed and volleyed, "Ah, you are their champion, Bolton." When it looked like he might respond angrily she tapped him with her fan letting it slide down his arm like a caress. "Do not let me ruffle your feathers, unless you want me to smooth them down for you," she chuckled. "To answer your question, I am very well, though I admit my nights can be restless. Perhaps, you have a cure for me." she whispered.

Thomas bit back the grin he almost revealed. The lady was clever, but he was not interested and knew trouble would come from furthering the conversation. He was about to make his regrets known when to his surprise and delight Arabella placed her hand on his arm.

Her possessive action astonished him, and to his amazement, also pleased him. Never in his life would he allow a debutante to take such a liberty, but with Arabella he found great satisfaction in broadcasting an alliance between them. Manners prompted him to introduce Arabella, until Lady Selby took the initiative and greeted, "Good evening, Miss Barrington."

"Good evening," Arabella returned before turning her attention to Thomas, "This is our dance, Bolton."

"Indeed, you will excuse us Lady Selby."

Thomas walked away with Arabella and inquired, "Did your partner offend you, Miss Barrington. You left the set early."

"No, but you looked like you were in need of rescue, so I abandoned him to come to your aid."

Arabella immediately cringed at her flimsy excuse. The sight of a voluptuous woman hanging on his every word drove her to his side, and by his insufferable grin he knew it. To add further to her mortification, she left her dancing partner alone on the floor without an explanation, so she could interrupt Thomas' intimate *tête-á-tête* with the fawning lady. *Heavens be! What will the gossipmongers say!*

Thomas took pity on her when her blushing cheeks lost all their color and before she could run away in horror, he said, "You were right to do so. I was in much need of rescuing."

And surprisingly enough, his words rang true. He would laugh at the revelation, if he did not think Arabella would mistake his outburst. She not only rescued him from Lady Selby, but from a marriage of convenience. He was resolute to live his life free of sentiment, but Arabella snuck in behind his defenses and captured his heart. In so doing, she offered him a glimpse of what marriage looked like with her by his side. He could no longer deny he loved her and wanted to spend the rest of his life with her.

The question was if she wished to spend her life with him. *Isn't she already reluctantly in love?* He decided it mattered not. He never failed to acquire something he wanted and he wanted Arabella. Tomorrow, he would see to it. Tonight, he would enjoy his dance.

Unfortunately, the next day and the days to follow kept him too busy organizing her protection detail and investigating Damburten's finances to pursue his own interests. There was no time to woo Arabella and it annoyed the dickens out of him the same could not be said for his competition.

Nathaniel was a constant source of news regarding Arabella's suitors. Ever since her successful debut, Nathaniel complained to Thomas during their morning rides about Arabella's numerous callers. He grumbled about all the bouquets smelling up his uncle's home. He said it was like being held hostage in a perfume bottle.

Thomas listened to all Nathaniel's grievances and soon owned a few of his own. He learned the Barrington's great-aunt, Lady Crosse, was having difficulty discerning which admirers were serious and eligible. Too many were young sons without title or fortune. Some were a prime catch and a few were fortune hunters trying to discover if Arabella was greatly dowered.

No names of the suitors were given, but Thomas knew Fairgrove and Sedgeworth were earnest in their courtships. He saw for himself the fruits of their labors. Arabella was equally in their company. She rode in their carriages in Hyde Park and parked along Berkeley Street to eat ices from Gunther's. Even so, he was glad she did not look like a woman enamored. More than once, the minx easily diverted from her swains, waved at him.

Arabella wanted a love-match and he was determined to be the one to give it to her. There was more than chemistry sparking between them. There was joy in seeing each other. Comfort in being near one another. Honor in caring for one another and contentment. She could not possibly love someone else; especially when they suited one another so well. He would have to disabuse her of the notion if she thought differently.

He laughed at his arrogance, knowing how she would react to such a declaration and that reminded him how their sparring of words was another wonderful element of their relationship. They were comfortable with one another to do and say as they pleased. They were free to be themselves knowing nothing they said or did would be used against them. Somehow over the course of knowing one another, they became each other's champion. Arabella would stand by his side and come to his aid, just as he would for her.

He was close to ridding them all of Damburten, and knew the sooner he did, the sooner he could profess his intentions. His investigations revealed the baron was in need of funds, having suffered great losses at the gaming tables. Damburten's property was not producing the income he needed, so he was looking to marry a well-dowered debutante.

Whitacker's young daughter seemed to be his mark and the reason why Damburten was attending the Whitacker Ball. Thomas would not let the baron come about through marriage. He made a morning call upon

Whitacker after Arabella's ball and presented his findings. At first, Whitacker stiffened at Thomas' impudence to interfere in his family business, but then he reviewed the evidence.

The report of Damburten's finances, or lack of them, made it clear what the baron sought. Whitacker disregarded the baron's motivation to marry for convenience to fill his coffer. After all, great alliances were made from contractual marriages, but learning of Damburten's reprobate lifestyle and the villainy of his deeds was not the kind of man he would align with his family. He certainly would not give his daughter into the care of a reprobate, nor to a man with no honor. Thomas did not mince words when he called Damburten a degenerate and murderer.

Whitacker thanked Thomas for the information. He confessed the baron was to attend his daughter's ball and he could not refuse him entry without causing a ruckus. He would not be the one to cause a scandal at his own ball. Even so, he assured Thomas he would not entertain any offer from the baron. He would give his daughter enough information regarding Damburten's character to convince her to steer clear of him. Thomas could ask for nothing more.

Chapter Nineteen

A footman dressed in Ketterling's livery stood at hand at the Whitacker's Ball, presumably to aid Lady Crosse, but in actuality was positioned to guard Arabella. He was diligent in his duties and watched all who came near her. He, along with a larger assembly of men and women, worked for Thomas and under his order stood guard to protect Arabella from Damburten. They were trained in the rudiments of covert observation and fighting.

Arabella did not mind how everything she did and with whom was under surveillance. As long as Damburten was alive, she and her family were in danger. The baron hated them for not selling Barrington Farm back to him and for the injuries his deranged mind placed at their door. Nathaniel was a prime target having saved Rebecca from his ill intent and for shooting him. No doubt, Damburten blamed all the Barrington siblings for his current financial struggles and for the taint to his good name.

Arabella's sixth sense when it came to Thomas made her search the Whitacker ballroom for him even before his name was called out in greeting. He looked amazing dressed in his formal black tailcoat and pantaloons. She was not the only lady appreciating his fine looks and form; but she was the only one for which he searched and that made her smile.

Something was different between them. The tension was gone. No words were exchanged to explain it, but Arabella's giddiness whenever she was in his company was nurtured by his look of admiration. His eyes and lips twitched in amusement. It was as though he knew a secret and she waited in anticipation for him to share it.

Her jubilant smile made Edward give her a pointed look. They were in friendly banter until Thomas arrived and he did not take kindly to being so easily forgotten. He untied the dance card strapped with a small pencil to her wrist and wrote his name on the first waltz before she realized what he did. He still held her dance card in his hand when Thomas joined them and smugly offered it to his friend.

Thomas took and gave the card a quick inspection before remarking, "I see you beat me in securing the first waltz, Fairgrove."

"The lady did not protest," retorted Edward glibly.

"She would not," replied Thomas looking at Arabella with admiration. He wrote his name in her card and deftly retied the card to her wrist before he turned his attention back to Edward.

"However," he informed, "I am most pleased you left the supper dance for me. It was quite generous of you, Fairgrove, for I will not only dance with Miss Barrington, but will have her company to enjoy my meal. I must thank you for the consideration."

Edward chuckled and with amusement retorted, "Your wit proves sharp, Bolton. Have I annoyed you, by chance?"

"You are beginning to do so, Fairgrove," he replied.

Edward grinned, took the hint to stop baiting his friend and immediately changed the topic by remarking, "I hope to see you at Adelaide's dinner, Bolton. It will be a small affair, but Miss Barrington promised to play and according to Adelaide will astound us all."

Arabella blushed and said, "Desist, my lord. You know I only play to please your sister. My skill is no more remarkable than any tutored debutante. Do not, I beg, set expectations that will leave Bolton disappointed."

Thomas informed Fairgrove, "I received my invitation and sent my response to attend." He assured Arabella, "you could never disappoint me, Miss Barrington, though you do vex me on occasion."

Edward chuckled. Arabella blushed at the implied sentiment. She could easily complain Thomas vexed her as well, bestowing unwavering care and affection in one moment, and then in another, treating her as someone of no import. She did not mind his momentary lapses from decorum, especially those times when he wrapped her up in his arms.

Arabella came alert from her woolgathering when Edward cleared his throat. She dared not look at Thomas lest she give away her romantic thoughts. Instead, she focused on Edward, remembering their first meeting and how she almost brought him to his knees using a defensive move on his hand. She thought him tall and handsome at their first meeting and since then, her opinion of him only grew.

He was paying her remarked attention and if her heart was not already engaged with Thomas, she might consider his overtures seriously. There were a number of aspects in his favor. He did not find fault with her forthright manner, nor her bold interest in self-defense and pistol shooting. He was fun to be around. He adored his sister and mother. She adored his sister and mother. They were well becoming good friends. Life with him would be tolerable.

"This is our dance, Miss Barrington," Edward informed offering his arm in escort when the strings announcing the waltz began to play. Arabella took Edward's arm and left Thomas behind.

Thomas watched them walk away and then looked at Arabella's guard disguised as a Ketterling footman. The man was far from the good looking lads usually dressed for such occasions. The uniform fit him tightly, but he owned brute strength and was more than capable of protecting

Arabella. The footman shook his head side to side to inform Thomas Damburten was not here.

Thomas' efforts to deny Damburten admittance to the Whitacker ball came too late. The invitations were already sent and their responses received by the time he met with the earl. Even so, their meeting produced the desired results.

At first, Whitacker took offense that Thomas had delved into his family's affairs, but he soon became appreciative. The earl held a strong affection for his shy little miss who dreamed of marrying a handsome and charming man. She was recently graduated from her finishing school and harbored expectations of a love-match. Whitacker's first priority was to marry her to a man with the means to care for her, but he was not so unfeeling to wed her to an unworthy and abusive man. After all, he did not settle fifty thousand pounds on his daughter to ensnare a snake. He wanted the eagle that soared above all others.

Thomas advised the earl to keep his daughter well-watched and close at hand until Dambuten lost interest. The notion the baron might do something to force a union enraged the earl, but he heeded Thomas' words and expressed his gratitude when Thomas took his leave.

Thomas wasted no time to seek out the baron's creditors and demand an audience with them. By the end of the day he had acquired all the baron's *debts of honor* and tradesmen's bills. He paid an exorbitant amount of money for them, but the power they wielded was worth it. Damburten now owed him a substantial amount of money. Without the funds to pay, Thomas could easily put Damburten in debtors' prison.

Everyone knew, without resource, there was little hope of leaving the cursed place once entering it. Plus, the taint of being placed there removed Damburten's cachet as *bon ton*. Thomas was betting Damburten would rather leave England than have his stature sullied. Of course, there was always the possibility a rich nabob would pull him out of the River Tick with a marriage of convenience. It was not uncommon for a wealthy merchant to raise his family's stature through marriage to a nobleman. For this class of newfound wealth, entering the elite parlours of Mayfair was more important than the character of a future son-by-marriage.

Thomas entered the Whitacker ballroom after taking supper with Arabella in one of the smaller rooms. He was beginning to believe Damburten might not come. And he was glad. He was enjoying himself and would hate for the evening to be ruined by the baron's attendance. Even Edward's insistent probes into his feelings for Arabella did not dismay him.

"Are you or are you not courting Miss Barrington?" pressed Edward. "For if you are, you best inform me before I offer her marriage."

Thomas looked at his friend wide-eyed, but did not have a chance to respond to Edward's incredulous proclamation because a marked hush drew his attention. Silence followed a cresting roll of chatter when Damburten entered the ballroom and by the look on the baron's face he did not like it.

Thomas' instincts told him to collect and remove Arabella from the premises. He looked at Edward who upon noting his friend's anxiety asked, "What is wrong?"

While Edward knew Damburten killed Arabella's father dishonorably in a duel he did not know of Damburten's assault on Rebecca or about the baron's hatred for her family. With no time to explain, he asked his friend, "Fairgrove, I need you to collect Miss Barrington from the retiring room and bring her home. I will tell Lady Crosse to meet you at the front door. The footman should be with Miss Barrington. Take him as he is charged to guard her. I will explain later."

Edward did not hesitate and left to collect Arabella. Thomas informed Lady Crosse her niece was waiting for her at the front door. Then, he turned his attention to Damburten. Tension filled the air. The baron walked up to Whitacker's daughter, made his salutation and requested a dance. The young lady explained her card was full, and when no one came to collect her for the next set, she blushed. Damburten asked her to take the floor with him, but she demurred, saying she needed to use the retiring room and left.

Damburten heard the whispers increase in volume and became aware of his peers' censure. No one held his gaze until his eyes met Thomas' and then silence ensued. The moment crackled like stepping upon an ice pond not yet solid. No one moved fearful to draw Damburten's rage. Thomas acknowledged Damburten with a nod, but the baron glared at him as if Thomas issued him a challenge. Perhaps he had, for he would not allow the villain to do harm to his family again and the Barringtons were his family. Satisfied he made his point, and knowing Arabella and her aunt were safely away, he turned and left.

Thomas told his coachman to take him to Ketterling House where he found Arabella, Nathaniel, William, Edward, and Lady Crosse in the drawing room. The scene was remarkably posed like a farce. Arabella sat in a winged chair in high distress coughing, while all the men and her aunt stood looking upon her with gaped-mouth concern.

Thomas strode forward and took the glass tumbler from Arabella's unstable hand and pushed it at Edward. Embarrassed, his friend had the wherewithal to take the glass, before explaining, "She was shaking so terribly I thought a tot of whiskey would settle her."

Thomas ignored Edward and began to massage Arabella's back. He bent over and whispered soft words of comfort until her coughing ceased.

Edward exclaimed with frustration, "Well, Bolton, there is no denying your interest in the lady now. I only wished you were forthcoming. Adelaide and my mama will be heartily disappointed."

His friend's declaration reminded him of Edward's intention to pay his addresses to Arabella. At the time, he was too astonished to speak. Then, Damburten arrived and he was compelled to find and protect her, but walking in to see Edward look at her as if it was his right to comfort and protect her, was more than he could tolerate.

Nathaniel did not appear surprised by Thomas' display, but his uncle frowned and ordered, "Unless you seek my niece's hand in marriage, Bolton, you best step away from her. I would hate to call you out for overstepping."

Thomas removed his hand and looked down into Arabella's eyes. He asked, "Will I do, Arabella?"

At first, his question confused her, but then she noted his concerned and beseeching eyes. She wanted to shout, "of course, you will do," but she was still too astonished to voice her thoughts.

"You will have to inform Sedgeworth, Bolton," complained Edward. "He will not be happy to hear your news."

"Have I made you unhappy, Fairgrove?"

Edward practically shouted, "Well, I am deuced annoyed after dancing attendance on the lady when all the time her heart was already engaged. Never saw such a reluctant courtship between two people who are obviously smitten."

Angry at his remark, Arabella glared at him and heatedly ranted, "Annoyed, my lord. Did you speak false in your compliments to me then? Do my brown eyes not beguile you? Is my fair skin not as creamy as milk? And what was it about my hair? Oh, yes, as velvety as chocolate. Perhaps, you made up these faradiddles to tolerate my company?"

Edward laughed. "Desist minx, you know very well I like spending time with you and my courtship was in earnest, even if my compliments were not. Who knows what could develop between us?"

Thomas glared at his friend and threatened, "Nothing could develop, Fairgrove. I might be slow to proclaim my intentions, but I never would allow someone else to marry Arabella without first professing my love to her." He moved before her and took her hands. He pulled her up from her seat and looked into her eyes. He pressed, "You did not answer my question, Arabella. I asked if I would do. I know you will only marry for love, so I guess I am asking if you love me?"

"I am not titled, Bolton," she stated anxiously remembering his parents' disappointment when Harry wed Rebecca. "You will make no great alliance with me."

"I beg to differ, but as for a title, you will have one upon marrying me." He asked again, "Do you love me?"

"I want to learn to shoot a pistol and ride a horse," she answered to remind him she was no common debutante. She had an independent nature; enjoyed adventure and owned opinions she openly stated. She did not want him to be disappointed in her after their marriage, nor did she want him trying to change her. He either accepted her as she was or not.

"Are we negotiating, Arabella?" Thomas asked with amusement. Leave it to Arabella to remind him of what marriage to her entailed. His wife would not fit the typical aristocratic model, but then he did not want one, he only wanted her.

Arabella grinned and Thomas fought to keep his reserve; especially knowing the display they were making. He did not need to hear she loved him publicly. He read her affection in her eyes and manner. Even more importantly, she trusted him, as he did her.

"We will discuss matters later in private, Miss Barrington," he said, reverting to protocol in addressing her. "I believe we entertained the men and your aunt enough." Thomas directed his question to Arabella's uncle, "Ketterling, may I come tomorrow to speak of settlements?"

"Do not think you can marry me without asking me, Bolton!" exclaimed Arabella tartly.

"I shall not," he replied amused, "but I shall not do so, until I inform my parents and have speech with your uncle."

Arabella pouted and said, "What if your parents disapprove? They were not happy with Harry's choice."

"Perhaps not at first, for all they knew of Rebecca was the gossip surrounding her name. They have taken you and your family's full measure. I do not think they will object and if they do, it is of no consequence. The choice is mine to make, which I have informed them on more than one occasion. Do not cry feeble, Miss Barrington. I will expect to wed the bold minx who opened the door to me when I first called at Barrington Farm."

"Then, you best release my hands to let me stand by your side. I mean to begin as I shall go on. Expect me to be your partner, not your property."

Thomas brought her hand to his lips and pressed a kiss to the back of it. He declared, "It is my greatest wish, Miss Barrington."

Arabella blushed and then, along with her aunt, retired for the evening. She was exhausted and expected a restless night in anticipation of learning what the earl and countess said of Thomas' marriage to her.

William inquired of Thomas, "Your intentions are honorable, Bolton? You will wed her even if Belcrave disapproves?"

"I will," he answered.

Nathaniel stepped forward and offered his hand in congratulations. Edward teased, "The lady has not agreed yet, Bolton," and received Thomas' glare for his taunting.

William inquired, "What did Damburten do at the Whitacker Ball?"

"He was not pleased by his reception. His options to wed a well-dowered lady might prove bleak now his finances are revealed. He will learn soon enough I was the one to inform Whitacker, and thus the *ton*; these matters are rarely held confidential. He most likely suspects me as I was the only one who did not shy away from his inspection. He will confront Whitacker to ask the reason behind his frosty reception and the earl will oblige him. I am sure Damburten will retaliate, and for that reason, I think we should wait to reveal my betrothal to your niece. I do not want her targeted for revenge. Your nephew is already in his sights as I expect he still wants the Barrington Farm."

Nathaniel confessed, "I do worry what he will try next to acquire my property. I wish I knew why he wants it so badly."

"I think he is insanely driven by a promise he made to his father," replied Thomas. "The reason 'why' does not matter, Barrington. Damburten is a threat to you and your family. I suggest you take an extended trip to visit your grandfather."

"And leave Arabella? Never!" he exclaimed.

"You are most at risk from Damburten. Rebecca is safely away with Harry and I can protect your other sister."

Nathaniel looked to his uncle for guidance.

"I think I agree with Bolton, Nathaniel," offered his uncle. "I admit I fear for your safety now Damburten is in Town."

"It will not be for long," explained Thomas. "I own Damburten's *debts of honor* and tradesmen's bills. I shall demand payment and unless Damburten finds himself a wealthy wife, he will have no choice but to negotiate with me."

Nathaniel asked, "What do you plan?"

"His written confession and immediate departure for America," explained Thomas. "I do not trust him. He is a constant threat to you and your sisters. Aside from a direct assault, he could charge you with attempted murder. He is underhanded enough to pay a minion to stand witness for him.

"The news you shot Damburten fed the rumor mill for months. Since coming to Town, the baron plays the magnanimous nobleman by not confirming one way or another whether you shot him, but that can change. I will see him disappear before he hurts any of you."

"You do all this because you want to marry Arabella?" asked Nathaniel.

"I will do anything to see her safe and happy," replied Thomas, "but do not think I care little for you or your sister. I call you family, after all."

"I expect to have a part in this," remarked Edward.

"Indeed," replied Thomas. "I shall ask you and Sedgeworth to continue dancing attendance on Arabella and watching over her when I am not near. I do not trust Damburten within a breath of her."

Chapter Twenty

Thomas arrived early the next morning at Belcrave House and sought out his father in the earl's study. His father always reviewed the Parliamentary initiatives before he left to take his seat, and while he listened to his peers' opinion on the merits of each bill, he relied on his own investigations and good sense to decide his vote. It was a behavior Thomas learned from him. Neither of them suffered fools gladly.

The moment he greeted his father and saw the earl's eyes alight, he knew he was to be pressed to marry. The worry over the earldom's succession was never far from the earl's mind, and his father took every opportunity to remind him of his duty. Unfortunately for the earl, Thomas, unlike Harry, lived independently of his father. He did not need an allowance. He held his own title, properties and wealth. Therefore, the earl held no power to bring him to heel.

His parents wanted the future of the succession secured with a grandson, so the news he paid his addresses to a lady would be happily received, until they learned it was Arabella he wished to wed. He did not doubt they held a fond regard for her. She lifted everyone's mood with her selfless help and good humor; however, they had opened their home and showed Arabella courtesy only because she was Rebecca's sister. They would not take kindly their hospitality allowed Miss Barrington to attach herself to their son, the heir.

Thomas expected to hear accusations of how she schemed to rise above her station. They would make her the villain and then remind him what was due of his station. No doubt, his mother was ready with a list of promising candidates from which he could choose a bride. It did not matter. At one time he was resigned to a marriage of convenience, but after knowing Arabella that concession was no longer an option. The idea of wedding any other lady was anathema to him. It was she or no one else.

"Thomas, I am glad you are here. Your mama and I wish to speak with you," Belcrave said in lieu of a proper greeting.

Thomas walked over to the bell cord and tugged it. When Dawson arrived he ordered the butler to inform the countess he was with the earl. The butler left and both the earl and Thomas waited. The earl looked as if he thought he would chase his son away if he spoke, so he shuffled some papers around his desk, clearing his throat on occasion. Thomas took a seat content to wait and used the time until his mother arrived to collect his words. He did not want a Cheltenham tragedy to ensue from his announcement.

His mother entered the study and he rose to receive her enthusiastic greeting. She looked to her husband who shuffled his papers once more before giving her a definitive nod to sit. Thomas helped his mother into a chair. The earl creased his brows.

This would not be the first time his parents said they wished to speak with him, only to badger him to marry. Usually, Thomas stiffened at the onset and then expressed in angry tones how the decision to wed was ultimately his choice to make. His current agreeable mood was discombobulating his parents evidenced by their unusual silence and rounded eyes.

"Shall I have Dawson provide tea or something stronger?" he asked into the quiet.

Belcrave asked, "Are we in need of something stronger?"

"Time will tell, father," Thomas replied. "I hope we might pop a bottle in celebration, regardless of the hour."

"Oh, Thomas!" exclaimed his mother, revived from her restrained mood. "You are to marry?"

"Indeed," he replied with a grin. His mother's effusive exclamation made it hard for him to remain sober. His father, the keen one, waited for more information, while his mother in her excitement asked, "For whom did you offer, Thomas? Is it the Barkley girl or maybe Cranston's?"

Thomas shook his head side to side.

"Oh, of course you would not want a green girl, but surely not someone on the shelf. Lady Margaret made a late debut because of the numerous deaths in her family. She is but one and twenty, a noted beauty and well-dowered."

Again, Thomas with a shake of his head replied no.

Emily opened her mouth again to guess, but her husband halted her with his hand. He said, "She played this game enough, Thomas. Why don't you tell us who will take your mama's place when I am gone?"

Thomas gave his answer in a steady calm voice. "I come to inform, not to receive your approval. I know what I want in a wife and what the earldom needs. I hope you will congratulate me, but if you cannot, I expect you to honor my betrothed with respect."

Belcrave almost shouted, "Do not condescend to me, my boy. Spit it out! If you are so sure of your choice, then there is no need to prevaricate."

Thomas smiled. "I am pleased to inform you, Miss Arabella Barrington consented to marry me."

Thomas entered Ketterling's study and accepted the viscount's greeting. However, Arabella's uncle soon scowled when Thomas presented him with formal documents and the viscount ascertained what they represented.

"You overstepped, Bolton," berated William.

"I am happy to amend anything you find lacking in the marriage settlements, Ketterling, but before you take umbrage I suggest you review them. I believe we are of like mind."

William returned to his desk and took his seat while waving his arm to Thomas to take the seat facing his desk. Moments, then minutes passed as William read through the documents. Marriage settlements were common among the peerage for securing a lady's financial future; especially in the event her husband died. Under law, everything a lady brought to the marriage, including herself, became her husband's property, as did her dowry unless contracted differently. It was not unheard for gentlemen to gamble away their wives' dowries, or to leave them at the mercy of their heirs should they die. Usually a father or a family trustee represented the lady's interests in negotiation with her betrothed. William with Nathaniel's approval stood as Arabella's guardian.

Yesterday, Thomas anticipated the grueling hour, or more, it would take to go over contractual points and decided he would rather spend that time with his betrothed than her uncle. So, he detailed the finances, property, and amenities he would settle on Arabella, had his solicitor write out the contract and presented it to William when he arrived.

He took great satisfaction when William's mouth gaped as he read through the contract and refrained from chuckling. He waited until William raised his head to look at him before he asked, "You are satisfied, Kettlering?"

The contract William read outlined in detail how Arabella's future was secure. The substantial amount of wealth and property Thomas settled on her guaranteed she would lack for nothing in terms of care, clothes, and transportation. Every consideration was made and specified, except the dowry William was prepared to give. Thomas suggested the money be given to Nathaniel, since his need was great. Thomas assured William he would match the sum and set it aside for any children his union with Arabella produced.

William rose from his seat and shook Thomas' hand, well-pleased his niece was to marry a man who truly cared for her welfare and happiness, before he confessed his only reservation. "What of your father, Bolton? Will Belcrave forbid you from marrying my niece?"

Thomas shook his head and explained. "Honor required me to inform my parents of my impending nuptials, but their opinion has no sway over me. They are well aware of my thoughts regarding marriage; the choice of wife is mine to make."

Satisfied his niece's future was secured, William told Thomas where to find Arabella. Thomas needed no further prompting. He turned and hastily made his way to William's garden.

The garden boasted of well-trimmed plants and trees. It was mapped out in squares bordered by gravel lanes. Some lanes led into arbors situated against the fence backing up to the lane for the mews. Stone benches were concealed within their recesses and it was in one of them, next to an arbor entwined with greenery and pink flowers, where Arabella stood woolgathering. Thomas never saw a more beautiful sight.

She stood in profile wearing a dark green pelisse over a sprig muslin dress trimmed with white lace at its hem. Even from his distance he could see she was distressed. He rushed forward and with each step the crunched gravel resounded like a bugle to announce his presence.

She turned to him with troubled eyes and asked, "Did my uncle give his consent?"

Thomas was glad her worry was of no account and drew her into a hug, before quickly allaying her fear. "The settlements are agreed upon and signed, Arabella, thereby giving me permission to pay you my addresses. You may marry me."

Arabella pushed away from him. Her fretful features turned cross as she scolded, "That is no proposal, Bolton!"

"Forgive me," Thomas responded as he released her, grinning at her fury. "Will you marry me?"

Arabella clenched her fists with arms akimbo and glared at him. She demanded, "Where are your professions of love?"

He retorted with amusement, "Where are mine?"

She explained heatedly, "I want to marry you. Doesn't that tell you how I feel?"

"I am offering," he retorted, his grin broadening into a smile. "Doesn't that tell you how I feel?"

Arabella pushed out her bottom lip in disappointment. This is not what she expected and queried, "Am I not to receive a flower or any symbol of affection?"

Thomas reached out to break the stem of the pink flower Arabella was staring at earlier and offered it to her. Then, he took her in his arms and kissed her soundly until her body relaxed into him. He broke the kiss and waited for her to regain her senses before he professed his love.

"I did not think I could ever fall in love, for that emotion takes trust and I had little in women. A disappointment in my *salad days* made me believe I was nothing more to them than a means to rank, property and wealth, and so my heart hardened.

"I think the first time you broke through my reserve was when you laughed over my mistaking you for a maid. Then, each time we battled, I realized you gave no import to my consequence. In fact, you thought me an insufferable, arrogant rake."

He grinned upon seeing in her gleaming eyes and growing smile how he spoke the truth. He continued, "I am not sure when my admiration of you turned into love, but my heart always knew you were the one. The moment you opened the door to me I delighted in your astonishment, and later upon learning your identity, I marveled at your wit and independent nature. You broke through my defenses and taught me I could trust in you. I love you Arabella. I want to marry and grow a family with you. I promise to always care, protect, and support you; and while I cannot promise you will not provoke me, or that I will let you have your way in all things, I can promise to love you all the days of my life and never forsake you. Will you marry me?"

Beaming from his profession of love, Arabella reciprocated, "I think I fell in love with you the first time you made me laugh." Seeing his eyes twinkle, she admitted, "Yes, I thought you a scoundrel, but I also saw your kindness and generosities to all those you love and were once under your protection."

Thomas raised his brows at the mention of protecttion and said, "Ah, I forgot you overheard my conversation with Mademoiselle Lavigne."

Arabella glared at him for mentioning his one-time mistress and then continued, "Yes, I did hear your *tête-à-tête*, but while I did not like to hear of your past dalliances, it was easy for me to understand why she wished to reconnect with you. It is not your title, not for me and I do not think it was for her, but for the man behind the title; a man full of strength, character, and resolve. A man unafraid to stand his ground and protect what belongs to him; and a man with so much compassion he looks after those incapable of looking after themselves. You treated me with respect and gentleness. I never feared anything in your company, Bolton, not even when *Jacques* captured and tied us up in that abominable cave. You have always been my hero and I have always longed to stay by your side. I love you and gladly accept your offer of marriage."

Her gleeful expression turned sober, prompting Thomas to ask, "What is wrong, Arabella. Are you unsure?"

"No, I just remembered your parents. I suspect they were not happy with your news."

He counseled, "Be patient. My parents must resolve their expectations. They thought to have a say in who became my countess, even though I warned them, more than once, the choice of wife is mine to make. They never heeded me, but they will come around as they did with Rebecca, so do not fret. Look yonder, your uncle waits to congratulate us. Let us be merry and if it pleases you, I shall take you out for a drive on Rotten Row since the social hour is near."

"Heavens!" exclaimed Arabella. "I almost forgot. Fairgrove shall arrive shortly to do just that. He brings his high perch phaeton. I do not believe there is room for three."

Thomas scowled and said, "If it wasn't for Damburten I would tell Fairgrove to go to the devil, but since I was the one to ask him to continue his attentions on you until I take care of Damburten, I cannot."

Arabella drew up on her toes and kissed Thomas on the cheek. "Thank you for taking care of me, Bolton."

He took her hand in his and said, "I have not forgotten your wishes, Arabella. I will see to your instructions regarding riding, shooting, and anything else that gives you pleasure, lest it puts you at risk."

"I never doubted it for a moment, Bolton. Do you suppose your parents will demand all the pomp and circumstance of a noble wedding?"

"It is your wishes that matter, Arabella. Do you want a large wedding?"

"Do you?"

"I have no desire to make a spectacle of myself unless it is your dream," he replied. "I dare say the Queen would give you Westminster Abby if you wanted it for our nuptials."

"No, Bolton. I do not want to be judged or put on display for all and sundry; and I certainly do not want my wedding to be discussed in every Mayfair parlour or read about in all the tabloids. I would prefer to marry with only family and friends for witnesses. Is there a small church in the village near your manor? My grandfather could attend without having to dress regally and so could my uncles."

Thomas' smile broadened watching Arabella's eye gleam in excitement. "Oh, Bolton!" she cried, "Do I dare be happy to have my greatest wish come true."

Thomas sobered immediately and asked, "What is your greatest wish, Arabella?"

"You," she replied with tears welling in her eyes. "To be loved by you."

"Then be happy, my love, for my heart is yours now and forever."

Ketterling came forward to intrude upon the intimate scene the moment he saw Arabella break out in tears. Concerned his niece was being pressed to accept

Thomas' addresses, he asked, "Is everything all right, Arabella? You need not accept Bolton's offer. You are most welcome to continue to live with me if you like."

Thomas' gasp made Arabella grin. Before he could roar what he thought of her uncle's suggestion, she went and gave her uncle a hug, then said, "All is well, uncle. *My cup runneth over.* My tears are of gladness at being loved and cherished. Congratulate us. I am to be married and heavens! I am to be a viscountess!"

Chapter Twenty-One

Thomas dismissed William's butler while he and Arabella waited for Fairgrove in Ketterling's entryway. He wanted a few more minutes with her before his friend arrived to pick her up. He took great satisfaction in helping Arabella into her redingote and to tying the ribbons of her bonnet just under her left ear. He could spend a whole day admiring her, but Arabella put a halt to his ridiculous notion when he remarked upon it. She swatted him for being silly and before he could retaliate with a kiss to the hand that hit him, a knock came.

He opened the door and Fairgrove immediately broke into an expansive smile at seeing Bolton play at butler. Thomas was not amused and wanted to wipe the smile from his friend's face, except he remembered Edward's magnanimity was keeping Arabella safe through his ruse of being Arabella's beau. It irked Thomas how much his friend was enjoying his part as swain.

He lifted Arabella onto her seat, while Edward climbed up to his own. Thomas stepped back to the sidewalk and watched as his friend tooled his showy high perch phaeton away. The moment Arabella turned from waving to him and faced forward, he set his thoughts on Damburten, rather than his disappointment in not being the one to drive her through Hyde Park.

It was time to bring the villain to account. The gossip concerning the baron's financial difficulties and his less than stellar character was starting to make the rounds among the *ton*. His name was becoming the brunt of any new offense mentioned. *Lost your purse? Perhaps, Damburten has it?*

The baron would not be pleased and there was no way of knowing how Damburten might strike back in retaliation. Thomas did not want Arabella caught in the crossfire, so he decided there was no better time than now to confront the baron. The absence of Damburten's door knocker surprised, but did not deter Thomas. He brought his Malacca cane up and rapped a tattoo on the door. No one answered. The house was closed without a servant to oversee it. Damburten was *at a stand.*

A townhome could not remain open without service, coal, or food. Most likely, the knowledge of Damburten's unpaid tradesmen's bills and dismissed servants was driving the Mayfair gossip. No lady of the realm liked to be uninformed, so they paid their servant's generously for a scandalous tidbit and then added their own twist to make them sound even more knowledgeable when they speculated with their peers.

Tonight was the Merryville Ball and Arabella was committed to attend it. He would have to remain vigilant and use all his resources to protect her, but tomorrow, he would order her to stay home. He cringed. Arabella would lose her temper at being told what to do, so he would have to remember to make his order a request.

Thomas stood near a potted fern in the Merryville ballroom across from where Arabella held court with her admirers. He was glad he did not alarm her with the latest news of Damburten, or else she would not be relaxed and enjoying herself. He wished he could say the same for himself. He did not like watching all the gentlemen preen like peacocks around her, offering witticisms and compliments to draw her attention. He kept his distance, too assured he would disperse her court of admirers with a sharp word and raised eyebrow.

Instead, he found comfort and amusement in the occasional glances she gifted him; especially because they notably annoyed Fairgrove and Sedgeworth. It was enough to appease him until the strings of the first waltz summoned him to her side. Without offering a greeting, he broke into the festive circle of her admirers and arrogantly took her hand. Without a by-your-leave, he escorted her away from her beaus to the dance floor. Fairgrove's chuckle and a number of the gentlemen's disgruntled re-marks pressed Arabella to comment.

"If I did not know you to be arrogant, Bolton, I might think you jealous. Does it bother you to see me ad-mired by others?"

"Not in the least, Miss Barrington," he lied as he guided her into position to begin their dance.

Grinning at his obvious denial, Arabella placed her hand on his shoulder and accepted his hand, while Thomas placed his other hand on her back to assume the proper waltz position. He glared at her teasing smile which only made it broaden.

"Minx," he retaliated, drawing her closer than the requisite twelve-inch rule between dancing couples. She did not complain, even knowing their closeness drew speculation upon them. *What does it matter? We are soon to marry.*

Then, as easily as a leaf floating through the air without hitch or hinder, they moved effortlessly around the floor. They danced without consideration for anyone else, but when the music ended, Thomas was alert to the growing whispers. He turned his attention from Arabella to his judging peers and almost exclaimed an oath from their blatant censure.

He blamed himself for letting his affection for Arabella show and his silent recrimination immediately hardened his features. His fierce anger quelled anyone from approaching him with questions about his obvious admiration for the Barrington gal. He escorted Arabella off the dance floor and returned her to her circle of admirers.

Sedgeworth scowled at him as did others amongst the group. Thomas knew he would have to beg his friend's forgiveness for playing him false. After all, it was his denial of owning any feelings for Arabella that prompted Sedgeworth to pursue her in earnest.

By now, the ballroom's volume was doubled with matrons voicing their thoughts on the couple. Many spoke loudly within Arabella's hearing with unkind remarks to make her cheeks crimson in embarrassment. Too many of them were outraged Bolton chose from among the common, instead of singling out one of their debutantes. Barbs were boldly voiced. More than one lady exclaimed how Arabella "reached too high."

The cruel remarks hurt Arabella; especially when one matron remarked, "Belcrave surely will not approve the match."

Arabella quickly excused herself when her vision clouded with tears to retire to the room set up for the ladies. Lady Crosse walked away with her and offered her great-niece some sage advice. She whispered, "Ignore them, Bella. They are all jealous because you succeeded where they could not and brought *up to scratch* the most eligible of bachelors."

"I did no such thing," gasped Arabella. "I simply fell in love and by the grace of God, Thomas did too!"

"Nevertheless," retorted Lady Crosse grinning, "it is a brilliant match."

Arabella laughed and then frowned when her aunt stopped in her tracks. "What is it, Aunt?"

"Fiddlesticks! I left my reticule on my seat," she replied. She immediately turned to command the footman following them, dressed in Ketterling's livery, to retrieve it. Lady Crosse did not know the man was ordered to guard Arabella, so took offense when the servant did not rush off to do her bidding.

"It is quite all right, Leo. Fetch her purse. I will retire with my aunt and be quite secure in the lady's room until you return."

It seemed like seconds, but assuredly it was minutes later when a maid entered the lady's room with news for Miss Barrington a man awaited her outside. Arabella grinned and told her aunt, "It is Leo returned. I shall collect your reticule and bring it to you."

Arabella followed the maid out and was surprised not to see Leo at hand. The maid shrugged her shoulders, begged Arabella's pardon and left. Arabella walked down the hallway thinking to see if Leo stepped aside, as to not hover near the door where a lady might take affront. She was dissuaded by the unlit sconces to venture further and turned to make her way back when she was grabbed from behind. An arm wrapped around her neck and before she realized what was happening, she was dragged back into the darkened hall.

She fought with her free hand to pull the assailant's arm from her neck, but with her other arm pinned against her side, her effort was futile. Each time she clawed at the arm pressing against her windpipe, the villain tightened his chokehold. She tried to recall what Thomas taught her, but she was afraid, much like a noose, her assailant's arm would hang her if her feet left the ground.

She was nearing unconsciousness when her conditioning from all her defense lessons took over. She leaned back and raised her knees to her chest to place all her weight in her assailant's hands. The shift unbalanced him and he was forced to loosen his grip, so as not to tumble. Arabella pulled back on his finger the moment her hands were free and turned out of his hold. Secure on her feet with him at her mercy she thought to kick him, but knew her shoes were too soft to produce any desired outcome.

Afraid she could not keep Damburten at bay for long she cried out for the one person who had always come to her rescue and as if heaven sent, she heard his reply. She let go of Damburten and ran just as she was instructed to do and was quickly wrapped up in familiar arms. Thomas had come and the relief she felt nearly buckled her knees.

Thomas quickly set her aside and chased after her assailant who turned tail to run away the moment Arabella released him. He was positive the villain was Damburten, but could not positively identify him since the sconces on the walls were extinguished and he did not catch him. He was furious Damburten got away and even more enraged the villain had put his hands on Arabella.

Thomas blamed himself for Arabella's near abducttion. If he did not let all the peerage see how much he admired Arabella, then Damburten would not have gone after her. He let his guard down by forgetting the baron was still received by Mayfair's *ton*. After all, too many noblemen lived on credit or on the whims of their parents' largesse to be discriminating, and without credible proof of Damburten's murderous villainy; he remained on the *ton's* guest lists.

Blood trumped wealth. After all Damburten could refill his coffer with a marriage to a well-dowered lady, an inheritance, or a windfall at the gaming tables and race tracks. There were too many ladies in need of a husband to discard an unmarried titled gentleman; especially those ladies who were in their second and third seasons. Lest not forget the upcoming heiresses from the merchant class who would willingly marry a titled man to raise their family's stature, regardless of character.

Fear kept Arabella from accepting the numerous invitations she received. Her regrets quickly stirred the gossip mill. Mayfair parlours and Gentlemen clubs speculated with relish over the reason behind her absences. One gentleman was heard to remark, "An incident at the Merryville Ball. A lady coming from the retiring room witnessed Miss Barrington being fought over by Bolton and another man."

The *on dit* grew into a fantastic tale of Bolton catching Arabella in the arms of another man. Her continued absence encouraged more speculation. Each passing day, the tale of betrayal grew. There were too many ladies ready to replace Arabella in Bolton's admiration to gladly believe the worst of her. They used her removal from society as proof of her guilt, embroiling the Barrington name in scandal once again.

A curt note for Thomas to present himself to Belcrave came within days. While not surprised to be summoned, he was startled to receive a blistering reckoning the moment he stepped into his father's study.

Belcrave complained his countess could not step foot outdoors without being bombarded with questions regarding the truth of Miss Barrington's imbroglio. The earl raged at Thomas for the indignity of having the family name again bantered about in Mayfair's parlours.

"Must we become fodder for the gossipmonger's again? Have we not suffered enough from Rebecca's scandal? Must you bring dishonor onto your family by allying yourself with a Barrington? One was more than enough to welcome into the family."

Belcrave was about to provide another example of his disgust when Thomas' patience broke at hearing his fiancée's name disparaged. His father did not even offer him a seat before he assailed him with a barrage of grievances and his nerves were already taut with worry. The only thing he could wrap his head around was keeping Arabella safe and ridding England of Damburten.

Thomas was schooled to be haughty, to not display his feelings when challenged; but as he described Damburten's attack on Arabella, his festering emotions erupted. In an uncommon show of sentiment, he raged, "I almost lost her to that villain's hands. Do you know what it feels like to watch the one you love being choked to death? Do you think I care a wit about gossip? Would you care what people said if you saw someone with their heavy hands squeezing mama's neck?"

Thomas did not wait to hear his father's response and left, leaving the door open in his wake. He hurried home hoping there was news of Damburten's location. Days passed, but finally the results he awaited were brought to him and he did not hesitate to act. He selected two of his most capable and strong men to accompany him.

He stopped by Ketterling House to inform Arabella he was on his way to confront Damburten. He announced as he entered the drawing room, "My men found him, Arabella. You and your family do not need to worry about that villain any longer. My men will place him on a ship departing for America on the morning's tide."

She rose from her seat, disbelieving his news and walked over to him and asked, "He will go?"

"Assuredly," replied Thomas, smoothing the worry lines from her forehead with his fingers. "He will choose America over debtor's prison; especially since I will settle him with funds to start his new life."

Arabella stepped back and raged, "It angers me that murderer receives anything, Bolton. Could you not, once you have his confession, have him tried?"

"Perhaps," he replied. "But it is difficult for a peer to pass judgement on another peer. They fear setting a precedence and one day seeing their own sorry hide held to account. Besides, Damburten might cry coercion and many would gladly believe him, rather than see one of their own hang."

She saw the truth in his words and turned the conversation to what else troubled her. She asked, "May I finally venture out of the house, then, Bolton?"

Thomas replied with empathy, "I ask you to wait until I see Damburten off, Arabella. I am on my way to his lodgings now and will return after my men take him away. They will stay with him, see him board, and not leave the dock until his ship sails."

"Thank you, Bolton," she said looking more worried than happy. She rose up on her toes and kissed his cheek."

Thomas wrapped her up in his arms and said, "Do not fret, love. I will see to it Damburten's villainy is done."

Chapter Twenty-Two

Thomas looked up at the tenement building where his people discovered Damburten took lodgings. The run-down building was a far cry from the baron's Mayfair townhome. A shout of "B'ware," came from an upper window in the tenement building and Thomas just managed to step out of range from the waste water raining down on the pavement. The unsightly puddle made him grimace. His servants offered up an apology, but he waved it off to stride forward into what looked like a den of iniquity.

The door to Damburten's lodging was slightly ajar and Thomas used his cane to push it open. Damburten did not look surprised to see him. The baron sat sprawled in a wooden chair next to a small wooden table with a glass tumbler of spirits in his hand. He wore no tailcoat, his vest was unbuttoned and the tails of an untied cravat hung around his neck. His eyes were bloodshot, his cheeks ruddy and his voice escaped in a drawl, "Congratulations, Bolton! You found me. I heard you were looking."

Thomas glared at him and replied, "You should have presented yourself and saved us both a lot of trouble. I will not waste words with you, Damburten. I give you two choices: exile or debtor's prison."

Damburten seethed, "You think you have the power?"

"Indeed," Thomas replied and took from his pocket a sheet of paper that listed all of Damburten's debts and IOUs. He had reconciled every tradesmen bill and promissory note. "You owe me now, Damburten, and I am ready to call in your debt should you decide to stay in England."

With a smirk, Damburten replied, "It appears I have little choice, but where am I to go? Belgium, Italy, France?"

"First, I will have your confession to Barrington's murder." Thomas supplied the paper, pen and ink, his servant handed him.

Damburten spewed, "You lost your wits if you think I shall give you any such thing, Bolton."

"Then, your choice is debtor's prison for I will not settle you abroad without it."

Damburten sat up and railed, "All right, but I do not see the point since the House of Lords will not try me."

"You need not worry as long as you stay out of England."

"There!" shouted the baron. He shoved his completed declaration of guilt at Thomas the minute he finished writing it.

Thomas read the confession to ensure it was an accurate accounting and then sanded the ink so it would not smear, before folding and placing it in his tailcoat pocket. Thomas signaled his men to collect Damburten. Each man grabbed one of the baron's arms, causing Damburten to shout, "Have you lost your mind, Bolton. I have business to attend before I can leave and items to pack."

"I will see your affairs are settled, but by the looks of it, the crown will take all you have in lieu of the taxes you owe, unless they appoint someone to take over your baronage. As for your clothes they will not fit in where you are headed."

"I am not dead, Bolton," railed the baron. "The baronship is mine and I will provide the next heir to govern it, but what do you mean? Where are you sending me?"

"America," replied Thomas. "I will settle you with a modicum of funds, but it will be up to you to find your way and employment."

"I am as blue-blooded as you, Bolton, and it is my God-given right to live as a nobleman."

You are getting more than you deserve," Thomas rebuked before turning and looking at his men. They gave their assurances with a nod Damburten would be gone by the morning tide. Thomas left, knowing his men would see his will done.

Thomas returned to Ketterling House to inform Arabella her family was free of Damburten and his villainy.

He was disappointed to find Lady Adelaide taking tea with her and was dumbstruck what to say other than to make his salutation.

His silence did not wash with Arabella. She put down the porcelain teapot and asked him, "It is done?"

"Yes."

Adelaide inquired, "What is done?"

"Nothing of import," replied Arabella, "except the news allows me to accept your kind invitation to walk. May I, Bolton? I have been cooped up for days and long for a stroll."

Thomas smiled and replied, "Yes, as long as Leo accompanies you."

"Of course," she responded, grinning.

Arabella asked Adelaide to wait while she went to retrieve her redingote, bonnet, and gloves. The day was cold and windy and Arabella hoped they could beat the rain before the overcast sky broke. For days the gloomy weather forecasted rain, but none had come.

At first, Adelaide was surprised to hear Arabella ask Bolton's permission to venture outside. A young lady only asked permission from someone who held authority over them. It made no sense to ask a friend, unless that person was more than a friend. Her sound reasoning made her angry. Adelaide looked up from her seat and glared at Thomas before inquiring, "Am I to congratulate you, Bolton? And in the process be disappointed not to call Arabella sister?"

"It is not publicly announced, but yes, Miss Barrington consented to be my wife," he answered.

"You are not worried my brother will call you out for your perfidy?" she queried, angry on her brother's behalf.

Thomas laughed and said, "Fairgrove is quite aware of my feelings, Lady Adelaide. You may sheath your sword for Edward is not suffering. His only regret is for you and your mama's disappointment."

"Very well," she responded contritely. "I shall still call you friend, but only if you love and cherish Arabella as she should be."

"It is my greatest desire and pleasure," proclaimed Thomas taking the lady's hand and proffering a kiss on her knuckles. Adelaide waved him off; annoyed she was not immune to his gallantry as she thought.

Arabella returned and Thomas saw them out the front door and on their way down the street. Comforted in knowing she was safe, he headed to his own townhome where he would wait until it was time to pick her up for Fairgrove's dinner.

The wind blew fierce against the ladies and Arabella's laughter flew up and away like a fluttering butterfly. Their flying skirts and flapping bonnets drew Adelaide to comment, "I am insane to suggest such an outing. Do you wish to return?"

"Not at all," replied Arabella. "I am thoroughly enjoying the adventure. I cannot thank you enough,

Adelaide. I feel revived as if the wind is carrying away all my burdens."

"You heard the gossip?" asked Adelaide. "I dare say it is a falsehood. Bolton does not look like he's been cuckold."

Affronted, Arabella asked tartly, "And if he did, would you believe it of me?"

"No," laughed Adelaide. "I only wished I heard your good news from you."

"You know I am to marry?"

"I asked Bolton and he did not prevaricate. I am happy for you Arabella, though I wished to call you sister. I hope I may still call you friend."

"The best of friends," Arabella replied. "Are you excited for tonight's dinner?"

"Indeed, I very much look forward to hearing you play."

Arabella swiped at the loose hairs flying in her face and after batting at them a number of times, took off her bonnet to secure them. To her astonishment, the wind grabbed her hat out of her hands and sent it flying. Leo called out he would retrieve it for her and Arabella laughed when the hat sailed away each time Leo swooped down to collect it.

Arabella pushed Adelaide to cross the street while she returned to help Leo and saw Thomas riding his mount hard towards her as if the devil was chasing him. The sight rooted her feet to the ground as she tried to hear what he was saying. No matter how hard she tried the wind carried his words away, much like her hat from Leo.

She struggled to keep her flying hair from covering her eyes, but the wind's power created havoc against her person and clothes. It was as if she stood on the bow of a ship during a gale and that notion brought clarity to what drove Thomas to collect her. He feared she would be caught in the brewing storm and wanted to bring her to the warmth and safety of her home.

She turned to tell Adelaide they needed to return to Ketterling House, but once again her windblown hair obstructed her view. No sooner did she push her hair aside than it flew back to cover her eyes. She would have laughed at her ineptitude except the shrill of Adelaide's scream frightened her beyond reason.

It took her a moment before she recovered from the terror of Adelaide's scream to think to use her arm to lift her hair away from her eyes. She shook as she saw what made her friend cry out in alarm. A great beast of a stallion with its massive hooves kicking up divots of dirt and dust was pounding down the lane towards her. Damburten sat upon the horse and was slapping his riding crop against his horse's rump to charge at her. Petrified, she froze.

Her only thought was of Thomas and how he was to bear witness to her death. The notion made her want to cry, but before she could, the ground fell away and the world flipped amongst the sounds of screams and chaos. She was wrapped up in Thomas' strong arm, her body held tight against his leg and horse, hanging like a rag doll. Thomas' stallion blew out his nose and swung his head when Thomas reined him in to stop.

His valiant steed began to prance in place in response to the whinnying and snorting of Damburten's horse. Thomas patted his horse's neck and then lowered Arabella to the ground. He quickly dismounted and wrapped her up in a backbreaking hug, dropping his reins, knowing his well-trained horse would not wander off. He took Arabella's head in his hands, carefully inspected her pale face, and asked, "Are you hurt?"

Arabella couldn't speak, but managed to answer, "No," with a shake of her head. Thomas wanted to hold and comfort Arabella's trembling body, but he had to deal with this latest attempt on her life. With an arm around her shoulders, he walked her over to a stunned Adelaide and told them to look after each other while he dealt with Damburten. Arabella's mind focused on the only relevant part of what happened. He saved her. Of course, he did. Didn't he always come to her rescue? He was her hero, after all, and the one person she could count on to be near whenever she needed him.

Leo was on the scene holding onto the baron's aggravated mount. Damburten was sprawled lifeless on the ground. Thomas began to move to the body already surrounded by spectators, until Leo informed, "Nothing you can do, my lord. Take the ladies home. I'll talk to the constable. Enough witnesses are here to tell how the gent was riding recklessly."

Thomas agreed and told Leo to send the constable to him if necessary.

Thomas escorted the ladies to Ketterling House, placed Adelaide in her carriage to go home, and then saw to comforting Arabella. He settled next to her on the sofa, wrapped his arm around her shoulders and drew her close. Arabella laid her head against his chest. She was once again shaken to the core, but her curiosity compelled her to ask, "How? How did you know I needed rescuing?"

"One of my men assigned to transport Damburten came riding hard to find me and tell me the baron escaped. My men were pushing him to enter a hackney when he shouted an absurd sum to anyone who got him free. A bunch of ruffians attacked my men; more for sport than anything.

"As soon as they escaped the brawl, they went in search of me. I immediately raced to find you and feared I might not reach you in time when I saw what Damburten planned. Dear Lord, Arabella, I do not think my heart can take too much more of you being in danger."

Thomas held her as she sobbed, her emotions overflowing from the fright she endured. He encouraged her to send her regrets to Fairgrove. Even Adelaide had suggested she do so, but Arabella refused. She said Damburten unsettled their lives enough and it was time to return to normalcy. Thomas supported her decision and left her in her aunt's and uncle's care.

The Earl of Belcrave waited for his valet to finish tying his cravat and make his exit before he turned to his wife to say, "I tell you, Emily, he left me speechless. I thought he would cry. Have you ever seen Thomas shed a tear?" The earl was recollecting his highly emotional conversation with his son.

"Not even in his short pants, Richard. He would suffer a hurt and bear it, puffing out his chest as you might do."

"Perhaps, now Damburten is dead and Arabella is no longer in need of protection, Thomas will marry suitably."

"He loves her, Richard," explained Emily. "His need for her is greater than her need to be protected."

"Nonsense," retorted the earl.

"You have not seen them together, Richard," countered Emily. "Their love is so strong it is nearly palpable. He will not forsake her."

"But Emily," he argued. "She has not the talents, nor the instruction to be the next Countess of Belcrave."

"You will estrange your son if you do not accept her. Take heed, my lord husband, in what you say this evening. Once words are spoken they can never be recalled."

Initially, when the earl received Fairgrove's dinner invitation he told his wife to send their regrets. He was not in good humor with his son, but then he learned Damburten died. He wanted to know if Damburten's death changed Thomas' plans to wed. He immediately dispatched a note to Fairgrove asking if he and his countess attending would upset their table numbers. Edward assured them it would not.

Arabella rose from her seat next to Lady Fairgrove when she saw the Earl and Countess of Belcrave enter the drawing room. Edward told her he extended the invitation after she and Thomas became betrothed. He did not reveal their initial regrets.

Arabella guessed Belcrave was not happy to call her daughter by his countenance and haughty demeanor, though she was not sure what Emily thought. She advanced to greet them, but was intercepted by Thomas who took her hand, placed it on his arm and smiled adoringly at her, before escorting her over to greet his parents.

Arabella put on her brightest smile and made her curtsies. She felt a pang of remorse when the earl scowled at her, but wanted to giggle when Thomas scowled right back at him. She turned her attention to Emily and found comfort in the lady's grin. Perhaps, all was not as bad as she thought.

Emily pulled Arabella away. Thomas was about to intervene, until he saw his mother shake her head. Her expression was not one of contempt, so he allowed Arabella to be taken away. He turned his attention to his father.

Emily drew Arabella down on a settee that only allowed seating for two and confessed, "I was not happy to hear the news, but I can see Thomas' mind is made up. I should have known by the way he looked at you and pro- tected you something was brewing; especially after I found the two of you alone in the drawing room. Belcrave is not pleased. He has expectations of a great alliance, but he will come about because he loves his children. I, on the other hand, believe you do Thomas a grave disservice in accept- ing his addresses."

"I beg to disagree," intervened Edward who heard the last of Emily's comments. Concerned at seeing Arabella cornered by Thomas' mother, he quickly joined their little *tête-á-tête* and surprised the both of them when he spoke, "I believe Arabella has done Bolton a great service in accepting his addresses and should my friend prove idiotic enough not know it, then myself and Sedgeworth would heartily offer for her hand. I tell you Miss Barrington, my mama will be in tears when the announcement of your betrothal to Bolton is made. She is most anxious to call you family and even now asks me to remind you to come tomorrow, so she can work on some embroidery with you."

Emily asked Arabella, "You embroider?"

Edward added, "And she paints and plays the piano, too."

Arabella laughed at Edward's attempt to champion her. Her laughter drew Thomas over to them. He remarked, "You lot are way too cheerful. What did I miss?"

"Your mother," informed Edward, "seems surprised to learn of Miss Barrington's many talents."

Thomas gave his mother a silent reprimand. Emily did not suffer the scold and rebutted. "Well, do not raise your hackles, Thomas. I did not know Miss Barrington received a lady's education. I suppose she speaks French?"

Arabella laughed and cheerfully said, "*Oui. Je parle couramment français. Y a-t-il quelque chose que vous voudriez que je dise ?*"

"I never thought you to be unkind," remarked Thomas to his mother, and to Arabella he said, "You need not say anything else in French to prove your fluency, Miss Barrington."

"Do not scold your mama, Bolton," rebuked Arabella. "Most likely she forgot my mama was the daughter of the then Viscount Ketterling and received the same instruction as any lady of the realm and used her knowledge to teach her daughters." Arabella directed her next response to Emily. "You will remember my grand-père, *Marquis du Benoît* is French and highly regarded by our queen."

"Now who is being unkind," laughed Emily. "Well, you set me straight, Arabella. No doubt, you will set society straight to your credentials, just as your sister did when she first arrived. I expect you will manage quite well when the time comes for you to wear my coronet, though I hope it will not be for a long time."

"Me too," remarked Arabella grinning.

Thomas and Edward walked off, uncomfortable with the emotions whirling between Arabella and Emily. The countess gave her future daughter-by-marriage a hug and said, "Our great expectations for Bolton blinded me and Belcrave. I trust you will forgive us?"

Arabella laughed and said, "There is no need. I am sure Bolton was top lofty when he made his announcement and gave neither you nor the earl a chance to voice your concerns. I would never see Bolton hindered or hurt."

"Thank you Arabella, and have no concern about Belcrave. He might be stubborn, but he is not inflexible. He will relinquish his former expectations and see Thomas, as did Harry, chose better than we ever could have for them."

"I hope so," replied Arabella.

The Earl and Countess of Belcrave entered their carriage after extending their gratitude for a lovely evening to the Earl of Fairgrove and his mother. It was a night of revelations and astonishments. Richard had looked at his son the moment Emily escorted Arabella away and asked, "You are determined to marry the gal?"

Thomas replied, "I am."

"You love her?"

And to that query, Thomas gave his father his broadest smile and said, "I do."

The earl did not bother to ask if Arabella loved him for it was obvious. Miss Barrington could not keep her eyes off his son and when Thomas returned her look, she blushed. Speaking about feelings quickly separated them. The earl sought a tot of whiskey and Thomas went to join

Arabella. The evening was filled with lively conversation, good food and later, as promised a performance by Arabella.

Richard broke the silence of the carriage and asked his wife, "Did you know she played exceptionally?"

"She is extraordinary, Richard," rebutted Emily. "I have not heard better."

"I think we might have misjudged her, Emily?"

"Blood tells, Richard. The Barringtons come from noble stock. Your son chose well. Do you approve?"

"Does it matter?"

"Not in his decision to marry, but yes, your approval matters to Thomas."

"He has it, Emily, I gave my acceptance to him earlier," Richard confessed. "It seems our fates are aligned with the Barringtons. Heaven help us if the brother comes calling. You don't think Charlotte will take a fancy to him."

Emily chuckled, "He will not want a girl out of the school room."

While the Earl and Countess discussed their daughter's upcoming Season, Thomas and Arabella made their way to Ketterling House. Thomas sat beside her in his closed town carriage and informed, "I shall procure a special license and then we will head to my manor and begin plans for our nuptials."

"It sounds lovely, Bolton," remarked Arabella.

"Don't you think it is time you called me Thomas," he suggested.

"Thomas," she whispered. "I cannot wait to start our life together."

"Nor I," he agreed and kissed her soundly.

Acknowledgements

I am very lucky to have an amazing photographer, Christina Brusaca, and cover models Nicole and Lawrence Sweeney III. Their tireless efforts to help create the perfect cover are very much appreciated. Christina has been my photographer for the past ten years and I am very thankful for her continued support and expertise.

Nicole and Lawrence were engaged to be married when they covered the award winning *Only a Captain Will Do*. They have three beautiful children and are expecting another baby. While they had fun characterizing a reluctant attraction for one another for this book's cover, they are far from reluctant in their love for one another.

A fun fact, Lawrence was directed to look away from the camera because unlike the book's hero, he is currently sporting a mustache and beard.

Thank you, Elizabeth Cooper and Chantal Vandemaële. I really appreciate your help to ensure the French dialogue was translated correctly.

As always, I want to acknowledge and thank my wonderful and ever-inspiring husband, children, grandchildren, my mom, and all my readers for their continued feedback and support. I couldn't do it without you.

About the Author

Teresa Sweeney takes great pleasure penning historical romance novels that focus on the charm, wit, and banter of courtship.

She is a Golden Leaf Award winner for her novel *Only a Captain Will Do* and a Golden Quill Finalist for her novel *The Reluctant Viscount.* Book One of The Barrington Saga: *A Reluctant Debut* was a Carolyn Readers' Choice Award Finalist and Holt Medallion Winner.

She dotes on her eight grandchildren and looks forward to welcoming another grandchild in 2025. She loves to read, write, and a myriad of other pursuits where she can use her creativity and imagination. Visit her website www.teresa-sweeney.com for the latest information on her novels.

www.ingramcontent.com/pod-product-compliance
Lightning Source LLC
Chambersburg PA
CBHW031335020726
47499CB00005B/1270